用對的方法充實自己，
讓人生變得更美好！

凱信企管

用對的方法充實自己，
讓人生變得更美好！

Daily English
Conversation
生活美語
帶著走

7大生活主題＋140篇情境會話＋1400個生活短句，英語會話能力三級跳！

① 情境分類清楚，貼近老外生活細節，循序漸近或按圖索驥學習都方便！

② 以實境模擬的方式來設計互動對話，非憑空想像，溝通更流暢；搭配音檔學習，如虎添翼！

③ 學習會話同時，擴充字彙量，並強化核心單字記憶，提升自行組建更多會話短句能力！

18 | 理髮店

TRACK058.

A: I didn't make an appointment. Is that ok?
B: That's fine. But you probably need to wait about 15 minutes.
B: Thank you for your ***patience***. How would you like your
A: I would like to have a ***wash*** and cut, but not
B: Do you want to have a ***perm***?
A: I'm too busy today, I don't have enough time.
B: Does the water temperature suit you?
A: It's a little bit too hot for me.

B: 可以，不過大概要等15分鐘左右。
B: 讓您久等了，你要怎麼剪你的頭髮？
A: 請幫我洗頭及剪髮，但不要剪的太短。
B: 要不要燙髮呢？
A: 今天我很忙，沒有時間。
B: 水溫可以嗎？
A: 稍微燙了點。

核心詞彙

Words&Phrases

patience	[ˋpeʃəns	名詞 耐心
hair	[hɛr]	名詞 頭髮
cut	[kʌt]	動詞 剪
wash	[wɑʃ]	動詞 洗
short	[ʃɔrt	形容詞 短的
perm		名詞 燙髮

④ 每一情境補充10句精準短句。因應狀況，隨機替換句子，英語溝通更靈活！

日常實用短句

- I'd like to have a haircut.
  我想要剪頭髮。
- Well, this is my first time here.
  嗯，這是我第一次來。
- How would you like your hair cut?
  你想剪成什麼樣？
- Just trim the fringe a little bit shorter.
  只要把瀏海修短一點。
- I want to color my hair.
  我想染頭髮。
- I am going to blow-dry your hair now.
  我現在要把你的頭髮吹乾。
- Can you make my hair look exactly like the woman's this picture?
  你可以把我的頭髮弄成跟照片裡的女人一樣嗎？
- How much do you charge for a shampoo?
  洗頭髮要多少錢？
- Will it take a long time?
  要很久嗎？
- It will be around 30 minutes.
  大概三十分鐘。

⑥ 自我驗收與複習：利用每一大主題學習結束後的關鍵單字總複習，檢視學習成效，扎實學習、定植記憶！

PART❸日常生活篇

你都記住了嗎？

從各篇「日常實用短句」裡整理出外國人常用的單字和片語，如果背起來了，就在前方空格打個勾吧！

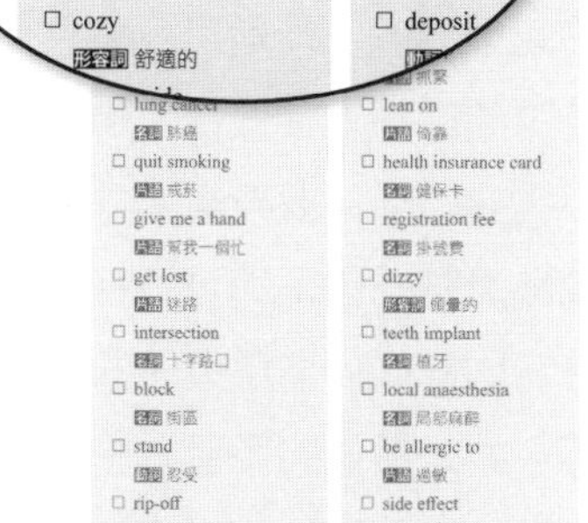

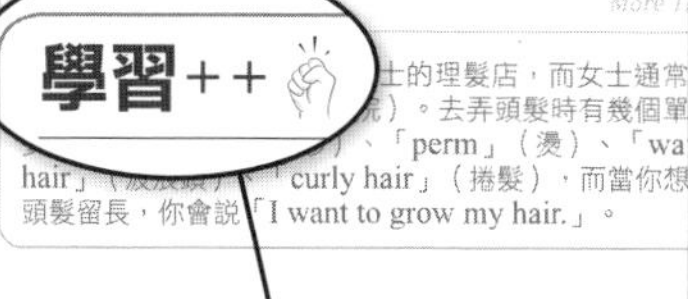

⑤ 同步補充更多關於異國文化資訊及相關學習內容；小小細節，大大關鍵！

全書音檔連結

因各家手機系統不同，若無法直接掃描，仍可以至以下電腦雲端連結下載收聽。

（https://tinyurl.com/yxau3yxm）

對學習英文者來說，除了應付考試的需求，能夠開口用流利的英語表達、溝通，亦是重要的學習目標；但這也因此常常讓學習者感到沮喪，因為學了那麼多年的英文，為什麼總有「詞彙或句子到用時方恨少」的窘境與哀傷？遑論至國外旅遊的溝通需求，甚至連在路上遇到外國人問路，都避之唯恐不急！「開口說英語」真是大多數的人死穴啊！

其實，英語口說的學習重點不在於要能講出多麼複雜的句型句子，或是用多麼漂亮的詞藻，就連老外在平時的生活裡都不會使用困難的句子來說話，我們當然就更不需要了；只要能掌握並理解你想要表達的內容，利用精準清楚的句子即可；時常短短的句子反而更易傳遞訊息。因此如何能用最短的時間，達到精準表達與溝通技巧，才是最佳的學習方法。

這本書在架構之初，即以小開本的方式設計，大小適中、輕巧好攜帶，不必擔心包包容量，隨時都能帶在身上利用零碎時間學習，英語口說能力定能三級跳！在單元設計，我以老外在生活裡最常見的場景及狀況來設定主題，並以實境模擬的方式來設計對話，因為生活是互動的，絕不是一個人自説自話；全書收錄的內容亦不是虛擬憑空想像的，而是使用頻率極高，同時最貼近老外生活的每一個細節來設計。學習者只要將每一個情境之下，容易聽到或是經常使用的語句學起來，每天練習一點點，熟悉了不同場合的應對方式，適時套用／替換短句，假以時日，你的英文一定也可以不假思索、流利的脫口而出。

另外，有鑑於在台灣有越來越多的外籍人士，所以第七章特別設計成「向老外介紹景點與文化篇」，不管是台北101大樓，或是日月潭的景點的英文都會在這一篇會話裡學到。下次再遇到老外就不用嚇得轉身逃開，從此擺脫不敢開口説英文的惡夢。

最後，要提醒所有學習者，學習時不要害怕犯錯，也不需追求完美，最大的重點就是：「大膽開口説」，唯有開口説，才更有機會從錯誤中進步，真正的學以致用，達到輕鬆説一口自然道地的英語的最終目標！

目錄
Contenes

Part 1 社交禮儀篇－音檔連結

因各家手機系統不同，若無法直接掃描，
仍可以至以下電腦雲端連結下載收聽。
（https://tinyurl.com/2p8de9vw）

PART 1

社交禮儀篇

01 見面寒暄

TRACK 001.

實境對話

A: How are you?
B: ***Not bad***. How ***about*** you?
A: I am very ***well***. ***Thank you***!
A: Nice to ***meet*** you!
B: Nice to meet you, too!
A: It has been ***a long time*** that we haven't seen ***each other***!
B: It ***really*** has been a long time!

A:你好嗎？
B:還可以，你呢？
A:謝謝！託你的福，很好！
A:很高興見到你！
B:我也很高興見到你！
A:久違了。
B:真是久違了。

核心詞彙

Words&Phrases

not bad	[nɑt bæd]	片語 還可以、還不錯
about	[əˋbaʊt]	介詞 關於
well	[wɛl]	形容詞 好的
thank you	[θæŋk ju]	片語 謝謝你、感謝
meet	[mit]	動詞 遇見、認識
a long time	[ə lɔŋ taɪm]	片語 很長一段時間
each other	[itʃ ˋʌθɚ]	片語 互相
really	[ˋriəlɪ]	副詞 真地

日常實用短句 Useful Sentences

- How do you do?
  你好嗎？
- How are you?
  你好嗎？
- How are you doing?
  你好嗎？
- How have you been?
  最近好嗎？
- I haven't seen you for ages.
  好久沒見到你了。
- Nice to meet you.
  很高興認識你。
- How's everything going?
  一切都還好嗎？
- I'm so glad to see you.
  真高興見到你。
- What's up?
  最近怎麼樣？
- What's new?
  最近如何？
- How's it going?
  一切都好嗎？
- Long time no see.
  好久不見。

學習++ More Tips

外國人見面時喜歡寒暄一番，通常他們都會說：「How are you?」，但是第一次見面的人則要用「How do you do?」（你好嗎？）或是說「Nice to meet you.」（很高興認識你！）。

02 介紹友人

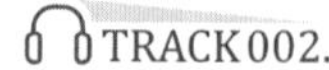

TRACK 002.

實境對話

Conversation

A: Shu-Yi, this is my ***friend*** Mary from New York. Mary, this is my sister, Shu-Yi.

B: Oh! I am so ***glad*** to meet you!

C: Me too, Mary.

A: ***Excuse me***. This lady is...

B: I'm really sorry. I should have ***introduced*** you to each other.

B: Mr. Ito. This is my ***colleague*** Ms. Kikuchi.

A: I'm very ***pleased*** to meet you.

C: I've ***heard*** your name for a long time.

A: 淑宜，這是我在紐約的朋友瑪麗。瑪麗，這是我的姊姊淑宜。

B: 哦，真高興見到妳！

C: 我也是，瑪麗。

A: 不好意思，請問這位是……？

B: 真抱歉，我應該幫您介紹才是。

B: 伊藤先生，這位是我同事菊池小姐。

A: 能認識妳，深感榮幸之至。

C: 久仰您的大名。

核心詞彙

Words&Phrases

friend	[frend]	名詞 朋友
glad	[glæd]	形容詞 高興的
excuse me	[ɪk`skjuz mi]	片語 不好意思
introduce	[ˌɪntrə`djus]	動詞 介紹

colleague	[ˋkɑlig]	名詞 同事
pleased	[plizd]	形容詞 高興的
hear	[hɪr]	動詞 聽

日常實用短句 *Useful Sentences*

- Peter, this is Michael.
  彼得，這是麥克。
- Have you met each other yet?
  你們見過彼此了嗎？
- John, let me introduce Sharon to you.
  約翰，讓我介紹雪倫給你認識。
- I'd like to introduce Owen.
  我要來介紹歐文。
- I'd like you to meet Emma.
  我要讓你來認識艾瑪。
- Allow me to introduce Mr. Potter.
  請讓我來介紹波特先生。
- Did you meet Polly, Anna?
  安娜，妳見過波麗了嗎？
- We haven't introduced ourselves, have we?
  我們還沒介紹我們自己，對吧？
- Cindy, meet Gary here.
  辛蒂，來見見蓋瑞。
- I'd like to introduce a coworker of mine.
  我想介紹一位同事。

學習++ *More Tips*

「introduce someone to someone」是「介紹某人給某人」的意思，是比較客氣的說法。除了在介紹友人的時候我們會用到這一句，在看大型晚會、表演的時候也會聽到「Let's introduce our host for tonight...」（讓我們來介紹今晚的主持人……）。

03 電話用語

TRACK 003.

實境對話

Conversation

A: Hello, Is Michiko in now?

B: I'm sorry, you have the wrong ***number***.

A: Oh, I'm really sorry!

A: Hello! Is this the Kumagaya ***residence***?

B: Yes, this is Kumagaya speaking.

A: Hello, this is Alan, I would like to ***speak to*** Cathy.

B: Sorry, Alan. She is not ***here*** now. Do you have any ***message*** for her?

A: I'll ***call*** again in 20 ***minutes***.

A: 喂，請問美智子在嗎？
B: 對不起，你打錯電話了。
A: 哦！真對不起。

A: 喂！這是熊谷家嗎？
B: 是的，我是熊谷。

A: 喂，我是亞倫，我想找凱西説話。
B: 對不起！亞倫，她現在不在這裡，你有什麼話要轉告嗎？
A: 20 分鐘後我再重撥一次。

核心詞彙

Words&Phrases

number	[ˋnʌmbɚ]	名詞 號碼、數字
residence	[ˋrɛzədəns]	名詞 住宅
speak to	[spik tu]	片語 跟……講電話
here	[hɪr]	副詞 在這裡
message	[ˋmɛsɪdʒ]	名詞 訊息、留言

call	[kɔl]	動詞 打電話
minute	[`mɪnɪt]	名詞 分鐘

日常實用短句 Useful Sentences

- This is Eric speaking.
  我是艾瑞克。
- May I speak to David, please?
  我可以跟大衛講電話嗎？
- Sorry, he's not here.
  不好意思，他不在這裡。
- May I take a message?
  您要留話嗎？
- Who's speaking?
  您是哪位？
- I'll call again later.
  我晚點再打。
- Hold on, please.
  請稍等。
- The line is busy.
  電話忙線中。
- May I leave a message?
  我可以留言嗎？
- He will return your call in the afternoon.
  他下午會回電給你。

學習++ More Tips

講電話的英文用語和一般講話的規則並不相通，比方說，當你要問「李小姐在嗎？」，你要說「Is this Miss Lee?」或是「Is Miss Lee there?」，而回答的那一方則要回答「Yes, this is Miss Lee.」（是，我就是。）、「Yes, this is she.」或是「This is Miss Lee speaking.」。

04 生日聚會

TRACK 004.

實境對話

Conversation

A: Oh! It has been a long time! ***Welcome***!

B: ***Happy Birthday***! This ***gift*** is for you.

A: ***It's*** very ***kind of*** you. May I open it now?

A: Oh, It's so beautiful. Just what I ***wanted***.

A: Please ***feel free to help yourself***.

A: Please ***relax*** and enjoy yourself!

A: Please come again!

A: 哦！好久不見，真歡迎你們來。

B: 生日快樂！這是給你的禮物。

A: 太謝謝你了。我可以現在打開嗎？

A: 哦，太漂亮了，這正是我一直想要擁有的東西。

A: 請享用，別客氣。

A: 請別拘束，隨便點。

A: 請再來玩！

核心詞彙

Words&Phrases

welcome	[ˋwɛlkɛm]	動詞 歡迎
happy birthday	[ˋhæpɪ ˋbɝθˏde]	片語 生日快樂
gift	[gɪft]	名詞 禮物
it's kind of sb.	[ɪts kaɪnd ɑv ˋsʌmˏbɑdɪ]	片語 ……人真好
want	[wɑnt]	動詞 想要
feel free to	[fil fri tu]	片語 隨意
help yourself	[hɛlp juɚˋsɛlf]	片語 自己來
relax	[rɪˋlæks]	動詞 放鬆

日常實用短句 Useful Sentences

- Happy birthday!
  生日快樂！
- Peter wants to throw a birthday party for his wife.
  彼得想為他老婆辦個生日派對。
- Help yourself.
  請自便。
- Enjoy the party.
  好好玩。
- He received the invitation card from Peter.
  他收到彼得的邀請卡。
- Blow out the candles.
  吹蠟燭。
- Have some drinks.
  喝點飲料。
- Make a wish, Julia.
  茱莉亞，許個願吧。
- Does anyone want more cakes?
  還有人想要蛋糕嗎？
- Wish you the best.
  祝福你。
- This is for you.
  這是給你的。
- Thank you. This is the best gift that I've got.
  謝謝，這是我收到最好的禮物。

學習++ More Tips

外國人喜歡辦「party」（派對），連小朋友的父母都會幫他們精心策劃一個有「games」（遊戲）、「present」（禮物）的「birthday party」（生日派對），而在收到禮物之後，外國人則有寫「thank you note／card」（感謝卡）的習慣，尤其是收到長輩的禮物。

05 感謝朋友幫忙

TRACK 005.

實境對話

Conversation

A: Oh, thank you so much, Bob. If you hadn't helped me last week, I wouldn't have ***finished*** the job ***on time***.

B: It's nothing. We are good friends and colleagues, aren't we? And you have often helped me.

A: It was such a difficult project. Without you, I wouldn't have ***completed*** it ***alone***. So I have to say thank you, ***anyhow***.

B: Glad I could help. If there's anything else I can do next time, please let me know.

A: I will. And you too.

A: 喔，非常謝謝你，鮑伯。上週如果不是你的幫忙，我就無法按時完成工作。

B: 沒什麼。我們是好朋友又是好同事，不是嗎？而且你也常幫我。

A: 那個計劃這麼困難，沒有你的話，我根本無法獨立完成。所以無論如何我還是要說謝謝。

B: 很高興幫得上忙。如果下次還有什麼我能效勞的，請讓我知道。

A: 我會的。你也是。

核心詞彙

Words&Phrases

finish	[ˋfɪnɪʃ]	動詞 完成
on time	[ɑn taɪm]	片語 準時
complete	[kəmˋplit]	動詞 完成
alone	[əˋlon]	副詞 單獨地
anyhow	[ˋɛnɪ͵haʊ]	副詞 無論如何

日常實用短句 Useful Sentences

- Thanks for your help.
  謝謝你的幫忙。
- You have been a good help.
  你幫了我一個大忙。
- I wouldn't accomplish this task without your help.
  如果沒有你的幫助，我無法完成這個任務。
- You're such a good friend.
  你真是個好朋友。
- You're so helpful.
  你對我真的很有幫助。
- How can I ever thank you enough!
  再怎樣都不夠感謝你！
- I'm glad that you can help.
  我很高興你能幫忙。
- No need to thank me.
  不用謝我。
- I'll probably need your help again soon.
  我可能很快就會再需要你的幫助了。
- I deeply appreciate your kindness.
  我真的非常感謝你的好心。

學習++ More Tips

當你說謝謝的時候，除了我們慣用的「thank you」、「thanks」之外，還可以說「I would like to express my gratitude to you.」（我想要跟你道謝。）、「I am much obliged to you.」（我非常的感謝你。）等等。

06 感謝朋友送禮

TRACK 006.

實境對話

Conversation

A: Happy birthday, Bob. This is for you.

B: Oh, thank you. It's very nice of you to ***remember*** my birthday. What is it?

A: A gift from all of my family. Open it and see what it is.

B: ***Good gracious***! You shouldn't have spent so much money for me. You are really too nice.

A: ***In fact***, all of our family would like to ***express*** our ***gratitude*** for your help when we moved to the new house in June.

B: Don't ***mention*** it. ***Piece of cake***.

A: But it was very helpful.

A: 生日快樂，鮑伯。這是給你的。

B: 哦，謝謝。你真好，還記得我的生日。這是什麼？

A: 我們全家人送你的禮物。打開看看。

B: 老天！你們不該為我花這麼多錢。你們真的太好了。

A: 其實，我們全家人都想謝謝你在六月時幫我們搬家 。

B: 哪兒的話。小事一樁罷了。

A: 但真的幫了很大的忙。

核心詞彙

Words&Phrases

remember	[rɪ`membɚ]	動詞 記得
good gracious	[gʊd `greʃəs]	片語 天啊
in fact	[ɪn fækt]	片語 事實上
express	[ɪk`sprɛs]	動詞 表達

gratitude	[ˋgrætə͵tjud]	名詞 感激之情、感謝
mention	[ˋmɛnʃən]	動詞 提起
piece of cake	[pis ɑv kek]	片語 小事一樁

日常實用短句 *Useful Sentences*

- Thanks for your gift.
  謝謝你的禮物。
- I really like it.
  我真的很喜歡。
- You're so sweet.
  你好貼心。
- May I open it?
  我可以打開嗎？
- What a lovely hat!
  好漂亮的帽子。
- This is the best gift I've ever got.
  這是我收過最好的禮物。
- This is a big surprise, thank you.
  這真是個大驚喜，謝謝你。
- This is exactly what I am looking for.
  這正是我想找的。
- You know me very well.
  你真的很了解我。
- I'm so moved.
  我真感動。

學習++ *More Tips*

我們通常會說：「Oh! My God!」（喔！我的天啊！），也可以比較含蓄的說：「Oh! My gosh!」，或是更優雅的感嘆「Good gracious!」（天啊！）。
「Piece of cake」是表示一件事很容易，不需要花什麼力氣就可以完成！

07 感謝朋友關心

TRACK 007.

實境對話

Conversation

A: ***What't the matter***, Bob? You ***look down***.

B: Nothing. Only that I ***failed in*** an ***interview*** for a job.

A: There are always two sides to everything. You can take it as an ***experience***. I know you will get a great job which you really want.

B: Thank you. I ***feel better*** now.

A: Take it easy. Let's go for a drink!

A: 怎麼了，鮑伯？你怎麼無精打采的。

B: 沒什麼。只是沒通過一個工作的面試。

A: 每件事都有兩面。你可以將它當成一次經驗。我知道你一定會找到一個你真正想要的工作。

B: 謝謝，我現在覺得好多了。

A: 放輕鬆點。我們去喝一杯吧！

核心詞彙

Words&Phrases

what's the matter	[hwɑts ðə ˋmætɚ]	片語 怎麼了
look	[lʊk]	動詞 看起來
down	[daʊn]	形容詞 情緒低落、消沉
fail in	[fel ɪn]	片語 失敗
interview	[ˋɪntɚˏvju]	名詞 面試
experience	[ɪkˋspɪrɪəns]	名詞 經驗
feel	[fil]	動詞 感到、感覺
better	[ˋbɛtɚ]	形容詞 更好的、較佳的

日常實用短句 *Useful Sentences*

- Thank you for your concern.
  謝謝你的關心。
- Thanks for staying with me when I needed help.
  謝謝你在我需要的時候陪在我身邊。
- Thanks from the bottom of my heart.
  打從心底感謝。
- I really care about you.
  我真的很關心你。
- Thanks you for listening to my complaints.
  謝謝你聽我抱怨。
- I'm very grateful.
  我真的很感激。
- I really appreciate your time.
  我真的很感謝你花的時間。
- You are so considerate.
  你真的很體貼。
- That's very nice of you.
  你人真的很好。
- I am thankful that you are always there for me.
  我很感謝你總是守候在我身邊。
- Thank you for your loving care.
  謝謝你真誠的愛護。
- I'm so glad that you're always by my side.
  我真的很開心你總是在我身邊。

學習++ *More Tips*

「look down in the mouth」是指看起來無精打采，而想要安慰朋友你就可以說：「Please cheer up.」（開心一點吧！），「Don't look so down! Be happy!」（別看起來那麼難過，開心一點嘛！）。

08 恭賀朋友升遷

TRACK 008.

實境對話 Conversation

A: Hi, Bob. I heard that you ***were promoted to*** Managing Director of your company.

B: Yeah, I was ***quite surprised***, too.

A: But it's not at all ***unexpected***. You always did such an ***outstanding*** job. Congratulations on your ***promotion***.

B: Thank you very much. I hope I'll ***be able to*** do better.

A: You ***certainly*** will.

A: 嗨，鮑伯。聽說你被升為公司的協理了。

B: 是啊，我自己也很意外。

A: 一點也不意外呢！你的工作一直都表現得很傑出，恭喜你高升。

B: 多謝了。希望我能做得更好。

A: 你會的。

核心詞彙 Words&Phrases

be promoted to	[bi prəˋmotɪd tu]	片語 晉升
quite	[kwaɪt]	副詞 相當地、頗
surprised	[səˋpraɪzd]	形容詞 驚訝的
unexpected	[ˏʌnɪkˋspɛktɪd]	形容詞 想不到的
outstanding	[ˋautˏstændɪŋ]	形容詞 傑出的
promotion	[prəˋmoʃən]	名詞 升遷
be able to	[be ˋebl̩ tu]	片語 能夠……
certainly	[ˋsɝtənlɪ]	副詞 無疑地

日常實用短句 Useful Sentences

- I'm so proud of you.
  我真為你感到驕傲。
- You deserve it.
  這是你該得的。
- Your hard work finally got paid off.
  你這麼努力工作終於有回報了。
- This promotion shows your impressive ability and accomplishments.
  這次升遷就代表你傑出的能力和成就。
- Let's go celebrate your promotion with a drink!
  讓我們去喝一杯慶祝你升職吧！
- Your hard work finally got recognized!
  你的努力終於受到賞識了。
- It's about time that the company recognized your efforts.
  你的付出也是時候受到公司的賞識了。
- I wish you the best in your future career.
  祝福你的前途一片光明。
- You are the most deserving person for this position.
  你應該是最配得上這個位置的人。
- For all your achievements, you deserve this promotion!
  依你的成就，你值得這個位置。
- Please accept our sincere congratulations on your recent accomplishments.
  請接受我們對你的成就最真摯的道賀。

學習++ More Tips

「Congratulations!」就是我們中文裡的「恭喜」，除了可以用來恭賀朋友升遷之外，有人生日、結婚或是中國人過年的時候都可以說「Congratulations!」。

09 恭賀朋友結婚

TRACK 009.

實境對話

Conversation

A: ***Congratulations on*** your ***marriage***. I have ***waited for*** years to ***say*** this ***sentence***. You're so beautiful today.

B: Thank you very much, and for coming today.

A: Where are you going for the ***honeymoon***?

B: We'***re going to*** Canada.

A: ***Bon voyage***!

A: 恭喜你們結婚了。我等著說這句話已經好多年了。妳今天好漂亮。

B: 多謝，還要謝謝你今天來。

A: 你們要去哪裡度蜜月？

B: 我們要去加拿大。

A: 一路順風。

核心詞彙

Words&Phrases

congratulations on	[kən͵grætʃə`leʃənz ɑn]	片語 恭喜……
marriage	[`mærɪdʒ]	名詞 婚姻
wait for	[wet fɔr]	片語 等候
say	[se]	動詞 說
sentence	[sɛntəns]	名詞 句子
honeymoon	[`hʌnɪ͵mun]	名詞 蜜月旅行
be going to	[bi `goɪŋ tu]	片語 正要去……
bon voyage	[bɑn `vɔɪɪdʒ]	片語 一路順風

日常實用短句 Useful Sentences

- Happy wedding!
  新婚快樂。
- Thank you for sharing our day.
  謝謝你來參加。
- A big congratulation to you both.
  給你們兩個特大號的祝福。
- From this day forward, may love and happiness fill your hearts.
  從今以後，希望你們的心裡充滿愛和幸福。
- You two are a very cute couple together.
  你們兩個是很可愛的一對。
- May your wedding day be filled with love and happiness.
  祝你的婚禮充滿愛和喜悅。
- What a sweet wedding!
  多可愛的婚禮啊！
- You're the most beautiful bride ever.
  你是最漂亮的新娘。
- Wish you both all the luck and happiness that life can offer.
  祝福你們生活充滿好運和喜悅。
- Wishing you lifelong happiness!
  祝你一輩子幸福快樂！

學習++ More Tips

以下是婚禮上一些角色的英文：「bride」（新娘）、「groom」（新郎）、「bride's maid」（伴娘）、「best man」（伴郎）。
「Bon voyage」是「一路順風」的意思，它其實原本是法文。

10 恭賀朋友得獎

TRACK 010.

實境對話

Conversation

A: Congratulations, Mary. I ***read*** in the ***newspaper*** that you won the ***National*** Scientist ***Award*** this year. I knew you would.

B: Oh, thank you, Bob. You're always a ***faithful supporter*** of my ***career***. Indeed, I got a lot of help from my colleagues. I really want to ***share*** this ***honor*** with them.

A: 恭喜你，瑪麗。我在報上看到，妳榮獲今年的國家科學家獎。我就知道妳會得獎。

B: 哦，謝謝你，鮑伯。你一直是我事業上的忠實支持者。其實我的同事也幫了很大的忙。我真想和他們一起分享這份榮耀。

核心詞彙

Words&Phrases

read	[rid]	動詞 讀
newspaper	[ˋnjuzˏpepɚ]	名詞 報紙
national	[ˋnæʃənḷ]	形容詞 國家性的
award	[əˋwɔrd]	名詞 獎項
faithful	[ˋfeθfəl]	形容詞 忠實的
supporter	[səˋportɚ]	名詞 支持者
career	[kəˋrɪr]	名詞 事業
share	[ʃɛr]	動詞 分享
honor	[ˋɑnɚ]	名詞 榮耀

日常實用短句 Useful Sentences

- Congratulations to you on winning the competition.
  恭喜你贏得這場比賽。
- I am really proud of your achievement.
  我真為你的成就感到驕傲。
- This was not an easy task to accomplish.
  這不是一件容易完成的任務。
- Keep up with the great work!
  繼續加油！
- You spent a lot of time on this, and the hard work finally got paid off.
  你花很多時間在這上面，而努力終於有成果了。
- How are you going to celebrate your success?
  你要怎麼慶祝這次的成功？
- You have completed a difficult task.
  你完成了一項困難的任務。
- Now that you have achieved your goal, what will you do next?
  現在你完成你的目標了，那下一步是什麼呢？
- Good job on beating out the rest of the competition.
  你打敗了其他對手，做得好。
- Tell us how you made it.
  告訴我們你是怎麼做到的。
- You completed what others could not.
  你做到了別人做不到的。

學習++ More Tips

祝賀朋友得獎的時候還可以說：「I am so happy for you.」（我真為你感到高興。）、「I am so proud of you.」（我真為你感到驕傲。）、「You really deserve this award.」（這個獎是你應得的。）等等。

11 慰問朋友生病

TRACK011.

實境對話

Conversation

A: I've heard that you are ***ill***. What's the matter?

B: This morning I felt tired and ***lack luster***.

A: You've been studying so hard for the ***final***. You probably ***got sick***.

B: That's right. I've hardly had ***a wink of sleep***.

A: ***Take a rest***. And you'll be okay Otherwise, you will have to ***see the doctor***.

B: I know. Thank you for coming.

A: 聽說你生病啦。怎麼了？

B: 今天早上覺得很累，而且沒有精神。

A: 你為了準備期末考太用功了。可能生病了。

B: 沒錯。我幾乎徹夜未眠。

A: 休息一下。就會好的。不然你就得去看醫生了。

B: 我曉得。謝謝你來。

核心詞彙

Words&Phrases

ill	[ɪl]	形容詞 生病的
lack	[læk]	動詞 缺少
luster	[ˋlʌstɚ]	名詞 精神、光采
final	[ˋfaɪnḷ]	名詞 期末考
get sick	[gɛt sɪk]	片語 生病
a wink of sleep	[ə wɪnk ɑv slip]	片語 小睡
take a rest	[tek ə rɛst]	片語 休息一下
see the doctor	[si ðə ˋdɑktɚ]	片語 看醫生

日常實用短句 Useful Sentences

- Get well soon.
  快好起來。
- Take good care of yourself.
  好好照顧自己。
- I hope you feel better soon.
  希望你很快好起來。
- I'm sorry to hear that you're sick.
  聽說你生病了，真遺憾。
- Do you feel better?
  好點了嗎？
- You need more rest.
  你需要多休息。
- I'm distressed to hear of your illness.
  我很難過聽到你生病了。
- Eat well and stay healthy.
  正常飲食，保持健康。
- You should take a good rest.
  你需要好好休息。
- I hope to see you up and about soon.
  我希望看到你趕快好起來。
- Best wishes for your recovery.
  祝你早日康復。
- I hope there is nothing serious of your sickness.
  我希望你的病沒有什麼大礙。

學習++ More Tips

「wink」當動詞的時候是指「眨（眼）」：「She winked her eyes.」（她眨了眨眼。）；當名詞的時候是指「眨眼」：「She gave me a knowing wink.」（她向我眨了眼表示她知道了。）。

12 慰問朋友失戀

TRACK012.

實境對話

Conversation

A: I've heard that you and your girl friend have ***broken up***.

B: Yes, we had a big ***quarrel*** two weeks ago.

A: If I were you, I would ***forget*** her and ***get over*** it soon. I've heard that she ***loses her temper*** easily, doesn't she?

B: That's right. So we quarreled a lot.

A: There must be somebody ***suitable*** for you waiting for you somewhere.

B: I hope you are right.

A: 聽說你和女朋友分手了。

B: 沒錯，我們兩星期前大吵了一架。

A: 如果我是你的話，就會很快忘掉她，從失戀中恢復。我聽說她很容易生氣，是不是？

B: 沒錯。所以我們經常吵架。

A: 一定還有適合你的人在某處等你。

B: 希望你說得對。

核心詞彙

Words&Phrases

break up	[brek ʌp]	片語 分手
quarrel	[ˋkwɔrəl]	名詞 爭吵
forget	[fɚˋgɛt]	動詞 忘掉
get over	[gɛt ˋovɚ]	片語 克服、恢復
lose one's temper	[luz wʌns ˋtɛmpɚ]	片語 發脾氣
suitable	[ˋsutəbl̩]	形容詞 適合的

日常實用短句 Useful Sentences

- I broke up with my boyfriend.
  我和男朋友分手了。
- Are you going to be ok?
  你還好嗎？
- I know how you feel.
  我知道你的感受。
- It must be tough for you.
  你一定很難熬。
- He is not the right person for you.
  他不是對的人。
- You deserve someone better.
  你值得更好的。
- She broke my heart.
  她傷了我的心。
- Next one will be better.
  下一個會更好。
- No one can be treated this way.
  沒有人應該被這樣對待。
- It is actually kind of pity.
  實在有點可惜。
- I feel sad for you.
  我替你感到難過。
- I am proud of your decision.
  我為你的決定感到難過。

學習++ More Tips

當情侶分手的時候，總是有一堆的解釋如：「We are not suitable for each other.」（我們不適合對方。）、「We are not compatible.」（我們不合適。）、「The fire just died between us.」（我們之間已經沒有感覺了。）、「I can not stand him any more.」（我不能夠再忍受他了！）等等。

13 慰問朋友工作不順

TRACK013.

實境對話

Conversation

A: How's it going these days?

B: I got a ***stern reprimand*** from my boss, because I lost a ***major account***. It was not ***on purpose***.

A: Certainly not. Nobody would lose a ***client*** on purpose. We all know you ***work*** very ***hard***. But sometimes, it's just ***unlucky***.

B: Thank you for saying that. I feel better now.

A: 最近怎麼樣？

B: 被老闆臭罵了一頓，因為我丟了一個大客戶。我又不是故意的。

A: 當然不是。沒有人會故意丟掉客戶。我們都知道你工作很努力。但有時候就是那麼倒楣。

B: 謝謝你那樣說。我覺得好多了。

核心詞彙

Words&Phrases

stern	[stɝn]	形容詞 嚴厲的、苛刻的
reprimand	[ˋrɛprəˌmænd]	名詞 譴責、訓斥
major	[ˋmedʒɚ]	形容詞 主要的
account	[əˋkaʊnt]	名詞 客戶
on purpose	[ɑn ˋpɝpəs]	片語 故意
client	[ˋklaɪənt]	名詞 客戶
work hard	[wɝk hɑrd]	片語 工作努力
unlucky	[ʌnˋlʌkɪ]	形容詞 倒楣、不幸運

日常實用短句 Useful Sentences

- What's bothering you?
  你在煩惱什麼？
- You should discuss with your boss for the problems that you have at work.
  你工作上遇到的問題，應該跟你的老闆討論。
- Pull yourself together.
  振作起來。
- You should have confident in your profession.
  你應該對自己的專業有信心。
- Tomorrow is another day.
  明天又是新的一天。
- Look at the bright side.
  看好的那一面。
- It's not the end of the world.
  又不是世界末日。
- Your co-workers should treat you with more respect.
  你的同事應該更尊重你一點。
- I think your boss has been unfair.
  我覺得你的老闆不公平。
- Take one step at a time.
  一步一步來。
- Things will get better.
  事情會更好的。

學習++ More Tips

以下是一些表達沒工作或是被炒魷魚的說法：「I got fired today.」（我今天被炒魷魚了。）、「I got laid off today.」（我今天被開除了。）、「I am out of work.」（我沒工作了。）、「I am unemployed.」（我沒工作了。）等等。

14 慰問朋友親人去世

TRACK014.

實境對話

Conversation

A: I was ***shocked*** to hear that your ***mother-in-law passed away*** last week. She was such a kind woman, and ***treated*** me as her own son.

B: Yeah. My wife still cannot accept it. She's so sad that she has not returned to work yet.

A: When will the ***funeral*** be?

B: Next Tuesday.

A: There's never anything that can be said to make it better, but I hope you will ***count on*** me for help ***if necessary***.

B: Thank you so much.

A: 聽到你岳母上週過世，實在很震驚。她實在是個親切的人，對我就好像對自己的兒子一樣。

B: 是啊。我太太仍然無法接受這個事實。她難過得到現在都還無法上班。

A: 葬禮什麼時候舉行？

B: 下星期二。

A: 現在說什麼也沒用，不過如果有需要，希望你儘管開口。

B: 太謝謝你了。

核心詞彙

Words&Phrases

shocked	[ʃɑkt]	形容詞 震驚的
mother-in-law	[ˋmʌðərɪnˏlɔ]	名詞 岳母、婆婆
pass away	[pæs əˋwe]	片語 過世
treat	[trit]	動詞 對待

funeral	[ˋfjunərəl]	名詞 喪禮
count on	[kaʊnt ɑn]	片語 依賴、指望
if necessary	[ɪfˋnɛsəˏsɛrɪ]	形容詞 如果必要的話

日常實用短句 Useful Sentences

- I'm so sorry to hear that.
  很遺憾聽到這個。
- A friend of mine just passed away last Saturday.
  我有一個朋友上個禮拜六過世了。
- He must be very devastated.
  他一定感到心力交瘁。
- Only close friends and family are invited.
  只會邀請親近的親朋好友。
- I am not in the mood to work.
  我沒心情工作。
- The funeral is on Sunday.
  喪禮在禮拜日。
- Let us know if there is anything we can do.
  有什麼需要我們幫忙的儘管說。
- Please be strong for the rest of your family.
  為了其他的家人，你要堅強起來。
- I'm so sorry for your loss.
  我很遺憾你所失去的。
- My thoughts and prayers are with you.
  我的關心和祈禱與你同在。

學習++ More Tips

當慰問朋友、親人去世的時候你可以說：「I am sorry.」（我覺得很難過、抱歉。）、「Please pull yourself together.」（請你保重自己）、「Please take care.」（請保重。）等等。

15 婚宴

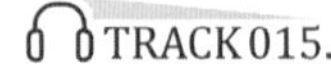

實境對話

Conversation

A: Congratulations, I am the ***bride***'s colleague. My name is Michiko. Nice to meet you!

B: Thank you very much! Please ***bring*** the ***red envelope*** over here.

A: It must be ***tough*** for you today!

B: Please sign your name.

A: You are the most beautiful bride!

B: Thanks for your ***compliments***!

A: May lots of ***blessings*** be with you both!

B: Thanks for attending our ***wedding feast***!

A: 今天真是非常恭喜，我是新娘的同事叫美智子。請多指教。

B: 非常謝謝您！紅包請拿到這邊登記。

A: 你今天辛苦了！

B: 請到這裡簽名。

A: 妳真是最美麗的新娘！

B: 謝謝妳的稱讚！

A: 祝你們永遠幸福！

B: 謝謝妳來參加我們的婚宴！

核心詞彙

Words&Phrases

bride	[braɪd]	名詞 新娘
bring	[brɪŋ]	動詞 帶
red envelope	[rɛd ˋɛnvə͵lop]	名詞 紅包
tough	[tʌf]	形容詞 辛苦的、費勁的

compliment	[ˋkɑmpləmənt]	名詞 恭維、讚美的話
blessing	[ˋblɛsɪŋ]	名詞 祝福
wedding feast	[ˋwɛdɪŋ fist]	名詞 婚宴

日常實用短句 *Useful Sentences*

- When is the wedding?
  婚禮在什麼時候？
- The wedding ceremony will be held in the chapel.
  婚禮會在教堂舉行。
- They'll have a honeymoon in Hawaii.
  他們會去夏威夷度蜜月。
- My best friend, Alex, is my best man.
  我的伴郎是我最好的朋友艾力克斯。
- My dad will walk down the aisle with me.
  我爸會牽我走紅毯。
- This is the most important day in my life.
  這是我人生中最重要的日子。
- The guests are here already.
  賓客們都到了。
- The dinner will start at 6:00 PM.
  晚宴會在六點開始。
- Let's toast the bride and groom.
  讓我們一起敬新娘和新郎。
- What a wonderful wedding!
  真棒的婚禮！

學習++ *More Tips*

「tough」原本的意思是「堅韌的、強壯的」，我們可以說：「He is a tough guy.」（他是一個強壯的人）；但在這裡表示「艱難的、費力的」，「This is a tough job.」（這個工作很困難。）。

16 道謝

TRACK016.

實境對話

Conversation

A: Thank you ***very much*** for your ***help***.
B: It's my ***pleasure*** to do ***something*** for you.

A: Thank you for ***helping me out***.
B: It's nothing. Don't mention it.

A: Thank you very much ***indeed***.
B: ***Not at all***.

A: It's very kind of you!
B: ***You are welcome***.

A: 很謝謝你的幫忙。
B: 能為你效勞，是我的榮幸。

A: 承蒙您的關照。
B: 小事一件，不足掛齒。

A: 誠摯地感謝你。
B: 哪裡，不要客氣。

A: 你人真好！
B: 別客氣。

核心詞彙

Words&Phrases

very much	[ˋvɛrɪ mʌtʃ]	片語 非常
help	[hɛlp]	名詞 幫助
pleasure	[ˋplɛʒɚ]	名詞 榮幸
something	[ˋsʌmθɪŋ]	名詞 某事
help sb. out	[hɛlp ˏsʌmˏbɑdɪ aʊt]	片語 幫……的忙
indeed	[ɪnˋdid]	副詞 真正地
not at all	[nɑt æt ɔl]	片語 別客氣
you are welcome	[ju ɑr ˋwɛlkəm]	片語 不客氣

日常實用短句 *Useful Sentences*

- Thank you.
  謝謝你。
- No sweat.
  沒什麼。
- Not at all.
  別客氣。
- Thanks a lot.
  真的很謝謝。
- Any time.
  不客氣。
- Thank you very much.
  非常謝謝你。
- I owe you one.
  欠你一次。
- I really appreciate it.
  我真的很感謝。
- So sweet of you.
  你真好。
- Thanks for your kindness.
  謝謝你的好心。
- I'm very grateful.
  我真的很感激。
- Don't mention it.
  不足掛齒。

學習++ *More Tips*

所謂禮多人不怪，當有人跟你表達謝意的時候，你也可以很客氣的回話「You're welcome.」（不客氣。）、「 Don't mention it.」（別提了。）、「My pleasure.」（我的榮幸。）、「Not at all.」（不會。）或是「No trouble at all.」（一點都不麻煩。）。

17 致歉

TRACK017.

實境對話

Conversation

A: Ah! I'm ***sorry***.
B: That's ok.

A: That's my ***fault***.
B: ***Don't worry***.

A: I do ***apologize***.
B: ***Never mind***.

A: I feel ***ashamed***, and have ***nothing to say***.
B: Everybody ***makes mistakes***.

A: 啊！對不起。
B: 沒關係。

A: 是我的錯。
B: 別擔心。

A: 實在很抱歉。
B: 別在意。

A: 我感到很羞愧，無言以對。
B: 每個人都會犯錯。

核心詞彙

Words&Phrases

sorry	[ˋsɑrɪ]	形容詞 感到抱歉的
fault	[fɔlt]	名詞 錯誤
don't worry	[dont wɝɪ]	片語 別擔心
apologize	[əˋpɑləˏdʒaɪz]	動詞 道歉
never mind	[ˋnɛvɚ maɪnd]	片語 別在意
ashamed	[əˋʃemd]	形容詞 羞愧的
nothing to say	[ˋnʌθɪŋ tu se]	片語 沒什麼好說

make mistake	[mek mɪˋstek]	**片語** 犯錯

日常實用短句 Useful Sentences

- Please accept my apology.
  請接受我的道歉。
- Please forgive me.
  請原諒我。
- I must apologize for being so careless.
  我一定要為我的粗心道歉。
- I'm sorry for giving you so much trouble.
  我很抱歉給你添這麼多麻煩。
- My apologies.
  我道歉。
- This is my mistake.
  是我的錯。
- That's the least I can do.
  這是我至少能做的。
- I beg you for your forgiveness.
  我請求你的原諒。
- Sorry the inconvenience.
  抱歉添麻煩。
- I'll make it up to you.
  我會補償你的。
- I am terribly sorry.
  我真的非常抱歉。
- I didn't mean it.
  我不是故意的。

學習++ More Tips

在跟別人致歉時，除了「I am sorry.」（我很抱歉。）之外，你也可以說「I apologize.」（我道歉。），或是說「Please forgive me.」（請原諒我。）。

18 付帳

TRACK 018.

實境對話

Conversation

A: I would like to ***pay*** my ***bill***.

B: Ok, Please wait a moment.

B: The ***total*** is one thousand five hundred and twenty dollars.

A: Do you accept ***credit cards***?

A: Let's ***go dutch***.

A: Let's share the bill.

B: ***Be my guest***.

B: Please ***keep the change***.

B: The ***receipt***, please.

A:我想買單。

B:是。請稍待。

B:總共一千五百二十元。

A:收信用卡嗎？

A:我們各付各的。

A:我們大家平均分攤。

B:我請客。

B:零錢不用找了。

B:請給我發票。

核心詞彙

Words&Phrases

pay bill	[pe bɪl]	片語 付帳
total	[ˋtotl̩]	名詞 總數、合計
credit card	[ˋkrɛdɪt kɑrd]	名詞 信用卡
go dutch	[go dʌtʃ]	片語 各付各的
be my guest	[bi maɪ gɛst]	片語 我請客

keep the change	[kip ðə tʃendʒ]	片語 不用找零
receipt	[rɪˋsit]	名詞 發票

日常實用短句 Useful Sentences

- This is my treat.
  我請客。
- Let's go Dutch.
  我們各付各的吧。
- Let me pay the bill.
  我付帳吧。
- Be my guest.
  我請客。
- It's on me.
  算在我的帳上。
- It's on the house.
  我請客。
- Let me get this one.
  讓我來付。
- We'd like the bill, please.
  麻煩給我們帳單。
- Could you give us separate checks?
  可以分開付嗎？
- Why don't you get it next time, John?
  約翰，下次再給你付吧。

學習++ More Tips

用餐付賬的時候，「waiter」（侍者）都會問你：「How would you like to pay?」（你想要如何付帳？），你可以用「credit card」（信用卡）、「cash」（現金）或是「check」（支票）。當你想請朋友的時候你就可以說：「This is my treat.」（讓我請吧！）、「It's on me.」（算在我的帳上。）、「Let me be the host today.」（今天讓我做東。）。

19 告辭

TRACK 019.

實境對話

Conversation

A: What a ***pity***! I ***have to leave*** now.

B: It's still ***early***! ***Why not*** stay here longer?

A: No. I don't want to ***bother*** you.

B: Not at all. If you have time, please come again!

A: Well, I need to say good-bye now.

B: Please ***take care***!

A: Please send my ***regards*** to the others.

B: Good-bye!

A: Good-bye!

A: 真遺憾，我不回去不行了。
B: 還早呢！多坐一會兒吧！
A: 不了，已經打擾太久了。
B: 哪裡的話，有空請再來玩！
A: 那麼，我現在得告辭了。
B: 請多保重。
A: 請向大家問好。
B: 再見。
A: 再見。

核心詞彙

Words&Phrases

pity	[ˋpɪtɪ]	名詞 可惜、遺憾
have to	[hæv tu]	片語 必須
leave	[liv]	動詞 離開
early	[ˋɝlɪ]	形容詞 早的
why not...?	[hwaɪ nɑt]	片語 為什麼不……？

bother	[ˋbaðɚ]	動詞 打擾
take care	[tek kɛr]	片語 保重
regard	[rɪˋgɑrd]	名詞 問候、致意

日常實用短句 Useful Sentences

- See you later.
  待會見。
- I got to go.
  我得走了。
- Thank you for your hospitality.
  感謝你的熱情款待。
- I must leave now.
  我得走了。
- I'm leaving.
  我要走了。
- I really have to go.
  我真的該走了。
- Catch you later.
  待會見。
- I hope to see you soon.
  希望很快見到你。
- I really had a great time.
  我玩的很開心。
- Give me a call sometimes.
  偶爾打個電話給我。

學習++ More Tips

當跟別人道別時，除了「goodbye」之外，我們還可以說「see you」，較口語的如「later」（see you later 的簡短說法）、「bye bye」，或是俏皮的說上一句俚語「See you later alligator.」（等會兒，見鱷魚先生。）。

20 用餐禮儀

TRACK 020.

實境對話

Conversation

A: Mr. Brown. This is our ***traditional*** seat for the guest of honor. Please sit down.

B: Thank you for giving me so much attention.

A: Our pleasure. Would you like to use ***chopsticks*** or a ***fork*** and a ***knife***?

B: While in Rome, do as the Romans do. I'll use the chopsticks.

A: Fine. ***Here you are***.

B: OK. I'll have a try. Wow, it's not that difficult to use chopsticks as my friend said.

A: You are doing great, Mr. Brown. Why not try our hand-pulled noodles with chopsticks?

B: OK. Big challenge.

A: 布朗先生。這是我國傳統的貴賓席。請上座。

B: 謝謝給我這麼多的關照。

A: 我們的榮幸。請問您是要用筷子呢，還是刀叉呢？

B: 入境隨俗。我就用筷子吧。

A: 很好。給您。

B: 嗯。我要試試看。哇，用筷子沒有我的朋友說的那麼難嘛。

A: 布朗先生，您做得很好呢。要不要用筷子嚐嚐我們的拉麵呢？

B: 好的。很大的挑戰啊。

核心詞彙

Words&Phrases

traditional	[trəˋdɪʃənl̩]	形容詞 傳統的
chopsticks	[ˋtʃɑpˏstɪks]	名詞 筷子

fork	[fɔrk]	名詞 叉子
knife	[naɪf]	名詞 刀
here you are	[hɪr ju ɑr]	片語 給你、拿去

日常實用短句 Useful Sentences

- That smells wonderful.
  聞起來很香。
- Excuse me. Could I have an extra fork, please?
  不好意思，能給我另一支叉子嗎？
- May I have some more juice, please?
  請給我多點果汁。
- Can I refill the coke, please?
  我可以續杯可樂嗎？
- Just relax and enjoy the meal.
  放輕鬆，好好享受這一餐吧。
- That fish really hit the spot.
  這魚正合我意。
- The steak was really good.
  牛排很好吃。
- Are you full, Steven?
  史帝夫，你飽了嗎？
- I wish I could eat more, but I'm stuffed.
  真希望我還能多吃點，但我真的飽了。
- Could we get this to go?
  我們可以把這個打包嗎？

學習++ More Tips

「try」一般做動詞用，如：「Let me try.」（讓我試試看！）；做名詞用時，則可說：「I'll have a try!」（我來試試看！）；若要鼓勵對方嘗試，可以說：「Why don't you give it a try?」（你為何不試試看呢？）。

PART ❶ 社交禮儀篇

你都記住了嗎？

從各篇「日常實用短句」裡整理出外國人常用的單字和片語，如果背起來了，就在前方空格打個勾吧！

☐ ages
名詞 很長時間

☐ allow me to...
片語 允許我……

☐ coworker
名詞 同事

☐ take a message
片語 （幫對方）留言

☐ leave a message
片語 （自己）留言

☐ hold on
片語 稍等

☐ throw a party
片語 舉辦派對

☐ invitation card
名詞 邀請卡

☐ make a wish
片語 許願

☐ accomplish
動詞 完成

☐ kindness
名詞 好意

☐ surprise
名詞 驚喜

☐ moved
形容詞 感動的

☐ concern
名詞 關心

☐ stay with me
片語 陪在我身邊

☐ considerate
形容詞 體貼的

☐ by my side
片語 在我身邊

☐ be proud of
片語 為……感到驕傲

☐ deserve
動詞 該得

☐ get paid off
片語 得到回報

☐ get recognized
片語 受到賞識

☐ sincere
形容詞 真誠的

☐ happiness
名詞 幸福快樂

☐ bride
名詞 新娘

☐ luck
名詞 好運

☐ competition
名詞 競爭、比賽

- ☐ achievement
  名詞 成就
- ☐ keep up
  片語 保持
- ☐ goal
  名詞 目標
- ☐ good job
  片語 幹得好
- ☐ take care
  片語 保重、小心
- ☐ distressed
  形容詞 憂傷的
- ☐ up and about
  片語 能起床走動的
- ☐ recovery
  名詞 康復
- ☐ tough
  形容詞 棘手的
- ☐ break one's heart
  片語 傷某人的心
- ☐ kind of
  片語 有點
- ☐ pity
  名詞 可惜
- ☐ pull oneself together
  片語 振作起來
- ☐ unfair
  形容詞 不公平
- ☐ get better
  片語 好起來
- ☐ devastated
  形容詞 身心交瘁的
- ☐ in the mood for sth.
  片語 有心情做某事
- ☐ loss
  名詞 損失
- ☐ ceremony
  名詞 儀式
- ☐ best man
  名詞 伴郎
- ☐ toast
  動詞 敬酒
- ☐ groom
  名詞 新郎
- ☐ forgive
  動詞 原諒
- ☐ mistake
  名詞 錯誤
- ☐ make up
  片語 補償
- ☐ my treat
  片語 我請客
- ☐ go dutch
  片語 各付各的
- ☐ separate
  形容詞 分開的
- ☐ hospitality
  名詞 好客
- ☐ give me a call
  片語 打電話給我
- ☐ refill
  動詞 再裝滿、續杯
- ☐ hit the spot
  片語 正如我意
- ☐ full
  形容詞 吃飽的
- ☐ to go
  片語 外帶

Part 2 娛樂消費篇－音檔連結

因各家手機系統不同，若無法直接掃描，仍可以至以下電腦雲端連結下載收聽。

（https://tinyurl.com/2arwryn7）

PART 2

娛樂消費篇

01 電影欣賞

TRACK 021.

實境對話 Conversation

A: Akiko, are you ***free*** tonight? I would like to ***invite*** you to ***see a movie***.

B: What's on tonight?

A: Avatar. It is ***the best selling*** and most popular movie this year.

B: When does it start?

A: 7:30 in the evening.

B: Ok! Let's go together!

A: Please give me two tickets ***in the middle***.

C: Ok. 300 dollars in total.

A: 昭子，妳今天晚上有空嗎？我想請妳一起去看電影。

B: 今晚在演什麼電影呢？

A: 阿凡達，它是今年最暢銷、受歡迎的電影。

B: 那麼幾點開始呢？

A: 晚上七點半。

B: 好啊！我們一起去吧！

A: 請給我兩張靠中間的票。

C: 好的，總共 300 元。

核心詞彙 Words&Phrases

free	[fri]	形容詞 有空的、自由的
invite	[ɪnˋvaɪt]	動詞 邀請
see a movie	[si ə ˋmuvɪ]	片語 看電影
the best selling	[ðə bɛst ˋsɛlɪŋ]	片語 最暢銷
in the middle	[ɪn ðə ˋmɪdl̩]	片語 在中間

日常實用短句 Useful Sentences

- Please switch off your cell phone.
  手機請關機。
- Would you mind exchanging seats with me?
  你介意跟我換個座位嗎？
- This movie is a box office hit.
  這部片票房很好。
- This movie got mixed reviews.
  這部片的評價毀譽參半。
- Who is the leading actor in this film?
  這部片的男主角是誰？
- Meryl Streep, the supporting actress in this film, is my favorite actress.
  這部片的女配角——梅莉史翠普，是我最喜歡的女演員。
- I prefer documentary films to feature films.
  我喜歡看紀錄片更勝於劇情片。
- This Ang Lee's film is a blockbuster of the year.
  這部李安的電影是今年的強檔影片。
- The leading actress' acting is really outstanding.
  女主角的演技真是出色。
- The cast of the movie isn't very strong but the story is impressing.
  這部電影的演員陣容不是很強，但是劇情很感人。

學習++ More Tips

去看電影最享受的莫過於一邊欣賞電影一邊吃著「popcorn」（爆米花）了。而約女生出去看電影時，可以用以下的句子：「Would you go to the movies with me?」（妳願意跟我去看電影嗎？）、「Do I have the pleasure to take you to the movies?」（我有榮幸請妳看電影嗎？）、「How about going to the movies tonight?」「妳覺得今晚去看場電影如何？」等等。

02 KTV

TRACK 022.

實境對話 Conversation

A: Folks, how about going to the KTV after work?

B: I'm an ***idiot musically***. I can't ***sing***.

C: Don't worry. KTV is lots of ***fun***. You can just relax and enjoy your drink.

(After work)

A: Alan, would you like to ***pick*** several ***songs*** first?

C: Well, English songs, Japanese songs, Mandarin songs and Taiwanese songs, which one should I start with?

C: How about this? Start with me, I'll sing a song of Gowai Mayomi's called"Lover".

A: 各位，下班後大家一起去唱 KTV 怎麼樣？

B: 我是個音樂白痴，不會唱歌。

C: 別擔心， KTV 很好玩，你在一旁喝飲料休息也可以。

（下班後）

A: 亞倫，你要不要先選幾首歌？

C: 嗯，英文歌、日文歌、國語歌還有台語歌，到底該從哪兒開始呢？

C: 這樣吧！由我先開始唱一首五輪真弓的「戀人」吧！

核心詞彙 Words&Phrases

idiot	[ˋɪdɪət]	名詞 白痴
musically	[ˋmjuzɪkḷɪ]	副詞 音樂上地
sing	[sɪŋ]	動詞 唱歌
fun	[fʌn]	名詞 樂趣
pick	[pɪk]	動詞 挑選

song	[sɔŋ]	**名詞** 歌曲

日常實用短句 *Useful Sentences*

- This music video is lousy.
  這支音樂錄影帶很瞎。
- Don't you snatch at my microphone.
  你別想要搶我的麥克風。
- I'll discontinue this song.
  我要把這首歌切掉。
- My throat is getting soar.
  我喉嚨越來越痛了。
- His husky voice is suitable for this song.
  他嘶啞的聲音很適合唱這首歌。
- I'm not familiar with the melody.
  我對這首歌的旋律不太熟。
- I've never heard this song before.
  我從來沒聽過這首歌。
- You have a beautiful voice.
  你的聲音很好聽耶。
- Sorry, I was off-key.
  抱歉，我走音了。
- You sang this song better than the original performer.
  你這首歌唱得比原唱還好。
- Do you mind that I insert a song?
  你介意我插播一首歌嗎？

學習++ *More Tips*

KTV 在台灣算是大家的娛樂消遣之一，而 KTV 在美國現在也慢慢興起了。當你想表達自己不會唱歌，除了直接說「I can't sing.」（我不會唱歌。）， 你還可以說「I can't carry a tune.」（我沒有音感。）。

03 歌劇欣賞

TRACK 023.

實境對話

Conversation

A: What's on at the National Theater now?

B: A very famous ***musical*** called"Cats".

A: ***What kind of*** story is it?

B: The world from a cat's ***point of view***.

A: Are kids also allowed to watch this ***show***?

B: That's the only musical kids are allowed to watch.

A: I'm worried about hardly understanding what they are singing.

B: Don't worry. They will be ***translated into*** Chinese and shown on the ***screen***.

A: 現在國家劇院正在上演什麼呢？

B: 一齣很有名的音樂劇，叫做「貓」。

A: 描寫什麼情節呢？

B: 由貓的角度來看世界。

A: 這個表演，小孩子也可以看嗎？

B: 這是唯一可以讓小孩子看的音樂劇。

A: 我擔心聽不懂他們在唱些什麼。

B: 別擔心，有中文字幕。

核心詞彙

Words&Phrases

musical	[ˋmjuzɪkḷ]	名詞 音樂劇
What kind of...?	[hwɑt kaɪnd ɑf]	片語 什麼樣的……？
point of view	[pɔɪnt ɑf vju]	片語 觀點
show	[ʃo]	名詞 表演、秀

translate into	[træns`let `ɪntu]	片語 翻譯成
screen	[skrin]	名詞 螢幕

日常實用短句 *Useful Sentences*

- We still have some time before the performance starts.
  離開演還有一段時間。
- I can't afford a box seat.
  我付不起包廂座位。
- The usher will show us to our seats.
  引座員會為我們帶位。
- It is the premiere of this musical in Taiwan.
  這是這齣音樂劇在台灣的首演。
- Did you switch off your cellphone?
  你關掉手機了嗎？
- Shall we buy a program?
  我們要買節目表嗎？
- We can go to the restroom during the intermission.
  我們可以在中場休息時去洗手間。
- The opera show will tour Asia.
  這場歌劇表演會在亞洲巡迴演出。
- The show is beyond my expectations.
  這場表演超乎我預期的精彩。
- I could hardly move my eyes away from the leading man.
  我幾乎無法把眼光從男主角身上移開。

學習++ *More Tips*

外國人對於「musical」（音樂劇）、「opera」（歌劇）、「Broadway show」（歌舞劇）、「plays」（舞台劇）都非常的欣賞與支持。

04 舞會

TRACK 024.

實境對話 Conversation

A: You ***dance*** very well!
B: Thanks!
A: ***Shall we*** dance ***together***?
B: Excuse me. I want to ***have a rest***.
A: Could I ***buy you a drink***?
B: No, thanks!
A: Would you mind if I ***take a seat*** here next to you?
B: No, I wouldn't. But my boyfriend will ***be back*** in a minute.

A: 妳舞跳得很好！
B: 謝謝！
A: 可以和你共舞嗎？
B: 對不起，我想休息。
A: 我請你喝一杯好嗎？
B: 不，謝謝！
A: 我可以坐在妳旁邊嗎？
B: 可以，但是我男朋友很快就回來了。

核心詞彙 Words&Phrases

dance	[dæns]	動詞 跳舞
Shall we...?	[ʃæl wi]	片語 我們可以……？
together	[tə`gɛðɚ]	副詞 一起
have a rest	[hæv ə rɛst]	片語 休息一下
buy sb. a drink	[baɪ `sʌm͵bɑdɪ ə drɪŋk]	片語 請……喝一杯
take a seat	[tek ə sit]	片語 坐下

be back	[bi bæk]	片語 回來

日常實用短句 *Useful Sentences*

- Is there a dress code?
  有服裝規定嗎？
- It's a costume party.
  這是個變裝舞會。
- No slippers or sandals.
  別穿拖鞋或涼鞋。
- Who's your prom date?
  誰是你畢業舞會的舞伴？
- Can you be my date?
  可以當我舞伴嗎？
- He's never a party-goer.
  他從來不是個愛參加派對的人。
- Just swing your body with the music.
  只要隨著音樂擺動身體就好了。
- It's a slow dance.
  這是首慢舞。
- Would you like to dance?
  你想跳舞嗎？
- Don't be such a wallflower.
  別當個壁花。

學習++ *More Tips*

外國人很喜歡辦「party」（舞會），而在舞會上想邀請女生跳舞你可以說：「Can I dance with you?」（我可以跟妳跳舞嗎？）、「May I have this dance?」（我可以跟妳跳支舞嗎？）、「Do I have the pleasure to dance with you?」（我有榮幸可以跟妳跳一支舞嗎？）。

05 餐廳用餐

TRACK 025.

實境對話

Conversation

A: Welcome! How many people do you have?

B: We have four people, could you give us the ***seats*** by the window?

A: Please ***have a look*** at the ***menu***.

B: Anything you would like to eat, Rie?

C: I would like to eat steak, medium, please.

B: Mr. Chen, What do you like to eat?

D: Anything is fine for me.

A: Are you ready to ***order*** now?

B: We ***are*** not ***ready*** yet.

A: 歡迎光臨！你們有幾位？
B: 我們共 4 位，請給我們靠窗的座位。
A: 請參考一下菜單。
B: 理惠，你想吃些什麼？
C: 我想吃牛排，五分熟。
B: 陳先生，你想吃什麼呢？
D: 我什麼都可以。
A: 決定好要點什麼了嗎？
B: 我們還沒有決定。

核心詞彙

Words&Phrases

seat	[sit]	名詞 座位
have a look	[hæv ə lʊk]	片語 看一下
menu	[ˋmɛnju]	名詞 菜單
order	[ˋɔrdɚ]	動詞 點餐
be ready	[bi ˋrɛdɪ]	片語 準備好

日常實用短句 Useful Sentences

- Are you ready to order?
  您準備點餐了嗎？
- What's today's special?
  今天的特餐是什麼？
- Do you care for anything to drink before you order?
  點餐前要不要喝點什麼？
- We'll skip the aperitif.
  我們不喝開胃酒了。
- Have you decided yet?
  您決定好要點什麼了嗎？
- What would you recommend?
  你推薦什麼菜呢？
- What would you like for your starter?
  前菜要吃什麼呢？
- I'll try that.
  我就試試那道菜吧！
- I think that should be enough.
  我想點這樣應該夠了吧！
- Their sandwiches are the best in town.
  他們的三明治是城裡最好吃的。
- I am not good at eating with chopsticks.
  我不太會用筷子吃東西。

學習++ More Tips

去餐廳用餐的時候，服務生會先問你要「smoking or non-smoking area」（吸煙或非吸煙區），接著幫你點餐的時候會問你「What would you like?」（你需要些什麼？），在吃「steak」（牛排）的時候，你可以選「rare」（三分熟）、「medium」（五分熟）、「medium-well」（七分熟）或是「well-done」（全熟的）。

06 速食店

TRACK 026.

實境對話

Conversation

A: Hey! Are you ready to order now?

B: I would like to have one McChicken Combo and two happy ***meals***.

A: One McChicken Combo and two happy meals, ***by the way***, do you want to have any other ***drinks***?

B: One coffee!

A: Would you like to ***eat in*** or ***take away***?

B: Take away, please.

A: One thousand dollars, this is your ***change*** seven hundred fifty dollars, Thank you!

B: Thanks!

A: 你好！準備好要點餐了嗎？

B: 請給我一客麥香雞套餐、兩個兒童餐。

A: 一個麥香雞套餐、兩個兒童餐，要不要其他的飲料？

B: 再給我一杯咖啡！

A: 請問要內用還是外帶？

B: 我要外帶。

A: 收您一千元，找您七百五十元，謝謝！

B: 謝謝！

核心詞彙

Words&Phrases

meal	[mil]	名詞 餐點
by the way	[baɪ ðə we]	片語 順帶一提
drink	[drɪŋk]	名詞 飲料

eat in	[it ɪn]	片語 內用
take away	[tek əˋwe]	片語 外帶
change	[tʃendʒ]	名詞 零錢

日常實用短句 *Useful Sentences*

- For here or to go?
  內用還是外帶？
- Meal number one for here.
  一號餐內用。
- A cheese burger to go.
  一個起司漢堡外帶。
- We can order takeout at the drive-thru.
  我們可以在得來速點餐外帶。
- Anything to drink?
  要飲料嗎？
- Anything else?
  還要些什麼嗎？
- Let me think.
  我想一下。
- What sauce would you like to have your nuggets with?
  您的雞塊要搭配什麼醬料？
- Here's your change.
  這是找您的零錢。
- Enjoy your meal.
  祝您用餐愉快。

學習++ *More Tips*

在國外的「fast food restaurant」（速食店）有「drive through」（得來速）的服務讓你不用下車就可以「take away」（外帶）；當然你也可以到店裡點餐，並在裡面享用「eat in」，或是「to go」（外帶）。

07 百貨公司

TRACK 027.

實境對話

Conversation

A: I am looking for a ***neck tie*** for an elderly male.

B: How do you like this one? It's a very popular ***style***.

A: This one is a little ***tacky***. I don't like it.

B: How about this one? It's very ***elegant*** and ***tasteful***.

A: OK! Please ***wrap*** it as a gift and ***attach a ribbon*** to it.

A: Is there any discount on this one?

B: Well, I'll give you a 5% discount.

A: 我要找年長男士用的領帶。

B: 這條怎麼樣？很受歡迎的樣式。

A: 這條有點俗氣，我不喜歡。

B: 這條如何呢？很高雅而且有品味。

A: 好吧！請幫我包裝成禮物，並繫上蝴蝶結。

A: 這個有打折嗎？

B: 那麼，給你打九五折吧！

核心詞彙

Words&Phrases

neck tie	[nɛk taɪ]	名詞 領帶
style	[staɪl]	名詞 樣式、款式
tacky	[ˋtækɪ]	形容詞 低俗的
elegant	[ˋɛləgənt]	形容詞 高雅的
tasteful	[ˋtestfəl]	形容詞 有品味的
wrap	[ræp]	動詞 包裝
attach a ribbon	[əˋtætʃ ə ˋrɪbən]	片語 綁蝴蝶結

日常實用短句 Useful Sentences

- When will the annual sale begin?
  週年慶何時開始？
- Everything is on sale!
  每樣東西都在特賣！
- You can buy one and get one free now!
  現在可以買一送一！
- I'd like to refund this shirt.
  我想退這件襯衫。
- Is this elevator going up or down?
  這台電梯是往上還是往下？
- It is fully loaded.
  電梯滿了。
- Let's use the escalator.
  我們搭手扶梯好了。
- The information center is on the ground floor.
  服務台在一樓。
- Let's go to the food court and feed ourselves.
  我們去美食街填飽肚子吧。
- There will be a clearance sale next week.
  下週會有個清倉特賣。
- We can save an extra 20%!
  我們可以另外再享八折優惠。
- Can I pay by gift certificates?
  我可以付禮券嗎？

學習++ More Tips

當你要「go shopping」（逛街）的時候，你可以詢問一下有沒有打折：「Is there a discount?」，或是跟店員要求比較便宜的價格：「Can I have a better price?」，「Can you lower the price?」（你可不可以降低價錢？）。

08 野餐

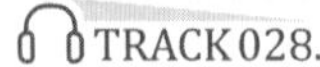

實境對話

Conversation

A: What a lovely day for an ***outing***! Shall we go somewhere?
B: How about ***going on a picnic*** in the Pinwheel ***Valley***?
A: Great! What shall we do there?
B: We can have a ***barbecue***.
A: A barbecue picnic? ***Don't bother***. Some sandwiches and drinks will do. Let's just play around and enjoy the ***sunshine***.
B: Fine. That sounds terrific. Let's go!

A: 多麼好的出遊日子！我們要不要去哪兒走走？
B: 到風車谷野餐怎麼樣？
A: 太棒了！在那裡要做什麼呢？
B: 可以烤肉。
A: 烤肉野餐？別麻煩了。帶點三明治和飲料就夠了。讓我們在那裡玩玩，享受陽光。
B: 好。聽起來好極了。走吧！

核心詞彙

Words&Phrases

outing	[ˋaʊtɪŋ]	名詞 遠足、郊遊
go on a picnic	[go ɑn ə ˋpɪknɪk]	片語 野餐
valley	[ˋvælɪ]	名詞 山谷
barbecue	[ˋbɑrbɪkju]	名詞 烤肉
don't bother	[donˋt ˋbɑðɚ]	片語 不用麻煩
sunshine	[ˋsʌn͵ʃaɪn]	名詞 陽光

日常實用短句 Useful Sentences

- What a beautiful day today!
  今天天氣真好！
- People crowded the whole picnic area.
  整個野餐區擠滿了人。
- Why don't we go on a picnic by the lake?
  我們何不去湖邊野餐呢？
- Please do not litter.
  請不要亂丟垃圾。
- I would like to take a nap on the grass.
  我想在草地上小睡一下。
- Don't pluck off the flowers over there.
  別摘那邊的花。
- There are too many mosquitoes here.
  這裡有太多蚊子了。
- Let's find a shade tree and enjoy our meal underneath.
  我們找一個能遮蔭的樹，並在底下享用餐點吧。
- Would you like some more tuna sandwiches?
  要不要再來點鮪魚三明治呢？
- I made the apple pie myself.
  這蘋果派是我自己做的。
- We should have brought some more juice.
  我們應該要多帶些果汁來的。
- We should definitely go on a picnic more often.
  我們真的應該常常野餐的。

學習++ More Tips

當你要表達一件事好極了，你可以說「That sounds terrific!」（聽起來好極了！），而「That is great!」（棒極了！）或是「Excellent!」（好極了！）、「That's awesome!」（太棒了！）等等都可以用來形容一件事或一個東西。

09 聽音樂會

TRACK 029.

實境對話 Conversation

A: Tonight, there's a concert performed by the National Experimental ***Orchestra conducted by*** a guest conductor, Mr. Yamata. They will perform Symphony No.8 by Dvorak.

B: Who is the piano ***soloist***?

A: Someone called"Komatsu", a female pianist.

B: Do you know why they chose Symphony No.8?

A: Well, I don't know. But the Eighth Symphony is really a ***masterpiece***, and it is unfamiliar to the local ***audience***.

B: I quite agree with you.

A: 今晚有場音樂會由國家實驗樂團演奏，客席指揮家山田先生指揮。他們將會演奏德弗札克的第八號交響曲。

B: 誰擔任鋼琴獨奏？

A: 有一位叫做「小松」的女性鋼琴家。

B: 你曉得他們為什麼要選德弗札克的八號交響曲呢？

A: 呃，不曉得。不過八號交響曲確實是個傑作，只不過本地聽眾比較陌生罷了。

B: 我非常贊同你的看法。

核心詞彙 Words&Phrases

orchestra	[ˋɔrkɪstrə]	名詞 管絃樂團
conduct by	[kənˋdʌkt baɪ]	片語 指揮
soloist	[ˋsoloɪst]	名詞 獨奏者
masterpiece	[ˋmæstɚˏpis]	名詞 傑作、名作
audience	[ˋɔdɪəns]	名詞 觀眾

日常實用短句 Useful Sentences

- Don't dress too casual to the concert.
  去音樂會別穿得太隨便。
- The tickets to the concert were all sold out.
  這場音樂會的票已經銷售一空了。
- This is my favorite symphony orchestra.
  這是我最喜歡的交響樂團。
- You're not supposed to bring food and drinks in here.
  你不該帶食物和飲料進來這裡的。
- The soprano sang two encores.
  那個女高音唱了兩首安可曲。
- The jazz trio will tour Europe and Berlin is the first stop.
  這支爵士樂三重奏將在歐洲做巡迴演奏，而柏林是第一站。
- The chorus is lucky to have the famous pianist accompany their singing.
  這支合唱團能請到這位名鋼琴家幫他們伴奏真是幸運啊！
- Are you going to present the conductor with a bouquet?
  你要獻花給指揮嗎？
- Can I check your playbill during the intermission?
  我可以在中場休息時間借看一下你的節目表嗎？
- I was totally carried away by the symphony music.
  我完全沉醉在那支交響樂中。
- All the audience stood up to applaud.
  所有觀眾都站起來鼓掌。

學習++ More Tips

「conduct」當動詞用的時候是「指揮」的意思，而當它當名詞的時候則有「舉止」、「行為」的意思。「She conducted the band at school.」（她在學校指揮樂團。）、「Your children have good conduct.」（你小孩的品行優良。）。

10 到健身房

TRACK 030.

實境對話

Conversation

A: Good afternoon. I haven't used this machine before. Would you ***demonstrate*** how to use it for me?

B: Sure. First, you sit on the ***cushion***. ***Adjust*** the height of the cushion. Then tighten the four straps.

A: Like this?

B: Right. Then ***stretch*** your arms, follow me! One-two-three-four...

A: It's not difficult.

B: Not at all. But you have to be very careful to avoid ***injury***. All right. I'll leave you alone. If you need me, please call me again.

A: Thank you.

A: 午安。我沒有用過這個機器。可否請你替我示範？
B: 當然。先坐在墊上。調整高度。然後綁緊那四條帶子。
A: 像這樣嗎？
B: 對了。然後伸展雙臂，跟著我做！一、二、三、四……
A: 不難嘛。
B: 一點也不難。但必須很小心，以免受傷。好。你自己做吧。如果需要我，請再叫我。
A: 謝謝。

核心詞彙

Words&Phrases

demonstrate	[ˋdɛmən͵stret]	動詞 示範
cushion	[ˋkʊʃən]	名詞 墊子
adjust	[əˋdʒʌst]	動詞 調整

stretch	[strɛtʃ]	動詞 伸直、展開
injury	[ˋɪndʒərɪ]	名詞 受傷

日常實用短句 Useful Sentences

- I forgot to bring my access card.
  我忘了帶通行證。
- You need a workout plan.
  你需要一個健身計畫。
- Charlie is a gym-goer.
  查理是個愛上健身房的人。
- I work out in the gym twice a week.
  我一星期上健身房健身二次。
- I'm sweating like a pig.
  我已經汗流浹背了。
- I'm beat.
  我累死了。
- Let's call it a day.
  今天就練到這兒為止吧。
- Working-out is how I keep in shape.
  我靠健身保持身材。
- I'll try the military press first.
  我先試試肩部推舉機。
- The treadmills are all taken.
  所有的跑步機都有人在用了。

學習++ More Tips

到健身房鍛鍊身體，一定要了解自己身體的「limit」（極限），而在運動前也絕對不可以忘了要做一些「warm-ups」（暖身操），這樣才不會有運動傷害！

11 餐廳裡

TRACK031.

實境對話

Conversation

A: I've ***reserved a table*** for two. My name is Lin.

B: Please ***follow me***, Mr. Lin.

A: Umm, is this a ***non-smoking area***?

B: Yes, it is. Would you like to wait for the other ***guest***, or would you like to order now?

A: I'll wait for a while.

A: This is the menu.

B: Thank you. What's your ***special*** today?

A: Chicken a la king. With corn ***soup*** and a cup of coffee.

B: Two, please.

A: 我訂了一個兩個人的桌子。我姓林。

B: 林先生，請跟我來。

A: 嗯，這是非吸煙區嗎？

B: 是的。你要等另一位客人，還是現在就點餐？

A: 我等一下好了。

A: 這是菜單。

B: 謝謝。今天的特餐是什麼？

A: 雞肉燴飯。附玉米湯和一杯咖啡。

B: 請給我們兩客。

核心詞彙

Words&Phrases

reserve a table	[rɪ`zɝv ə `tebl̩]	片語 訂桌
follow me	[`falo mi]	片語 跟我來
non-smoking area	[ˏnɑn `smokɪŋ `ɛrɪə]	名詞 非吸煙區
guest	[gɛst]	名詞 客人

special	[ˋspɛʃəl]	名詞 特餐
soup	[sup]	名詞 湯

日常實用短句 Useful Sentences

- Do you have a reservation?
  您有訂位嗎？
- We need a table for four.
  我們要一張四個人的餐桌。
- We are a group of four.
  我們有四個人。
- The house is full now.
  餐廳現在客滿了。
- We don’t have a free table at the moment.
  我們目前沒有空桌。
- Your table is ready.
  您的桌子已經準備好了。
- Who’s going to pick up the tab?
  哪一位要結帳呢？
- I’ll take it.
  我來買單。
- Let me treat you this time.
  這次我請客。
- Do you want separated bills or just one single bill?
  您要分開結帳還是一起結？

學習++ More Tips

到餐廳點餐時，「waiter」（侍者）會問你說：「May I take your order now?」（我可以為你點餐了嗎？），你也可以問「What's your recommendation?」（你有什麼建議？），而在最後結帳時，你可以說：「Check, please.」或是「May I have the bill?」。

12 逛書店

TRACK 032.

實境對話

Conversation

A: I'd like to buy some books for my five-year-old daughter. What would you recommend?

B: For five-year-old children, ***picture books*** are suitable. Have you read"Snow White and the Seven ***Dwarfs***"or"Sleeping Beauty"to her?

A: Yes, already.

B: How about"The Lion King"?

A: ***Not yet***. Can a girl of her age ***understand*** it?

B: I think so. Children ***nowadays*** seem to be much more ***clever*** than in our time.

A: 我想買幾本書給我五歲的女兒。你推薦什麼書好？

B: 給五歲的小孩的話，圖畫書比較合適。你有沒有唸《白雪公主》、《睡美人》給她聽過？

A: 已經唸過了。

B: 《獅子王》呢？

A: 還沒有。像她這個年齡的孩子聽得懂嗎？

B: 我想可以。現在的小孩好像比我們那個年代的聰明多了。

核心詞彙

Words&Phrases

picture book	[ˋpɪktʃɚ bʊk]	名詞 圖畫書
dwarf	[dwɔrf]	名詞 侏儒、矮子
not yet	[nɑt jɛt]	片語 還沒
understand	[ˏʌndɚˋstænd]	動詞 理解、懂
nowadays	[ˋnaʊəˏdez]	副詞 現今、時下
clever	[ˋklɛvɚ]	形容詞 聰明的

日常實用短句 Useful Sentences

- Could you help me find a magazine?
  可以幫我找一本雜誌嗎？
- Where is the fiction area?
  小說區在哪裡？
- What's the title or the author's name?
  書名或作者名字是什麼？
- Cook books are in the nonfiction section.
  食譜書在非小說區。
- It's on the rack of bestsellers.
  它在暢銷書架上。
- You can find it on bestseller section.
  你可以在暢銷書區找到那本書。
- I can't find it anywhere.
  我到處都找不到。
- I'll check it on the computer for you.
  我幫你在電腦上查一下。
- Sorry, it's not available now.
  抱歉，這本書現在缺貨。
- When will the book come in?
  這本書何時會進來？
- You can come back in two days.
  你可以兩天後再過來。
- Could you inform me when it comes in?
  書來的時候可以通知我嗎？

學習++ More Tips

現在的書店應該都會將書分門別類，如「fiction」（小說、虛構類）、「non-fiction」（非小說）、「poetry」（詩集）、「science」（自然）、「magazines」（雜誌）等，你只要到各區去找自己需要的書就可以了！

13 玩樂器

TRACK 033.

實境對話

Conversation

A: Hi, Tina. I want to ***learn*** a ***musical instrument***. Which do you think is the best for me to learn?

B: I think the ***bamboo flute*** may be the easiest one. ***In addition***, it's easy to carry.

A: What else would you suggest?

B: And the most popular and satisfying musical instrument is guitar. You can ***make*** great ***progress at the beginning***.

A: Oh, it's so cool to see others singing songs while ***playing guitar***.

A: 嗨，蒂娜。我想學一種樂器。你覺得我最適合學什麼呢？
B: 我覺得或許竹笛是最容易學的。而且，它也方便攜帶。
A: 你還能建議什麼其他的嗎？
B: 還有最流行也最容易產生滿足感的樂器就是吉他了。你在初級階段就可以取得很大的進步。
A: 噢，看到別人邊彈吉他邊唱歌真是太酷了。

核心詞彙

Words&Phrases

learn	[lɝn]	動詞 學習
musical instrument	[ˋmjuzɪkḷ ˋɪnstrəmənt]	名詞 樂器
bamboo flute	[bæmˋbu flut]	名詞 竹笛
in addition	[ɪn əˋdɪʃən]	片語 而且
make progress	[mek ˋprɑgrɛs]	片語 進步
at the beginning	[æt ðə bɪˋgɪnɪŋ]	片語 一開始
play guitar	[ple gɪˋtɑr]	片語 彈吉他

日常實用短句 Useful Sentences

- When did you start playing the guitar?
  你何時開始彈吉他的？
- My sister plays the flute beautifully.
  我妹妹長笛吹得很好聽。
- The guy living upstairs is beating the drums again.
  樓上那傢伙又在打鼓了。
- Can you play a song for us after dinner?
  晚飯後能不能為我們彈奏一曲？
- You shouldn't practice playing the violin this late.
  你不應該這麼晚還練習拉小提琴。
- Don't worry. The practice room is soundproofed.
  別擔心，這間練習室有加隔音設備。
- Jack has a gift for music.
  傑克很有音樂天賦。
- Do you want to join our band?
  你要不要加入我們的樂團？
- Our band needs a guitarist.
  我們的樂團需要一個吉他手。
- The sound of the bass clarinet is appealing to the ear.
  低音豎笛的聲音真是動聽啊。
- The cello is out of tune.
  大提琴走調了。
- I like saxophone the best among all the musical instruments.
  所有樂器中我最喜歡薩克斯風。

學習++ More Tips

「Perhaps not.」表示「大概沒有。」是用來附和對方前一個否定句或否定疑問句。如「A: It isn't that cool, isn't it?」，「B: Perhaps not.」（「它沒那麼酷，不是嗎？」，「大概是吧。」）如果前面的句子是肯定句或肯定疑問句，則不需要加「not」。

14 美容院

TRACK 034.

實境對話

Conversation

A: What would you like to be done with your ***hair***?

B: I'd like to have my hair ***dyed***.

A: All or ***streaked***?

B: Are the prices the same?

A: No, streaking is even more expensive, but some feel it is more ***stylish***.

B: let me try it this time.

A: Which color do you like? Here are the color samples. You would expect much darker ***tones*** on your hair.

B: This one, please.

A: 你的頭髮要怎麼做？

B: 我想要染髮。

A: 整頭染還是挑染？

B: 價格都一樣嗎？

A: 不同，挑染甚至更貴。但有些人覺得會比較時髦。

B: 那這次我試試這種。

A: 你喜歡什麼色？這裡是顏色的樣本。真正染上後可能顏色會稍微深一點。

B: 這個吧。

核心詞彙

Words&Phrases

hair	[hɛr]	名詞 頭髮
dye	[daɪ]	動詞 染色
streaked	[ˋstrikɪd]	形容詞 有條紋的

stylish	[ˋstaɪlɪʃ]	形容詞 有型的
tone	[ton]	名詞 色調

日常實用短句 Useful Sentences

- Please layer the hair.
  請幫我剪層次。
- I'd like a hair treatment.
  我要護髮。
- Just shampoo my hair today.
  我今天只要洗頭就好。
- You need a haircut.
  你該剪頭髮了。
- Would you like me to thin out the side?
  要我幫你把兩邊頭髮打薄嗎？
- Please shave my sideburns.
  請幫我剃鬢角。
- I just want to trim off the split ends.
  我只想修剪分叉的髮尾。
- My hair needs a perm.
  我的頭髮要燙了。
- Do you need something to read while I'm shampooing your hair?
  我幫您洗頭時，您要看些什麼嗎？
- Do you have a particular hair stylist you like?
  你有特別想指定的設計師嗎？

學習++ More Tips

「beauty parlor」（美容院）是給女生做頭髮用的，通常男生會去的是「barber's」（理髮店）。當你請你的「hairdresser」（美髮師）幫你設計新的頭髮時你可以說：「Could you style my hair?」，或是「I need a new hairdo.」（我需要新的髮型。）。

15 打牌

TRACK 035.

實境對話

Conversation

A: Hi, Linda, what are you doing now?

B: Nothing. I feel so ***bored***.

A: So do I. Let's do something. Do you know how to ***play cards***?

B: Actually, I ***am*** very ***good at*** playing cards.

A: Wow, why not play together?

B: There is a very special and interesting card game. But it needs four people to play.

A: ***In that case***, let's ask Mary and Nancy to ***come over***.

B: Good idea. Let's do it right now!

A: 嘿，琳達，你現在幹嘛呢？

B: 沒幹什麼。我覺得好無聊哦。

A: 我也是。我們做點什麼吧。你會打牌嗎？

B: 事實上，我非常擅長打牌。

A: 哇，那為什麼不一起玩呢？

B: 我知道一種非常特別又有趣的打法。但要四個人才夠啊。

A: 那樣的話，我們叫瑪麗和南茜過來吧。

B: 好主意。馬上行動！

核心詞彙

Words&Phrases

bored	[bord]	形容詞 無聊的
play cards	[ple kɑrdz]	片語 打牌
be good at	[bi gʊd æt]	片語 擅長……
in that case	[ɪn ðæt kes]	片語 既然那樣
come over	[kʌm `ovɚ]	片語 過來

日常實用短句 Useful Sentences

- They whiled away the whole weekend playing cards.
  他們玩牌消磨了一整個週末。
- Black Jack is the only card game that I play.
  21 點是我唯一會玩的撲克牌遊戲。
- Can you explain the rules of this card game for me?
  你可以跟我説明玩這個撲克牌遊戲的規則嗎？
- Do you know how to play a bridge?
  你知道怎麼打橋牌嗎？
- How many people does it require to play Big Two?
  要多少人才能玩大老二？
- Big Two is a four players' card game.
  大老二是四個人玩的撲克牌遊戲。
- The first one to get rid of all the player's cards to a discard pile will be the winner.
  第一個將手上的牌都丟出去的人就贏了。
- Do you get it?
  你聽懂了嗎？
- Do you know that you can play card games online now?
  你知道現在可以線上玩撲克牌遊戲了嗎？
- My luck is in.
  我運氣來了。
- It's your call.
  該你叫牌了。

學習++ More Tips

「be good at V-ing」是表示「擅長做……」的片語，如：「I am good at playing cards.」（我很會玩牌。），介係詞「at」後面也可以接一般名詞，如：「He's especially good at card games.」（他特別擅長撲克牌遊戲。）。

16 園藝

TRACK036.

實境對話

Conversation

A: Bree, your garden is so beautiful.

B: Thank you for your compliment.

A: Could you tell me what those flowers are?

B: Of course. They are purple roses.

A: How could you make your garden so ***vital***?

B: I'***m interested in gardening***. Beside, these flowers are like my own kids. I ***take*** good ***care of*** them and hope they ***grow*** well. That's all.

A: Wow. ***No wonder*** you have the most beautiful garden in the neighborhood.

A: 布莉，你的花園可真美。

B: 謝謝你的讚美。

A: 可不可以請你告訴我那些是什麼花？

B: 當然可以啦。那些是紫薔薇。

A: 你是怎麼樣把花園呵護得這麼有生氣啊？

B: 我對園藝有興趣。除此之外，這些花就像我自己的孩子。我用心照顧它們，並希望它們能夠長得好。如此而已。

A: 哇，難怪你的花園會是這一區最漂亮的。

核心詞彙

Words&Phrases

vital	[ˋvaɪtḷ]	形容詞 生氣勃勃的
be interested in	[bi ˋɪntərɪstɪd ɪn]	片語 對……有興趣
gardening	[ˋgɑrdṇɪŋ]	名詞 園藝
take care of	[tek kɛr ɑv]	片語 照顧
grow	[gro]	動詞 生長

no wonder	[no ˋwʌndɚ]	**片語** 難怪

日常實用短句 *Useful Sentences*

- I'm looking for some gardening know-how.
  我正在找一些園藝知識。
- How often do I have to water them?
  我多久為它們澆一次水？
- The trees need clipping.
  這些樹需要修剪一下了。
- Did you apply fertilizer to these plants?
  你有為這些植物施肥嗎？
- I use organic fertilizers only.
  我只用有機肥料。
- Are roses perennial?
  玫瑰是多年生植物嗎？
- You should prune every branch that did not bear fruit.
  你應該把沒結果的枝都剪掉。
- I'm thinking about growing some asparagus in my garden.
  我考慮在花園種點蘆筍。
- They don't need any special care.
  它們不需要任何特別的照料。
- This flower seeds in the winter.
  這種花在冬天結果。
- Should I use pesticides?
  我應該用殺蟲劑嗎？

學習++ *More Tips*

「no wonder」是表示「難怪、原來如此」的意思。如：「No wonder they are so beautiful.」（難怪它們這麼美。），同樣的一句話，也可以說：「So that's why they are so beautiful.」（原來這就是為什麼它們會這麼美麗的原因。）。

17 在海邊

TRACK 037.

實境對話

Conversation

A: Wow, the sea!

B: Why do you look so excited?

A: Because this is the first time that I ***get*** so ***close to*** the sea! I have always wanted to come to the ***beach*** since I was a child.

B: First time? No wonder you are so happy.

A: The sea is so ***unlimited*** that it makes me forget all the troubles.

B: That's why I often come here. So why don't you come here more ***frequently***?

A: I will. Let's ***go for a walk along*** the beach.

A: 哇，是海耶！
B: 你為什麼看起來那麼激動啊？
A: 因為我第一次這麼親近大海啊！我從小就一直想來海邊。
B: 第一次？難怪你那麼高興呢。
A: 大海是如此的遼闊，讓我忘記所有的煩惱。
B: 這也是我常到海邊來的原因。那麼你為什麼不常來呢？
A: 我會的。我們沿著海邊散個步吧！

核心詞彙

Words&Phrases

get close to	[gɛt klos tu]	片語 與……親近
beach	[bitʃ]	名詞 海灘
unlimited	[ʌnˋlɪmɪtɪd]	形容詞 無邊無際的
frequently	[ˋfrikwɛntlɪ]	副詞 經常地
go for a walk	[go fɔr ə wɔk]	片語 去散步

along	[əˋlɔŋ]	**介係詞** 沿著

日常實用短句 Useful Sentences

- Let's take a sunbath.
  我們來做個日光浴吧。
- Look at her tan!
  看她曬得古銅色的皮膚！
- Let me put on some suntan lotion first.
  讓我先擦個防曬油。
- My skin sunburns easily.
  我的皮膚很容易曬傷。
- I don't want to get a sunburn.
  我可不想被曬傷。
- Is it waterproof?
  這是防水的嗎？
- Don't litter on the sand.
  別在沙灘上丟垃圾。
- Let's go surfing.
  我們去衝浪吧。
- He is actually a landlubber.
  他其實是個旱鴨子。
- Leave your beach sandals under the parasol.
  把你的海灘拖鞋留在遮陽傘下吧。
- That bikini girl is such an eye candy.
  那個比基尼女郎真養眼。

學習++ More Tips

「go for a walk」表示「去散步」，也可以表示成「take a walk」（散步）。如：「Shall we go for a walk after dinner?」（我們晚飯後要不要去散個步？），同樣的用法變化，「go for a swim」表示「去游泳」，如：「Let's go for a swim now.」（咱們現在去游個泳吧！）。

18 滑雪

TRACK 038.

實境對話

Conversation

A: Oh, God! Are you OK?

B: I am fine. I just had a ***sudden tumble***. Thank you.

A: Anyway, be careful next time. I guess it's your first ***skiing***. Am I right?

B: That's right. ***Apparently*** it is not as easy as I thought it would be.

A: It is easy, but it's necessary to learn some ***basic skills*** at the beginning. Otherwise, you might ***get hurt*** easily while skiing.

B: You are right. I was too ***negligent***.

A: 噢，天哪！你還好吧？

B: 我沒事。我只是突然摔了一跤。謝謝。

A: 不管怎樣，下次小心哦。我猜這是你第一次來滑雪吧。我說對了嗎？

B: 沒錯。顯然它沒我以為的那麼容易。

A: 它是很簡單，不過一開始有必要先學一些滑雪基本技巧。否則，你在滑雪的過程中可能會很容易受傷。

B: 你說的沒錯。是我太大意了。

核心詞彙

Words&Phrases

sudden	[ˋsʌdn̩]	形容詞 突然的、意外的
tumble	[ˋtʌmbl̩]	名詞 跌倒
ski	[ski]	動詞 滑雪
apparently	[əˋpærəntlɪ]	副詞 顯然地
basic skill	[ˋbesɪk ˋskɪl]	名詞 基本技巧
get hurt	[gɛt hɝt]	片語 受傷

negligent	[ˋnɛglɪdʒənt]	形容詞 粗心的

日常實用短句 *Useful Sentences*

- I feel excited about going skiing tomorrow.
  明天要去滑雪讓我感到好興奮。
- The ski lift will take us up there.
  滑雪電纜車會帶我們到那上面去。
- The ski runs are for advanced skiers.
  這些滑雪道是給滑雪高手們使用的。
- And those ski runs are for beginner.
  而那些滑雪道是給新手們使用的。
- They will give you a skiing lesson on the bunny hill.
  他們會在一個約三十度的坡地上教你滑雪。
- We're going to have a good time skiing.
  我們將會滑雪滑得很愉快。
- He is very fond of ski jumping.
  他很熱中跳臺滑雪。
- Can I hire ski boots here if I don't have my own ones?
  如果我沒有滑雪靴的話，可以在這裡租借嗎？
- They go skiing in Japan every winter.
  他們每年冬天都去日本滑雪。
- We can spend out winter vacation in a ski resort in California.
  我們可以在加州某一個滑雪勝地去度寒假。

學習++ *More Tips*

「as... as...」是「如同……一樣」的片語，是比較級的一種表示法。如：「It is not as easy as I thought it would be.」（它沒我原先以為的那麼容易。），也可以拿兩個名詞來做比較，如：「Skiing is not as easy as skating.」（滑雪不像溜冰那麼簡單。）。

19 泡溫泉

TRACK 039.

實境對話

Conversation

A: Jim, there is a new opened ***hot spring spa*** which is very popular these days. Would you like to go with me?

B: Good idea! How much do they ***charge***?

A: NT 800 for three hours ***per*** person.

B: OK. I can ***afford*** it. By the way, have you ever been there before?

A: I've been there twice. It's really ***comfortable*** and relaxing.

B: Really? Good, I'll go there with you.

A: 吉姆，最近有一家新開幕的溫泉會館很受歡迎呢。你想不想跟我一起去呢？

B: 好主意啊！他們怎麼收費？

A: 一個人三小時八百台幣。

B: 好，我還付得起。對了，你曾經去過嗎？

A: 我去過兩次，那裡真的很舒服很令人放鬆喔。

B: 是嗎？好，那我也跟你去感受一下吧。

核心詞彙

Words&Phrases

hot spring	[hɑt sprɪŋ]	名詞 溫泉
spa	[spɑ]	名詞 溫泉浴場
charge	[tʃɑrdʒ]	動詞 收費
per	[pɚ]	介係詞 每一
afford	[əˋford]	動詞 負擔
comfortable	[ˋkʌmfɚtəbl̩]	形容詞 舒服的

日常實用短句 *Useful Sentences*

- Do I have to be naked?
  我必須脫光光嗎？
- Are there any rules of taking a bath in a hot spring?
  泡溫泉有什麼規定嗎？
- Japanese hot springs are all enjoyed naked.
  日本溫泉都是要裸身泡的。
- Can I wear my swimsuit?
  我可以穿著泳衣嗎？
- You can bring a small towel with you to enhance your privacy.
  你可以帶一條小毛巾遮一下隱私部位。
- Make sure you keep the towel out of water.
  一定不要把毛巾放入水裡。
- Rinse your body before entering the hot spring.
  進入溫泉之前先沖洗身體。
- Nothing is better than soaking in a hot spring in chilly winter.
  沒什麼比在寒冷的冬天泡溫泉還要更棒的了。
- Hot springs often have a very high mineral content.
  溫泉通常有很高的礦物含量。
- Hot springs have medical value because of their curative effects on human bodies.
  溫泉因為對人體有治療效果而具醫療價值。

學習++ *More Tips*

「hot spring」指的是「溫泉」，「hot spring spa」指的是「溫泉會館」，而「hot spring bath」則可以表示為「泡溫泉」的意思。如：「Having a hot spring bath in winter is really relaxing.」（冬天泡個溫泉真是讓人放鬆啊。）。

20 上網聊天

TRACK040.

實境對話

Conversation

A: What are you doing, Peter?

B: I am ***surfing the Internet***.

A: Internet again? What's so interesting about Internet? ***What on earth*** are you doing in front of the computer ***day and night***?

B: Millions of things. I can check e-mails, look up information or play ***online games***. But mostly I ***chat with*** my friends from ***all over the world***.

A: Wow, it sounds interesting.

B: Come on! Just have a try. You'll like it.

A: 彼得，你在幹什麼呢？

B: 我在上網啊。

A: 又是網路？網路到底有什麼好玩的？你日日夜夜地坐在電腦前面究竟在做些什麼呀？

B: 能做的事情太多了。收信、查資料或是玩線上遊戲，不過我大部分都是在跟我世界各地的朋友聊天。

A: 哇，挺起來蠻有趣的。

B: 來試試吧！你會喜歡的。

核心詞彙

Words&Phrases

surf the Internet	[sɝf ðə ˋɪntɚ͵nɛt]	片語 上網
What on earth...?	[hwɑt ɑn ɝθ]	片語 到底……？
day and night	[de ænd naɪt]	片語 日日夜夜
online game	[ˋɑn͵laɪn gem]	名詞 線上遊戲
chat with	[tʃæt wɪð]	片語 和……聊天
all over the world	[ɔl ˋovɚ ðə wɝld]	片語 世界各處

日常實用短句 Useful Sentences

- What's the topic of this chat room?
  這個聊天室的主題是什麼？
- Is it free?
  這是免費的嗎？
- Don't give away your personal information.
  別洩漏你的個人資料。
- Just message me directly.
  直接傳訊息給我就好了。
- How do I send instant messages?
  我要如何傳送立即訊息？
- Is there a chat room for sports?
  有聊運動的聊天室嗎？
- The guy keeps messaging me dirty jokes.
  那傢伙一直傳黃色笑話過來。
- I'm going to ask my net friends out.
  我要約網友出來。
- He's offline.
  他離線了。
- It's easy to stay in touch with my friends.
  它讓我易於和朋友保持聯絡。
- Can I invite friends to the chat room?
  我可以邀請朋友進聊天室嗎？
- How to create my own chat room?
  要怎麼自設聊天室？

學習++ More Tips

「make friends」是「交朋友」的意思，如：「I like to make friends with different kinds of people.」（我喜歡和不同類型的人交朋友。），另一個類似的片語是「meet people」（認識人），如：「You can meet a lot of interesting people in online chat rooms.」（你會在線上聊天室認識很多有趣的人。）。

PART❷娛樂消費篇

你都記住了嗎？

從各篇「日常實用短句」裡整理出外國人常用的單字和片語，如果背起來了，就在前方空格打個勾吧！

- ☐ switch off
  片語 關掉
- ☐ box office hit
  片語 很賣座
- ☐ leading actor
  名詞 男主角
- ☐ supporting actress
  名詞 女配角
- ☐ documentary film
  名詞 紀錄片
- ☐ blockbuster
  名詞 強檔電影
- ☐ cast
  名詞 （電影）卡司
- ☐ lousy
  形容詞 討厭的
- ☐ snatch
  動詞 搶
- ☐ husky
  形容詞 嘶啞的
- ☐ off-key
  形容詞 走音的
- ☐ insert a song
  片語 插播一首歌
- ☐ box seat
  名詞 包廂座位
- ☐ intermission
  名詞 中場休息
- ☐ tour
  動詞 巡迴演出
- ☐ expectation
  名詞 預期
- ☐ dress code
  名詞 服裝規定
- ☐ costume party
  名詞 變裝舞會
- ☐ prom date
  名詞 畢業舞會的舞伴
- ☐ party-goer
  名詞 社交聚會常客
- ☐ wallflower
  名詞 壁花
- ☐ aperitif
  名詞 開胃酒
- ☐ starter
  名詞 開胃菜、第一道菜
- ☐ takeout
  名詞 外帶
- ☐ drive-thru
  名詞 得來速
- ☐ annual sale
  名詞 週年慶

- ☐ on sale
  片語 拍賣
- ☐ buy one get one free
  片語 買一送一
- ☐ information center
  名詞 服務台
- ☐ ground floor
  名詞 一樓
- ☐ clearance sale
  名詞 清倉拍賣
- ☐ gift certificate
  名詞 禮券
- ☐ litter
  動詞 亂丟
- ☐ take a nap
  片語 小睡一下
- ☐ pluck off
  片語 摘取
- ☐ sold out
  片語 賣光
- ☐ encore
  名詞 安可曲
- ☐ bouquet
  名詞 花束
- ☐ applaud
  動詞 鼓掌
- ☐ access card
  名詞 通行證
- ☐ work out
  片語 運動健身
- ☐ sweat
  動詞 流汗
- ☐ call it a day
  片語 結束一天的工作
- ☐ keep in shape
  片語 保持身材
- ☐ treadmill
  名詞 跑步機
- ☐ pick up the tab
  片語 付帳
- ☐ available
  形容詞 可買到的
- ☐ beat the drums
  片語 打鼓
- ☐ soundproof
  動詞 給（房屋等）裝隔音設備
- ☐ out of tune
  片語 走調
- ☐ saxophone
  名詞 薩克斯風
- ☐ layer the hair
  片語 打薄頭髮
- ☐ shampoo
  動詞 洗頭髮
- ☐ trim
  動詞 修剪
- ☐ split end
  名詞 分岔的髮尾
- ☐ get rid of
  片語 擺脱
- ☐ Big two
  名詞 大老二
- ☐ know-how
  名詞 實際知識、竅門
- ☐ eye candy
  片語 能吸引注意力的視覺元素
- ☐ dirty joke
  片語 黃色笑話

Part 3 日常生活篇－音檔連結

因各家手機系統不同，若無法直接掃描，仍可以至以下電腦雲端連結下載收聽。

（https://tinyurl.com/24js7yjd）

PART 3

日常生活篇

01 道歉

TRACK 041.

實境對話 Conversation

A: Have you ***brought*** the book you ***borrowed from*** me ***last time***?
B: Oh, no. How ***stupid***! I forgot it on my ***desk***. Oh, sorry.
A: Oh, it's ***all right***.
B: It's only eight o'clock. ***Perhaps*** I should go home and ***fetch*** it.
A: It's quite all right.

A: 你上次跟我借的書帶來了沒？
B: 啊，沒有。我怎麼那麼笨！忘在桌子上。對不起。
A: 喔，沒關係。
B: 現在才八點鐘。或許我應該回家一趟，把書拿來。
A: 真的沒關係。

核心詞彙 Words&Phrases

brought	[brɔt]	動詞（bring 的過去式與過去分詞）帶來
borrow from	[ˋbɑro frɑm]	片語 從……借入
last time	[læst taɪm]	片語 上一次
stupid	[ˋstjupɪd]	形容詞 蠢的
desk	[dɛsk]	名詞 書桌
all right	[ɔl raɪt]	片語 沒關係
perhaps	[pɚˋhæps]	副詞 或許、可能
fetch	[fɛtʃ]	動詞 去拿來

日常實用短句 Useful Sentences

- Sorry.
  抱歉。
- I feel really sorry.
  我真的很抱歉。
- It's my fault.
  是我的錯。
- I apologize.
  我道歉。
- My bad.
  我的錯。
- I feel terribly sorry about that.
  我對於那件事感到非常得抱歉。
- Sorry to have kept you waiting.
  抱歉讓你久等了。
- I'm terribly sorry that I forgot to do the homework.
  我非常抱歉沒有做作業。
- Sorry for being rude.
  失禮了，真抱歉。
- Please excuse my bad memories.
  請原諒我不好的記性。
- My apology.
  我錯了。

學習++ More Tips

在表達歉意的時候，除了可以說：「I am sorry.」之外，你也可以說：「I apologize.」，「Please forgive me.」（請原諒我。）。在這裡的「terribly sorry」是非常抱歉的意思。「terribly」本來是「可怕的」，但在這裡卻是「非常地」的意思：「 He is terribly sick.」（他病得非常的重。）。

02 拜訪朋友

TRACK 042.

實境對話

Conversation

A: Good evening, Miss Ton. ***May I*** introduce my brother, Tom?

B: How do you do, Mr. Wang? Miss Wang's ***often*** mentioned you. I am happy to ***know*** you.

C: Nice to meet you, Miss Ton.

C: I ***hope*** I'll see a great deal of you ***from now on***.

B: It's my pleasure.

A: I have to go now Tom, would you ***stay*** here and chat with Miss Ton?

C: It would be a pleasure.

A: 晚安，唐小姐。我可以介紹我弟弟湯姆嗎？

B: 幸會，王先生。王小姐時常提到你，很高興認識你。

C: 唐小姐，我也很高興認識妳。

C: 我希望以後能常常見到妳。

B: 歡迎之至。

A: 我得走了。湯姆，你要留下來和唐小姐聊天嗎？

C: 榮幸之至。

核心詞彙

Words&Phrases

May I...?	[me aɪ]	片語 我可以……？
often	[ˋɔfən]	副詞 經常
know	[no]	動詞 知道、認識
hope	[hop]	動詞 希望
from now on	[frɑm naʊ ɑn]	片語 從現在起
stay	[ste]	動詞 停留

日常實用短句 Useful Sentences

- Hello. Here is a little something for you.
  哈囉。這小東西是要送你的。
- You're so sweet.
  你真好。
- I haven't seen you for a long time.
  我好久沒看到你了。
- How have you been lately?
  你最近好不好呢？
- Thanks for the delicious dinner.
  謝謝你美味的晚餐。
- It's so nice of you to come around.
  你能過來真好。
- Welcome to my house.
  歡迎到我家來。
- What a cozy house.
  好舒適的房子啊。
- Make yourself at home.
  別拘束。
- You made it.
  你總算來了。
- You look great!
  你看起來真美！
- Thanks for inviting me.
  謝謝你邀請我。

學習++ More Tips

「a great deal」是指很多，已經數不清楚的意思，例如：「He has a great deal of money.」（他有很多的錢。）、「She gave me a great deal of support.」（她給了我許多的支持。）。

03 借車&借錢

TRACK043.

實境對話

Conversation

A: Hi, Tony. Could you ***lend*** me one thousand dollars? I left my wallet at home.

B: You always say that. Well, here you are.

A: Thank you. I ***promise***, it's the last time.

A: Would you mind giving me a ***push***? My car has ***stalled***.

B: ***Never mind***. If you are ***in a hurry***, why don't you take my car?

A: Oh, I'd be much ***obliged*** if you'd let me borrow your car for today.

B: Don't mention it.

A: 嗨，湯尼。可不可以借我一千元？我把錢包放在家裡了。
B: 你總是那麼說。算了，拿去吧。
A: 謝謝你。我保證，這是最後一次。
A: 你不介意幫我推一推車吧？我的車發不動了。
B: 不要管它了。如果你趕時間，為什麼不用我的車？
A: 哦，如果今天能借你的車，真是感激不盡。
B: 這沒什麼。

核心詞彙

Words&Phrases

lend	[lɛnd]	動詞 借出
promise	[ˋprɑmɪs]	動詞 答應
push	[pʊʃ]	動詞 推
stall	[stɔl]	動詞 使動彈不得
never mind	[ˋnɛvɚ maɪnd]	片語 不要管了

in a hurry	[ɪn ə ˋhɝɪ]	片語 趕時間
obliged	[əˋblaɪdʒd]	形容詞 感激的

日常實用短句 Useful Sentences

- Could you lend me your car?
  你可以借我車嗎？
- My car is in the garage.
  我的車在車庫裡。
- I'm wondering if you could lend me some money.
  我在想你是不是能借我一點錢。
- When do you need it?
  你什麼時候要用？
- May I borrow some money from you?
  我可以跟你借錢嗎？
- How long will you need the car for?
  你車子要用多久？
- Take your time.
  不用急著還。
- I am very tight with money now.
  我現在手頭很緊。
- Can I make monthly payments?
  我可以每月攤還給你嗎？
- What is the interest rate?
  利息多少？

學習++ More Tips

「borrow」與「lend」的中文解釋都是「借」，但實際上它們的用法式有差別的。「borrow」是跟人家借東西；而「lend」則是把東西借給別人。「May I borrow your pen?」（你可以借我你的筆嗎？），「I lend you my pencil.」（我把我的筆借給你。）。

04 搭便車

TRACK 044.

實境對話

Conversation

A: Hi, Bob. Which ***road*** do you usually take to the office?

B: A30, and then, I ***turn*** on to Hoping Road.

A: Would you mind ***picking*** me ***up on*** your ***way to*** the office tomorrow?

B: Of course not. Where are you living now? And where should I pick you up?

A: I'm living near the Hoping Hospital. So if it is ***convenient*** for you...

B: That is all right. Why don't you wait for me in front of the Hoping Hospital at eight thirty?

A: It's very kind of you.

A: 嗨，鮑伯。你上班通常都走哪條路？
B: 通常都走 A30 公路，然後轉到和平路上。
A: 你介意明天上班途中，讓我搭你的便車嗎？
B: 當然不介意。你現在住在哪裡？我要在哪裡讓你上車？
A: 我住在靠近和平醫院的地方。如果你方便的話……
B: 沒關係。你何不八點半在和平醫院正前方等我？
A: 你真好。

核心詞彙

Words&Phrases

road	[rod]	名詞 路
turn	[tɝn]	動詞 轉彎
pick up	[pɪk ʌp]	片語 接送
on one's way to	[ɑn wʌns ˋwe tu]	片語 在某人去……途中
convenient	[kənˋvɪnjənt]	形容詞 方便的

日常實用短句 Useful Sentences

- Can you give me a ride?
  你可以載我一程嗎？
- Can I hitch a ride?
  我可以搭便車嗎？
- You can just drop me off at the intersection.
  你可以在路口放我下車。
- Do you mind giving me a lift home?
  你介意開車載我回家嗎？
- It's very nice of you to give me a ride.
  你能載我一程真是太好了。
- Do you need a ride home?
  需要載你回家嗎？
- Can you drop me off at the airport on your way to work?
  你去上班的路上能在機場放我下車嗎？
- Can I catch a ride with you?
  我可以和你一起搭車嗎？
- Which direction are you heading to?
  你要往哪個方向去？
- Since we are going the same way, do you mind if I share a taxi with you?
  既然我們要往同一個方向，你介意我們共乘一台計程車嗎？
- Hope it's not too much of an inconvenience.
  希望不會造成太大不便。
- Hope it is not out of your way.
  希望你不會不順路。

學習++ More Tips

在外國電影中常常會看到有人在路邊豎起大拇指，搭人家便車，這就叫做「hitchhike」。在國外也流行「car pool」，也就是一個媽媽或爸爸負責開車接送好多家的小朋友上下學，或是上班族也有這樣的搭便車。

05 請勿吸菸

TRACK 045.

實境對話 Conversation

A: Excuse me. But this is a non-smoking area.

B: I'm sorry.

A: If you'*d like to* smoke, you can go ***outside***.

B: How do I get outside?

A: Go ***straight*** and ***turn right immediately*** after the ***secretary***'s office, and then you will ***find*** your way.

B: Thank you. Sorry for your ***inconvenience***.

A: 抱歉，這裡是非吸菸區。

B: 對不起。

A: 如果你想抽菸，可以到外面去。

B: 要怎麼出去？

A: 直走，過了祕書室後馬上右轉，你就會看到指標。

B: 謝謝，抱歉造成你的不便。

核心詞彙 Words&Phrases

would like to	[wʊd ˋlaɪk tu]	片語 想要……
outside	[ˋaʊtˋsaɪd]	名詞 外面
straight	[stret]	形容詞 直的
turn right	[tɝt raɪt]	片語 右轉
immediately	[ɪˋmidɪɪtly]	副詞 立刻、馬上
secretary	[ˋsɛkrəˏtɛrɪ]	名詞 祕書
find	[faɪnd]	動詞 找到
inconvenience	[ˏɪnkənˋvinjəns]	名詞 不便之處

日常實用短句 Useful Sentences

- No smoking, please.
  請不要抽菸。
- Please don't smoke in the restaurant.
  請勿在餐廳裡吸菸。
- Do you mind if I smoke here?
  你介意我在這裡抽菸嗎？
- Smoking is banned in most of the public places.
  大部分的公共場所都禁止抽菸。
- There's a non-smoking sign here.
  這裡有個非吸菸區的標示。
- Smoking is bad for health.
  抽菸對健康不好。
- Second hand smoke is also dangerous to your health.
  二手菸也會對你的健康有害。
- Smoking increases the risk of lung cancer.
  抽菸提高產生肺癌的風險
- Smoking is not permitted on all airplanes.
  所有飛機上都禁止抽菸。
- Non-smokers are easily irritated by the cigarette smoke.
  不抽菸的人很容易被煙霧嗆到。
- I've already quit smoking.
  我已經戒菸了。

學習++ More Tips

現在的餐廳與許多公共場合都會分「smoking or non-smoking area」（吸菸或非吸菸區）。如果在不該抽菸的公共場合有人抽菸，你可以含蓄的跟他們說：「Would you mind putting out that cigarette?」（你介不介意把菸熄掉？），或是說：「Do you mind?」（你介意嗎？），但這句話的語氣不是那麼的客氣。

06 請求幫忙

TRACK 046.

實境對話

Conversation

A: Would you do me a favor?

B: Sure, if I can.

A: Good. How about going to the ***deli*** across the street and buying me some food?

A: And then post this letter in the ***post box***, which you can find ***around the corner***.

B: All right. ***What else***?

A: And then find a ***parking space*** for me. Here's my car key. Right now it is ***double-parked*** in front of the building.

B: OKay.

A: 可不可以幫我個忙？

B: 當然，如果我做得到的話。

A: 好，那麼可否請你到對街的熟食店，幫我買點東西吃？

A: 然後再幫我把這封信投到轉角口的郵筒。

B: 好。還有呢？

A: 然後幫我找個停車位，這是我的車鑰匙。車子現在並排停在大樓前面。

B: 好的。

核心詞彙

Words&Phrases

deli	[ˋdɛlɪ]	名詞 熟食店
post box	[post bɑks]	名詞 郵筒
around the corner	[əˋraund ðə ˋkɔrnɚ]	片語 轉角
What else...?	[hwɑt ˋɛls]	片語 還有其他……？

parking space	[ˋparkɪŋ spes]	名詞 停車位
double-park	[ˋdʌbḷ park]	動詞 並排停車

日常實用短句 Useful Sentences

- Could you give me a hand?
  你可以幫我個忙嗎？
- My pleasure.
  我的榮幸。
- Help me, please.
  請幫幫我。
- Do you mind if I use the ladder?
  你介意我用這個梯子嗎？
- Thank you for your help.
  謝謝你的幫忙。
- I appreciate your time and effort.
  感謝你的時間與付出。
- How can I help you?
  有什麼能幫忙的嗎？
- Can you help me?
  你能幫我嗎？
- I wonder if you could tell me how to get to the supermarket.
  我在想你是不是能告訴我超市怎麼去。
- I'm glad I can help.
  我很高興能幫得上忙。

學習++ More Tips

當你請求幫忙的時候除了說：「Could you do something for me?」（你可以幫我做一件事嗎？），還可以婉轉的說：「Would it be too much trouble if you helped me to...?」（你若是幫我……會不會很麻煩？）。

07 問路

實境對話

Conversation

A: Excuse me. Could you show me how to ***get to*** the National Palace Museum?

B: Ok. You go south three ***blocks***. On your ***right hand side***. You will see a huge Chinese palace style ***building***. That's it.

A: I am lost. Is there a ***subway station*** around here?

B: Yes. You go this way until you get to the next ***traffic light***. The subway ***entrance*** is just over there.

A: 對不起，能不能告訴我怎麼去故宮博物院？

B: 可以。從這裡向南走 3 條街區，右邊的大中國宮殿式建築物即是。

A: 我迷路了。這附近有地下鐵車站嗎？

B: 是的。就從這裡穿過去，走到下一個交通號誌，地下鐵入口就在那裡。

核心詞彙

Words&Phrases

get to	[gɛt tu]	片語 到達
block	[blɑk]	名詞 街區
right hand side	[raɪt hænd saɪd]	片語 右手邊
building	[ˋbɪldɪŋ]	名詞 建築物
subway station	[ˋsʌb͵we ˋsteʃən]	名詞 地下鐵車站
traffic light	[ˋtræfɪk laɪt]	名詞 紅綠燈
entrance	[ˋɛntrəns]	名詞 入口

日常實用短句 Useful Sentences

- I got lost.
  我迷路了。
- Where do you want to go?
  你想去哪裡？
- Excuse me, how can I get to the movie theater?
  不好意思，電影院該怎麼去？
- Walk along this street and turn right at the first intersection.
  沿著這條路走，然後在第一個交叉口右轉。
- Go down the road, walk two blocks and you'll see it.
  往這條路走兩個街口，你就會看到了。
- You will have to take the bus.
  你必須搭公車。
- Where is the nearest bus stop?
  最近的公車站牌在哪裡？
- Is there any landmark there?
  那裡有任何路標嗎？
- Could you point me to the right direction, please?
  請問你可以告訴我正確的方向嗎？
- You're walking in the opposite direction.
  你走反方向了。
- I'd rather go by taxi.
  我寧願搭計程車去。

學習++ More Tips

到陌生的國家旅遊若是迷路就糟糕了，所以這裡有幾句實用的英文可以當成你在迷路時候的救星：「I am lost.」（我迷路了）、「Can you help me?」（你可以幫我嗎？）、「Can you show me the way?」（你可以告訴我路嗎？）、「How can I get to...?」（我如何才能到達……？）。

08 提出抱怨

TRACK 048.

實境對話 Conversation

A: I ***ordered*** a computer and paid for it last week. But it hasn't been ***delivered so far***.

B: I'm sorry. Can I have your order number?

A: Got it. It's 00351.

B: Sorry, miss. The model you ordered has been ***out of stock*** for two weeks.

A: It's ***none of my business***, but I think your salesman should have ***informed*** me.

B: I'm terribly sorry. Could you leave your telephone number so I can call you after I check the ***situation*** with the shipping department?

A: 我上週訂了一部電腦，還付了錢。但到現在都還沒送來。

B: 對不起，請問你的訂貨編號是多少？

A: 找到了，是 00351。

B: 小姐，很抱歉。你所訂的型號已經缺貨兩週了。

A: 那不關我的事，可是我覺得你的業務員應該通知我啊。

B: 真的很抱歉，你可否留下電話號碼，等我跟出貨部門弄清楚狀況，再打電話給你。

核心詞彙 Words&Phrases

order	[ˋɔrdɚ]	動詞 下訂
deliver	[dɪˋlɪvɚ]	動詞 運送
so far	[so fɑr]	片語 目前為止
out of stock	[aʊt ɑv stɑk]	片語 缺貨
none of my business	[nʌn ɑv maɪ ˋbɪznɪs]	片語 不關我的事

inform	[ɪn`fɔrm]	動詞 通知
situation	[ˏsɪtʃʊ`eʃən]	名詞 情況

日常實用短句 Useful Sentences

- I believe that you can do better.
  我相信你可以做得更好。
- Are you kidding me?
  你是在開玩笑嗎？
- You will have to re-do it
  你必須重做。
- I can't stand it anymore.
  我無法再忍受了。
- It's a rip-off.
  這是冒牌貨。
- Please turn the music down a little bit. Thanks.
  請把音樂關小聲一點，謝謝。
- This is not what I expected.
  這不是我想要的。
- Have you tried your best?
  你已經盡力了嗎？
- Stop nagging me.
  不要再唸我了。
- You need to watch your attitude.
  你必須注意你的態度。

學習++ More Tips

「got it」的用法很多，比方說，當有人跟你解釋一個題目然後問你懂了沒：「Do you get it?」（你懂了嗎？），「Yes, I got it.」（我懂了。）；或是當有人說：「Did you get the keys?」（你有沒有拿鑰匙？），「Got it.」（拿了。）。

09 到郵局寄物

TRACK 049.

實境對話

Conversation

A: I want to send this small ***parcel*** to Canada.

B: By ***airmail*** or ***surface mail***?

A: How different are the rates?

B: Your parcel weights 420 grams. So it's 213 dollars ***by air***, or 69 dollars ***by sea***.

A: By sea, please.

B: Please ***fill out*** this form, and then take your parcel to the counter on my ***left hand side***.

A: All right. Thank you very much.

A: 我想把這個小包裹寄到加拿大。

B: 空運還是海運？

A: 郵資有什麼差別？

B: 你的包裹重 420 公克。所以空運是 213 元，海運則是 69 元。

A: 那就寄海運吧。

B: 請填好這張單子，然後把包裹拿到我左手邊的櫃檯。

A: 好的，非常謝謝。

核心詞彙

Words&Phrases

parcel	[ˋpɑrsḷ]	名詞 包裹
airmail	[ˋɛr͵mel]	名詞 航空信件
surface mail	[ˋsɝfɪs mel]	名詞 普通平信
by air	[baɪ ˋɛr]	片語 空運
by sea	[baɪ ˋsi]	片語 海運
fill out	[fɪl aʊt]	片語 填寫
left hand side	[lɛft hænd saɪd]	片語 左手邊

日常實用短句 Useful Sentences

- I want to mail these cards.
  我想寄這些卡片。
- Where can I buy stamps?
  我在哪裡買得到郵票？
- How much is the postage?
  郵資多少？
- It will be NT$10 dollars.
  總共 10 元。
- I want to send this parcel to US.
  我想寄這個包裹去美國。
- By air or surface?
  空運還是海運？
- How much would it cost to ship this parcel by air?
  空運這個包裹要多少錢？
- Let me weight it for you.
  我來幫你秤重量。
- How do you like to send it?
  你想要怎麼寄？
- I'd like a receipt.
  我要發票。
- It takes 7 days by airmail.
  空運要 7 天時間。
- I want to send this document by registered mail.
  這個文件我要寄掛號。

學習++ More Tips

到郵局的時候，你還需要用的句子有：「I need to buy some stamps.」（我需要買一些郵票。）、「I want to air mail this letter.」（這封信我想寄航空件。）、「I need to send parcel by express.」（我需限時專送這個包裹。）。

10 到銀行存款

TRACK050.

實境對話

Conversation

A: I'd like to open a ***savings account***.

B: We have general ***current*** accounts, and special current accounts.

A: What's a special current account?

B: With a special current account one had to have at least 200,000 dollars in the account ***at any time***. But the ***interest rate*** is higher than that of a general current account.

B: While with the general current account there's no ***minimum balance***.

A: A general current account seems like just the thing for me.

A: 我想開個存款帳戶。

B: 我們有一般活期存款，和特別活期存款。

A: 特別活期存款是什麼？

B: 特別活期存款的帳戶必須隨時保持二十萬元以上。但它的利息比一般活期存款帳戶高。

B: 而一般活期存款帳戶沒有最低金額限制。

A: 一般活期存款帳戶大概比較適合我。

核心詞彙

Words&Phrases

savings account	[ˋsevɪŋz əˋkaunt]	名詞 存款帳戶
current	[ˋkɝənt]	形容詞 通用的
at any time	[æt ˋɛnɪ taɪm]	片語 在任何時候
interest rate	[ˋɪntərɪst ret]	名詞 利率
minimum balance	[ˋmɪnəməm ˋbæləns]	名詞 最小餘額

日常實用短句 Useful Sentences

- I'd like to open an account.
  我想開一個戶頭。
- Do you want to open a checking account?
  你要開支票戶頭嗎？
- Can you give me some suggestions?
  你可以給我些建議嗎？
- Checking and savings account.
  支票帳戶和存款帳戶。
- Fill out the forms, please.
  請填好這些表格。
- May I see your ID, please?
  我可以看你的身分證嗎？
- How much do I need to deposit to open an account?
  開戶要存多少錢？
- What is the annual interest rate?
  年利率是多少？
- How much do you want to deposit today?
  你今天要存多少錢？
- Here's your passbook and bank card.
  這是你的存簿和金融卡。
- You may use the ATMs to deposit and withdraw money.
  你可以用 ATM 領錢或存錢。

學習++ More Tips

當你要把錢存到銀行裡，「存」的英文除了用「save」還可以用「deposit」，「I want to deposit my money in the bank.」（我想把我的錢存在銀行裡。），而把錢從銀行提出所用的單字則要用「withdraw」，「I withdraw my money from the bank.」（我從銀行裡把我的錢提出來。）。

11 搭捷運

TRACK 051.

實境對話

Conversation

A: How long will it take to go to the zoo ***by taxi***?

B: It ***depends on*** traffic. But why don't you use the Rapid Transit System?

A: Oh, I haven't been to this city for years. Has the ***construction*** of the Rapid Transit System been completed?

B: Yes. You can take the Brown Line. Its main ***terminal*** is the zoo.

A: Are the trains safe and comfortable?

B: Well, I should say so, though the trains seem to ***swing unsteadily*** when they go very fast.

A: 坐計程車去動物園得花多少時間？

B: 那要看交通狀況。但你為什麼不搭捷運去？

A: 哦，我很多年沒來這個城市了。捷運系統已經完工了嗎？

B: 是啊！你可以搭棕線，它的終點就是動物園。

A: 車子安全、舒服嗎？

B: 恩，可以這麼說，雖然車子行駛得很快時，車身好像有點搖擺不穩。

核心詞彙

Words&Phrases

by taxi	[baɪ ˋtæksɪ]	片語 搭計程車
depend on	[dɪˋpɛnd ɑn]	片語 視……而定
construction	[kənˋstrʌkʃən]	名詞 建設、建造
terminal	[ˋtɝmən!]	名詞 終點站
swing	[swɪŋ]	動詞 搖晃
unsteadily	[ʌnˋstɛdɪlɪ]	副詞 不穩地

日常實用短句 *Useful Sentences*

- You should change trains at Taipei Main Station.
  你要在台北車站換車。
- No eating, drinking and smoking.
  請勿飲食及吸菸。
- Watch your head.
  小心你的頭。
- For your safety, please hold on to handrails at all times.
  為了安全，請隨時抓著扶手。
- Get a grip.
  抓緊。
- The next station is Long-shan Temple.
  下一站是龍山寺。
- Violators will be fined up to NT$7500.
  違規者會被罰高達台幣 7500 元。
- You can buy your ticket from a ticket vending machine.
  你可以在自動售票機買車票。
- Mind the platform gap.
  小心月台間隙。
- Yield seats to elderly, infirm passengers, and women with children.
  讓座給老人、行動不便的乘客還有帶小孩的婦女。
- Is this train bound to Dam Shui?
  這班車是往淡水的嗎？
- Do not lean on doors.
  不要倚靠車門。

學習++ *More Tips*

在台灣的捷運叫做「MRT」(Mass Rapid Transportation)，而英美國家則有「subway」（地下鐵）。

12 診所

TRACK 052.

實境對話

Conversation

A: What's wrong with you?

B: I have a ***fever***. I have a ***headache*** and ***diarrhea***.

A: Let me check your ***temperature*** and ***blood pressure***.

A: ***Are*** you ***allergic to*** any kinds of medicine?

B: Not at all.

A: Please take this ***prescription*** to the ***drugstore*** and have them filled it for you.

A: 你覺得哪裡不舒服呢？

B: 我在發燒，而且頭很痛，也拉肚子。

A: 我替你量量體溫和血壓。

A: 你對什麼藥物會過敏嗎？

B: 完全不會。

A: 請拿這個處方去藥房配藥。

核心詞彙

Words&Phrases

fever	[ˋfivɚ]	名詞 發燒
headache	[ˋhɛd͵ek]	名詞 頭痛
diarrhea	[͵daɪəˋriə]	名詞 腹瀉
temperature	[ˋtɛmprətʃɚ]	名詞 溫度
blood pressure	[blʌd ˋprɛʃɚ]	名詞 血壓
be allergic to	[bi əˋlɝdʒɪk tu]	片語 對……過敏
prescription	[prɪˋskɪpʃən]	名詞 處方
drugstore	[ˋdrʌg͵stor]	名詞 藥房

日常實用短句 Useful Sentences

- May I have your health insurance card, please?
  請給我你的健保卡，好嗎？
- Have you ever been here before?
  之前有來過嗎？
- The registration fee is NT$50 dollars.
  掛號費 50 元。
- If you don't have health insurance, there will be a full charge.
  如果你沒有健保，就必須全額負擔。
- I'll take your temperature first.
  我先會幫你量體溫。
- Please wait here and we will call your name.
  請在這裡稍後，我們會叫你的名字。
- What is your symptom?
  你有什麼症狀？
- I need to make an appointment for next visit.
  我要先預約下一次的門診。
- There will be an additional fee for medication.
  藥物另外收費。
- Here is your prescription.
  這是你的處方箋。
- Hope you get well soon, Mr. Wu.
  吳先生，希望你趕快好起來。
- If the discomfort continues in the next 24 hours, please give us a call.
  如果接下來 24 小時還是不舒服，請打電話過來。

學習++ More Tips

除了上述的「diarrhea」（拉肚子）、「fever」（發燒），我們較常發生的一些症狀有「running nose」（流鼻水）、「cold」（感冒）、「flu」（流行感冒），而表達方法則是「I have a running nose.」（我流鼻水。）。

13 看醫生

實境對話 Conversation

A: What's the matter with you, Mr. Wang?

B: Well, I have a sore throat and a ***cough***. And it's hard for me to ***breathe*** through my nose.

A: Do you have a headache?

B: Yes, my head pounds. And I had a fever yesterday.

A: How is your ***appetite***?

B: Very bad. I do not want to eat anything, even my favorite chocolate pie.

B: Will you ***give*** me ***a shot***?

A: No, no. But here is your prescription. You need to take some pills.

A: 哪裡不舒服，王先生？

B: 嗯，我喉嚨痛，還咳嗽，而且鼻塞呼吸困難。

A: 頭痛不痛？

B: 也很痛。昨天還發燒。

A: 胃口怎麼樣？

B: 很差。不想吃任何東西，即使我最喜歡的巧克力派也是。

B: 要不要打針？

A: 不，不用。不過必須吃點藥，這是處方。

核心詞彙 Words&Phrases

cough	[kɔf]	名詞 咳嗽
breathe	[brið]	動詞 呼吸
appetite	[ˋæpəˏtaɪt]	名詞 胃口
give a shot	[gɪv ə ʃɑt]	片語 打針

日常實用短句 Useful Sentences

- What's wrong with you?
  你怎麼了？
- I have a terrible headache.
  我頭非常痛。
- Aren't you feeling well?
  你不舒服嗎？
- I have no appetite.
  我沒有胃口。
- I'm a bit under the westher.
  我有點不舒服。
- Take the medicine on time.
  準時吃藥。
- You will get better soon.
  你很快就會好起來了。
- I'm feeling much better now.
  我現在覺得好多了。
- I need to take your temperature.
  我必須幫你量體溫。
- How long have you been feeling like this?
  你已經這樣多久了？
- Since last night.
  昨天晚上開始。
- I'm still feeling dizzy.
  我還是覺得很暈。

學習++ More Tips

在國外看醫生，醫生都會開一個「prescription」（處方），讓你到「pharmacy」（藥房）去買藥。而國外的「drug store」（藥房）有一些藥可供名眾自由採買，但有一些則是需要醫生的「prescription」才能買到的。

14 牙醫診所

TRACK 054.

實境對話

Conversation

A: Could you check my ***teeth*** for me?

B: Please open your month ***wide***, let me have a look.

B: ***Which one*** is ***painful***?

A: Here.

B: You have a ***cavity***.

B: Please ***rinse*** your ***mouth***.

B: I will ***fill*** the cavity for you.

A: 請你檢查一下我的牙齒。

B: 請張大嘴巴，我看一下。

B: 哪一顆牙齒你覺得疼痛呢？

A: 這裡。

B: 這個牙齒被蛀了。

B: 請漱漱口。

B: 我替你把它補起來。

核心詞彙

Words&Phrases

teeth	[tiθ]	名詞 牙齒
wide	[waɪd]	副詞 很大地
which one...?	[hwɪtʃ wʌn]	片語 哪一個……?
painful	[ˋpenfəl]	形容詞 疼痛的
cavity	[ˋkævətɪ]	名詞 蛀牙
rinse	[rɪns]	動詞 漱、沖洗
mouth	[maʊθ]	名詞 嘴巴
fill	[fɪl]	動詞 補、填滿

日常實用短句 Useful Sentences

- I've got a toothache.
  我牙痛。
- How long do I have to wait?
  我要等多久？
- I can't eat anything.
  我什麼都不能吃。
- You will need root canals.
  你需要抽神經。
- Perhaps you need teeth implants.
  或許你需要植牙。
- Before the teeth implant procedure, you need to take anti-inflammatory.
  在植牙之前，你必須先吃消炎藥。
- This procedure requires 3 separate visits.
  你需要來三次。
- Local anaesthesia will be used to numb the area before the procedure.
  在手術之前會先做局部麻醉。
- Here is the pamphlet that shows you the correct way of brush teeth.
  這個小冊子可以教你怎麼正確的刷牙。
- Remember to brush your teeth after every meal!
  記得要在每一餐之後刷牙。
- Don't be scared. It will be over in no time!
  不要害怕，很快就結束了。

學習++ More Tips

當你牙疼、牙齒蛀了，你可以說「I have a cavity.」，而現在極為普遍的牙套的英文則是「braces」，牙醫叫做「dentist」，而專門矯正牙齒的醫生則叫做「orrhodonist」。假牙除了可以說是「fake teeth」，也可以用「denture」來表示。

15 藥房買藥

TRACK 055.

實境對話

Conversation

A: I have a ***sore throat***. I think I've ***caught a cold***. Could I have some ***medicine***?

B: These are for colds. But if you do not feel better tomorrow, you'd better see the doctor. The doctor will give you a prescription.

A: I'd like to buy ***eye drops***.

B: Which brand do you like?

A: I'm not sure. Are they all the same?

B: No. Some are for general use. The others are for specific ***ailments***.

A: I only need one for general use.

A: 我喉嚨痛，大概是感冒了。可以買一點藥嗎？

B: 這些是治感冒藥，但如果你明天還沒有覺得比較好，最好去看醫生。他會給你開處方。

A: 我想買眼藥水。

B: 你喜歡什麼牌子的？

A: 不曉得，都一樣嗎？

B: 不，有些是一般使用的，有些則是特殊治療用。

A: 我只需要一般用的。

核心詞彙

Words&Phrases

sore throat	[sor θrot]	片語 喉嚨痛
catch a cold	[kætʃ ə kold]	片語 感冒
medicine	[ˋmɛdəsn̩]	名詞 藥物
eye drops	[aɪ drɑps]	名詞 眼藥水
ailment	[ˋelmənt]	名詞 疼痛、疾病

日常實用短句 Useful Sentences

- I want to buy some medicine for diarrhea.
  我要買一些腹瀉的藥。
- Are you allergic to any drugs?
  你有對什麼藥過敏嗎？
- Take a good rest for a few days.
  好好休息幾天。
- Be sure to follow the instructions.
  一定要遵照指示。
- There may be some side effects.
  可能會有些副作用。
- I am also looking for some pain killers.
  我也在找些止痛藥。
- You can't obtain these pills without a prescription.
  如果沒有處方箋就不能拿這些藥。
- Here is the prescription from my doctor.
  這是醫生給我的處方。
- Can you suggest an ointment for my backache?
  你能推薦我一些擦背痛的藥膏嗎？
- Make sure you put the medicine out of children's reach.
  務必把藥放在孩子們拿不到的地方。
- How should I take the pills?
  我要怎麼服這些藥？
- Take two tablets every four hours.
  每四個小時吃兩片藥。

學習++ More Tips

在國外「pharmacy」和「drug store」都是「藥房」的意思，它們和台灣的藥房不一樣的，就是他們除了有賣「drug、medicine」（藥）之外，它們還像一個小的超市，賣許多的日用品呢！

16 圖書館

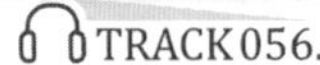

實境對話

Conversation

A: Is there a city ***library*** around here?
B: Yes, it's just next door to Central Station.
A: Is it open weekends and holidays?
B: Yes. It's open ***all year round***.
A: Are ***foreigners*** also able to use this library?
B: Of course. You just show your I.D. to them, then you may go in.
A: If you got a ***library card***, how many books are you allowed to borrow at one time?
B: You may borrow up to 10 books at one time. The ***time limit*** is three weeks.

A: 請問這附近有市立圖書館嗎？
B: 有，在中央車站的隔壁。
A: 在周末或假日也開放嗎？
B: 是的，整年都不休息。
A: 這個圖書館，外國人也可以使用嗎？
B: 當然可以，你只要給他們看你的身分證就可以進入了。
A: 若有借書證的話，最多可以借幾本書呢？
B: 一次可以借出 10 本，期限 3 周。

核心詞彙

Words&Phrases

library	[ˋlaɪˏbrɛrɪ]	名詞 圖書館
all year round	[ɔl jɪr raʊnd]	片語 全年
foreigner	[ˋfɔrɪnɚ]	名詞 外國人
library card	[ˋlaɪˏbrarɪ kɑrd]	名詞 借書證

time limit	[taɪm ˋlɪmɪt]	名詞 時間限制

日常實用短句 *Useful Sentences*

- How do I check out books?
  我要怎麼外借書？
- There's a Children's Story Time on Saturday afternoon.
  星期六下午有兒童故事時間。
- There is a fine if you don't return the books on time.
  如果你沒有準時還書會罰款。
- Please be quiet around other readers in the library.
  在圖書館內的其他閱讀者旁邊請安靜。
- Get ready for reading activities in the library on Fridays.
  請準備好禮拜五在圖書館的閱讀活動。
- Keep the volume to a minimum to avoid disturbing others.
  請保持最低音量以避免打擾其他人。
- You need a get a library card to check out books.
  你必須有借書證才能外借書。
- How do I get library card?
  我要怎麼得到借書證？
- Is there a limit on the number of items I can check out?
  有限制可以外借幾本書嗎？
- How long can the books be checked out each time?
  書一次可以借多久？
- Can I check out the same item again?
  我可以再借一次同樣的書嗎？

學習++ *More Tips*

外國人很喜歡閱讀，並且很注重閱讀的品質，而去圖書館借書也算是他們生活的一部份。「I.D.」是「identification」（身分確認）的縮寫，而「ID card」也就是我們所謂的身分證。

17 洗衣店

TRACK 057.

實境對話

Conversation

A: What can I do for you, Sir?
B: Could you ***clean*** this ***jacket*** for me?
A: Do you want it ***dry-cleaned***?
B: Ok, can you ***remove*** this ***stain***?
A: I'll ***do my best***.
B: When will it ***be ready***? And how much is it?
A: It should be ready ***around*** 3p.m. The total is 250 dollars. Thank you!

A: 歡迎光臨，請問我可以為您做什麼呢？
B: 想請你替我洗這件夾克。
A: 需要乾洗嗎？
B: 好吧，這個汙點洗的掉嗎？
A: 我盡力試試看。
B: 大概幾點會好呢？洗衣費多少錢呢？
A: 大約下午三點可以好。全部 250 元，謝謝！

核心詞彙

Words&Phrases

clean	[klin]	動詞 清洗
jacket	[ˋdʒækɪt]	名詞 夾克
dry-clean	[draɪ klin]	動詞 乾洗
remove	[rɪˋmuv]	動詞 移除
stain	[sten]	名詞 污漬
do my best	[du maɪ bɛst]	片語 我盡力
be ready	[bi ˋrɛdɪ]	片語 準備好

around	[əˋraund]	副詞 附近、大約

日常實用短句 *Useful Sentences*

- My coat needs to be dry-cleaned.
  我的外套需要乾洗。
- There is a laundromat just around the corner down the street.
  就在這條街的轉角有一間自助洗衣。
- It takes me about two hours to finish my laundry.
  我洗一次衣服要花兩個小時。
- Each wash takes about three dollars in coins.
  洗一次衣服要差不多三塊錢。
- Before the second rinse cycle, I will add the fabric softener.
  在洗衣機運轉第二次之前，我會加點柔軟精。
- I always use the dryer to dry my clothes.
  我通常會用烘乾機把我的衣服烘乾。
- Separate your clothes into dark and light colors and wash them separately.
  把深色和淺色的衣服分開洗。
- The drying machine is not working properly.
  烘乾機稍微有點故障。
- Some people wash the delicates separately.
  有些人會把纖薄衣服分開洗。
- I love the smell of freshly washed clothes.
  我喜歡洗過的衣服那種清新的味道。

學習++ *More Tips*

當你單身或是有無法自己處理的衣物時，洗衣店是最方便不過的了。在衣服標籤上的洗衣方式我們常會看到的英文包括：「dry clean」（乾洗）、「tumble dry」（烘乾）、「iron」（燙）、「hand wash」（手洗）……等。只要多留意一下，衣服就可以保存更久一些。

18 理髮店

TRACK 058.

實境對話

Conversation

A: I didn't make an appointment. Is that ok?

B: That's fine. But you probably need to wait about 15 minutes.

B: Thank you for your ***patience***. How would you like your ***hair cut***?

A: I would like to have a ***wash*** and cut, but not too ***short***, please.

B: Do you want to have a ***perm***?

A: I'm too busy today, I don't have enough time.

B: Does the water temperature suit you?

A: It's a little bit too hot for me.

A: 沒有預約也可以嗎？

B: 可以，不過大概要等 15 分鐘左右。

B: 讓您久等了，你要怎麼剪你的頭髮？

A: 請幫我洗頭及剪髮，但不要剪的太短。

B: 要不要燙髮呢？

A: 今天我很忙，沒有時間。

B: 水溫可以嗎？

A: 稍微燙了點。

核心詞彙

Words&Phrases

patience	[ˋpeʃəns]	名詞 耐心
hair	[hɛr]	名詞 頭髮
cut	[kʌt]	動詞 剪
wash	[wɑʃ]	動詞 洗
short	[ʃɔrt]	形容詞 短的
perm	[pɝm]	名詞 燙髮

日常實用短句 Useful Sentences

- I'd like to have a haircut.
  我想要剪頭髮。
- Well, this is my first time here.
  嗯，這是我第一次來。
- How would you like your hair cut?
  你想剪成什麼樣？
- Just trim the fringe a little bit shorter.
  只要把瀏海修短一點。
- I want to color my hair.
  我想染頭髮。
- I am going to blow-dry your hair now.
  我現在要把你的頭髮吹乾。
- Can you make my hair look exactly like the woman's in this picture?
  你可以把我的頭髮弄成跟照片裡的女人一樣嗎？
- How much do you charge for a shampoo?
  洗頭髮要多少錢？
- Will it take a long time?
  要很久嗎？
- It will be around 30 minutes.
  大概三十分鐘。

學習++ More Tips

「barber shop」指的是給男士的理髮店，而女士通常會去「beauty salon」（美容院）。去弄頭髮時有幾個單字要學會的：「trim」（修）、「perm」（燙）、「wavy hair」（波浪頭）、「curly hair」（捲髮），而當你想把頭髮留長，你會說「I want to grow my hair.」。

19 照相館

TRACK 059.

實境對話

Conversation

A: Please ***develop*** this ***film*** for me.

B: I'll do it.

A: When do you think it will be ready?

B: In three hours you may come to ***collect*** your ***photos***. Here is your receipt.

A: By the way, could you please give me two ***batteries*** this size?

B: Welcome! May I help you, Sir?

A: I come to pick up my photos, this is the receipt.

B: Please wait a moment...Here they are!

A: 請你幫我沖洗這卷底片。

B: 好的。

A: 大概什麼時候會好呢？

B: 你大約 3 個小時後可以來取件，這是你的存根。

A: 另外，請你給我兩顆這樣大小的電池。

B: 歡迎光臨，有什麼需要服務的嗎？

A: 我來拿相片，這是我的存根。

B: 請稍後一下……啊！這個就是。

核心詞彙

Words&Phrases

develop	[dɪˋvɛləp]	動詞 沖洗相片
film	[fɪlm]	名詞 底片
collect	[kəˋlɛkt]	動詞 領取
photo	[ˋfoto]	名詞 照片
battery	[ˋbætərɪ]	名詞 電池

日常實用短句 Useful Sentences

- Do you know any good photography studios?
  你知道有什麼好的照相館嗎？
- Alicia is a popular photographer.
  艾莉西亞是個很受歡迎的攝影師。
- My family takes the family photos twice a year.
  我們家每年會拍兩次全家福照片。
- I need a passport photo taken.
  我需要去拍護照用的照片。
- I need extra prints of these photos.
  我要多洗這些照片。
- I need to get this picture enlarged.
  我要放大這個圖片。
- Do you take photos for newborns?
  你幫新生兒拍照嗎？
- Do you have a preferred photographer?
  你有比較想要的攝影師嗎？
- I prefer to have the originals on CDs.
  我想要把底片存在 CD。
- Most pictures are taken with a digital camera nowadays.
  現在大部分的照片都是數位相機拍的。
- Digital files make printing pictures quick and easy.
  數位檔案讓沖洗照片更快更簡單。
- Do you like your pictures glossy or matted?
  你想要你的照片是亮面或非亮面的？

學習++ More Tips

我們最常犯的一個錯就是把「洗照片」直接翻譯成「wash film」，而正確的說法應該是「develop the film」。外國人在照相的時候，喜歡說「Say cheese.」，因為，當你說「cheese」的時候嘴巴向兩側咧開，看起來就像在笑。

20 超市購物

TRACK 060.

實境對話

Conversation

A: Excuse me, young lady, we have free samples now. Do you want to try?
B: Well, ***not bad***. How much for one ***kilo***?
A: One kilo for 350 dollars.

A: What are you ***looking for***?
B: I can't find the ***pet food***.
A: It's at the ***end*** of this aisle.

A: I would like to take that ***fish***. Could you ***double bag*** it?
B: No problem!

A: 小姐，這裡有試吃，妳要不要試試看？
B: 嗯，還不錯，一公斤賣多少錢呢？
A: 一公斤 350 元。

A: 請問您在找什麼？
B: 我找不到寵物食品。
A: 在這條通道的最末端。

A: 我要這條魚，能幫我裝兩層袋子嗎？
B: 沒有問題！

核心詞彙

Words&Phrases

not bad	[nɑt bæd]	片語 不錯
kilo	[ˋkilo]	名詞 公斤
look for	[lʊk for]	片詞 尋找
pet food	[pɛt fud]	名詞 寵物食品
end	[ɛnd]	名詞 盡頭、末端
fish	[fɪʃ]	名詞 魚

double	[ˋdʌbl̩]	副詞 雙重地
bag	[bæg]	動詞 裝入袋中

日常實用短句 *Useful Sentences*

- Let's get a shopping cart first.
  我們去拿個手推車。
- I need to buy some eggs.
  我需要買些蛋。
- What's on sale today?
  今天什麼有特價？
- You can buy three and get one free.
  可以買三送一。
- I'm looking for toothpastes.
  我在找牙膏。
- They are on isle C.
  它們在 C 區。
- It's a good deal if you buy them with coupons.
  如果你用折價券買這些很划算。
- I need to do some grocery shopping in the market.
  我需要去市場採買一些雜貨。
- You can buy all things at a time in the supermarket.
  你可以在超市一次購足。
- Two bottles of coke are only 1 dollar.
  兩瓶可樂只要一元。
- Mom spent NT$ 300 on fruit.
  媽媽買了三百塊的水果。
- How about some milk?
  要不要買牛奶？

學習++ *More Tips*

「kilo」是「kilogram」（公斤）的簡短說法。不過在英國、美國，他們比較習慣用「pound」（磅），作為秤重量的單位。

21 家庭及工作

TRACK061.

實境對話

Conversation

A: I have my own ***consulting*** company now.

B: Oh, great! What kind of consulting company?

A: Accounting and management consulting.

B: How many ***employees*** do you have? Are you busy?

A: Five people, including myself. I usually work over fourteen hours a day. Janet always asks me to come home earlier, and not to be so tired. I know she ***is concerned about*** my health. I had a ***gastric ulcer*** last year. She was ***frightened***.

B: Take care!

A: 我現在有自己的顧問公司。

B: 哦，好棒！什麼樣的顧問公司？

A: 做會計和管理顧問的。

B: 你有多少員工？忙不忙？

A: 有五個人，包括我自己。我每天工作通常都超過十四小時。珍妮老是叫我早點回家，不要太累。我知道她關心我的健康。我去年還胃潰瘍呢！她嚇壞了。

B: 保重啊！

核心詞彙

Words&Phrases

consulting	[kən͵sʌltɪŋ]	形容詞 顧問的
employee	[͵ɛmplɔɪˋi]	名詞 員工
be concerned about	[bi kənsɝnd əˋbaut]	片語 關心
gastric ulcer	[ˋgæstrɪk ˋʌlsɚ]	名詞 胃潰瘍
frightened	[ˋfraɪtn̩d]	形容詞 受驚的

日常實用短句 Useful Sentences

- There are four people in my family.
  我們家有四個人。
- My dad is chubby.
  我爸有點胖胖的。
- My mom goes hiking every Sunday.
  我媽每個禮拜日會去健行。
- We usually have a family trip once a year.
  我們通常一年會去一次家族旅行。
- I have been working for the bank for two years.
  我已經在銀行工作兩年了。
- My father is an engineer.
  我爸是個工程師。
- I am looking for a job now.
  我現在在找工作。
- My mom works part-time in the bakery.
  我媽在麵包店兼差。
- My brother is at college.
  我弟在念大學。
- He majors in science.
  他主修科學。

學習++ More Tips

「How's it going?」是相當口語的一句問候語，有「過的如何啊？」、「你好嗎？」的意思。除了這一句之外，你還可以說「How is everything?」（一切好嗎？）、「What's up?」（最近在幹嘛？），都是很好的問候方式。

22 談論運動

TRACK 062.

實境對話

Conversation

A: Lack of exercise ***results in*** unhealthy people.

B: I have no other choice. My apartment is too small to ***do exercise***.

A: No excuse! You can do some ***calisthenics*** exercises every night before you sleep.

B: Yes, I know. But I am so tired after work that I ***fall asleep*** immediately when I hit the bed. Besides, I prefer outdoor activities.

A: Such as?

B: For example, baseball and basketball. But my problem is I am often unable to find enough people to ***organize*** a baseball team. And you know, one-man basketball is quite boring.

A: 缺乏運動讓現代人不健康。

B: 我沒有別的選擇啊。我住的公寓太小，沒辦法做運動。

A: 別找藉口了。每天晚上睡覺前，你可以做柔軟體操啊。

B: 對，我知道。但下班後實在太累，我一碰到床就會睡著了，況且我比較喜歡戶外的運動項目。

A: 譬如呢？

B: 譬如：棒球和籃球。但問題是我時常找不到足夠的人可以組織棒球隊。還有你知道，一個人打籃球也很無聊。

核心詞彙

Words&Phrases

result in	[rɪˋzʌlt ɪn]	片語 導致
do exercise	[du ˋɛksɚˏsaɪz]	片語 做運動
calisthenics	[ˏkæləsˋθɛnɪks]	名詞 體操

fall asleep	[fɔl ə`slip]	片語 睡著
organize	[`ɔrgə͵naɪz]	動詞 組織

日常實用短句 *Useful Sentences*

- What sports do you like?
  你喜歡什麼運動？
- Do you play hockey?
  你會打曲棍球嗎？
- I like to go jogging in the morning when the air is fresh.
  我喜歡在空氣清新的早上晨跑。
- I usually play tennis twice a week.
  我通常一個禮拜會打兩次網球。
- Sit-ups and push-ups are my two least favorite daily exercises.
  仰臥起坐跟伏地挺身是我每天至少會做的兩項運動。
- I learned to play golf lately.
  我最近在學打高爾夫。
- Do you follow any sports?
  你有在做什麼運動嗎？
- Do you want to go to the gym with me on the weekend?
  你周末想和我去健身房嗎？
- Exercises and nutritious foods are essential for maintaining a good health condition.
  運動和營養飲食是保持健康的必需。

學習++ *More Tips*

外國人非常重視運動，常常上「gym」（健身房）去「work out」（練身體），可以強健和美化身體的線條。他們也相當注重戶外的活動，如「jogging」（慢跑）、「hiking」（健行），或是一些球類的運動如：「baseball」（棒球）、「football」（足球）等。

23 討論嗜好

TRACK063.

實境對話 Conversation

A: Hi, how do you spend the weekend usually? Do you have any special ***hobbies***? I'd like some suggestions on how to spend my ***free time***.

B: Well, it depends on the person. But as for me, if I do not go out, I usually spend my time working on ***puzzles***.

A: Puzzles? How ***unique*** they are! You must have a very good ***memory*** to solve puzzles.

B: Perhaps. But patience is more important.

A: I'm not patient enough to sit in front of the desk all day, just to solve a puzzle.

B: Then, you could try some small ones.

A: 嗨，你通常都怎麼過週末？有什麼特殊的嗜好嗎？請給我一點建議看如何打發空暇時間。

B: 呃，那要看人。我的話，如果不出去，通常都在玩拼圖。

A: 拼圖？好特別啊！你得有很好的記憶才能玩拼圖。

B: 或許吧。但耐心更重要。

A: 要我整天都坐在桌前拼好一幅拼圖，實在沒什麼耐心。

B: 那你可以試試比較小的拼圖。

核心詞彙 Words&Phrases

hobby	[ˋhɑbɪ]	名詞 嗜好
free time	[fri taɪm]	名詞 空閒時間
puzzles	[ˋpʌzl̩s]	名詞 拼圖
unique	[juˋnik]	形容詞 獨特的
memory	[ˋmɛmərɪ]	名詞 回憶

日常實用短句 Useful Sentences

- What's your hobby?
  你的嗜好是什麼？
- I collect bottles.
  我收集瓶子。
- I really don't have one.
  我還真的沒有。
- I would like to learn fly-fishing.
  我想學用假繩釣魚。
- I want to take up a new hobby like riding a bike.
  我想要進行一項新的嗜好，譬如騎腳踏車。
- My mother does quilting in her spare time.
  我媽媽在閒暇時間會縫紉。
- Hiking is a great way to enjoy the outdoors.
  健行是可以享受戶外生活的好方法。
- I like going to movies, especially comedies.
  我喜歡去看電影，特別是喜劇片。
- Since I love food, I like to try different restaurants.
  因為我很喜歡食物，我會去試不同的餐廳。
- You should come to the recreation center with me if you want to learn skating.
  如果你想學溜冰，你應該跟我去活動中心。
- The recreation center provides many activities and programs.
  活動中心提供很多活動和節目。

學習++ More Tips

加入俱樂部或者是健身房不可以用「add」這個動詞，而是要用「join the club」、「join the gym」或是「 join the school team」（加入校隊）；「add」則適用在「add some salt into the soup.」（在湯裡面加些鹽巴。）。

24 邀請客人

TRACK 064.

實境對話

Conversation

A: Mike and I are going to ***throw a housewarming party***. We'd like you to come. Are you available next Sunday?

B: Yes, I am. What time will the party ***begin***?

A: 5 P.M. next Sunday, at my new house. I'll give you the ***address*** later on.

B: OK. I get it! Is there anything I can ***bring*** for you?

A: Don't bother. We've got everything.

B: Fine. I will be ***looking forward to*** the party on next Sunday.

A: 麥克和我想辦一個喬遷派對。我們想邀請你參加。你下周日有空嗎？

B: 有啊！派對幾點開始呢？

A: 下周日下午五點，在我們的新房子，稍後我會給你地址。

B: 好的，我知道了！有什麼我可以幫忙帶的嗎？

A: 不用麻煩了，我們什麼都準備了。

B: 那好吧，我會期待下週日的派對的。

核心詞彙

Words&Phrases

throw a party	[θro ə ˋpɑrtɪ]	片語 開派對
housewarming	[ˋhausˏwɔrmɪŋ]	名詞 喬遷慶宴
begin	[bɪˋgɪŋ]	動詞 開始
address	[əˋdrɛs]	名詞 地址
bring	[brɪŋ]	動詞 帶
look forward to	[luk ˋfɔrˏwɚd tu]	片語 盼望

日常實用短句 Useful Sentences

- We'll have a swimming party on Sunday evening.
  禮拜日晚上我們要辦一個泳池派對。
- Please join us if you can.
  如果可以的話請來參加。
- I'd love to come.
  我想去。
- Should I bring anything?
  我要帶什麼嗎？
- Some soft drink will be good.
  一些軟性飲料就可以了。
- I'll send out the invitation cards as soon as possible.
  我會盡快寄出邀請卡。
- Do you know that Jacky Chang is going to have a concert?
  你知道張學友要開演唱會嗎？
- Are you interested?
  你有興趣嗎？
- I might not have time to go.
  我可能沒時間去。
- I'd love to, but I can't make it on that day.
  我很想，但是那天不行。
- Maybe next time.
  下次吧。

學習++ More Tips

「throw a party」是「舉行派對」的口語用法，也可以改成「give a party」（舉辦派對）。如：「They are going to throw a housewarming party.」（他們即將舉辦一個喬遷派對。）。或是「We're giving a farewell party for John.」（我們將要為約翰舉行歡送會。）。

25 招待訪客

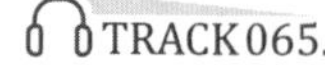

實境對話

Conversation

A: Your house is ***gorgeous***. I love the ***decoration***!
B: Thank you. Would you like something to drink? Coffee or tea?
A: Tea, please.
B: Would you like your tea with ***honey*** or lemon?
A: Ur...honey, please.
B: Here is your tea. I have some very ***tasty cookies***. You must have to try them.
A: Good. Thank you for your ***warm reception***.

A: 你的房子真漂亮。我好喜歡這裝潢！
B: 謝謝。要不要喝點東西呢，咖啡或茶？
A: 喝茶吧。
B: 你的茶要加蜂蜜還是檸檬呢？
A: 呃……蜂蜜吧，麻煩你。
B: 這是你的茶。我有些很美味的餅乾。你一定要試試看。
A: 好啊。謝謝你熱情的招待。

核心詞彙

Words&Phrases

gorgeous	[ˋgɔrdʒəs]	形容詞 漂亮的
decoration	[ˏdɛkəˋreʃən]	名詞 裝潢
honey	[ˋhʌnɪ]	名詞 蜂蜜
tasty	[ˋtestɪ]	形容詞 美味的
cookie	[ˋkʊkɪ]	名詞 餅乾
warm	[wɔrm]	形容詞 熱情的
reception	[rɪˋsɛpʃən]	名詞 招待

日常實用短句 Useful Sentences

- Please have something to drink.
  請喝點東西吧。
- These snacks are prepared just for you.
  這些點心是為你準備的。
- These gifts are for the children.
  這些禮物是給孩子們的。
- Please enjoy the dinner!
  請好好享用晚餐。
- Let me show you around the house.
  我帶你參觀一下房子。
- Please help yourself to some more.
  請多拿一點。
- There are plenty more.
  還有很多。
- Can I get you something to drink?
  要幫你拿點喝的嗎？
- Would you like something to eat?
  你想吃什麼嗎？
- Try some of these tasty appetizers.
  試試看這些美味的開胃菜。
- Can I take your coat for you?
  我可以幫你把外套掛起來嗎？
- Be at home.
  當自己家。

學習++ More Tips

到別人家中做客時，禮貌上要讚美對方的房子，如：「Your apartment is beautiful!」（你的公寓好漂亮。），若要給具體的稱讚，可以讚美其裝潢或是屋內的擺設，如：「You must have spent a lot of time furnishing the house.」（你一定花了不少時間佈置這房子吧。）。

26 買化妝品

實境對話 Conversation

A: Good afternoon. How can I help you?
B: I'd like to buy a ***lipstick***.
A: We have ***various types*** of lipsticks. Is there any specific ***color*** that you prefer?
B: I want a ***light pink*** one.
A: What about this one?
B: I am afraid it's a little too ***dark***.
A: How about this one? It's the lightest one.
B: Oh, that's what I want. I'll take it.

A: 午安，請問需要什麼？
B: 我想買支口紅。
A: 我們有各種不同類的口紅。你有特別喜歡什麼顏色的嗎？
B: 我想要淺粉色的。
A: 這款怎麼樣？
B: 我覺得它有點太深了。
A: 那麼這款呢？這是顏色最淺的了。
B: 噢，那正是我想要的。我買下了。

核心詞彙 Words&Phrases

lipstick	[ˋlɪpˏstɪk]	名詞 口紅
various	[ˋvɛrɪəs]	形容詞 多樣的
type	[taɪp]	名詞 種類
color	[ˋkʌlɚ]	名詞 顏色
light	[laɪt]	形容詞 淺色的
pink	[pɪŋk]	名詞 粉紅色
dark	[dɑrk]	形容詞 深色的

日常實用短句 *Useful Sentences*

- Can I try this lotion?
  我可以試用這個乳液嗎？
- What's your skin type?
  你是什麼種類的膚質？
- I have very sensitive skin.
  我的皮膚很敏感。
- Do you want to try this newest lip gloss?
  你要試試看這個最新的唇蜜嗎？
- This will suit your skin tone.
  這個會很搭配你的膚色。
- Can I try?
  我可以試試看嗎？
- Do you have any perfume samples?
  有任何的香水樣品嗎？
- Oh, I like this color.
  哦，我喜歡這個顏色。
- I'll take it.
  我買了。
- What does mascara do?
  睫毛膏是幹嘛用的？
- It makes your eyelashes look longer.
  它讓你的睫毛看起來更長。
- This eye cream can ease the wrinkles in two weeks.
  用這罐眼霜兩個禮拜可以撫平皺紋。

學習++ *More Tips*

「prefer」是表示「較喜歡」的意思。購買化妝品時，要清楚的將自己的喜好告知店員，好方便他幫你找到適合的款式，如：「I prefer peach to claret.」（我喜歡桃紅色勝過紫紅色。）。

27 買首飾

TRACK 067.

實境對話

Conversation

A: Can I help you, sir?

B: I'd like to buy a ***necklace*** for my wife.

A: We have many ***selections*** of beautiful necklaces. Which kind of ***materials*** do you want?

B: I'd like a ***pearl*** necklace, which I think is more elegant.

A: What do you think of this pearl necklace?

B: It looks beautiful. How much is it?

A: 500 dollars. No discount.

B: Oh, ***dear***! That's too ***expensive***.

A: 需要我幫忙嗎？先生。

B: 我想給我的妻子買條項鏈。

A: 我們有很多漂亮的項鏈可以選擇。您想要哪種材質的呢？

B: 我想買條珍珠項鏈，我覺得它更顯高雅。

A: 你覺得這條珍珠項鏈怎麼樣？

B: 它看起來很漂亮。多少錢啊？

A: 五百美元。沒有折扣。

B: 噢，天哪！它太貴了。

核心詞彙

Words&Phrases

necklace	[ˋnɛklɪs]	名詞 項鍊
selection	[səˋlɛkʃən]	名詞 選擇
material	[məˋtɪrɪəl]	名詞 材料
pearl	[pɝl]	名詞 珍珠
dear	[dɪr]	感嘆詞 天啊、哎呀
expensive	[ɪkˋspɛnsɪv]	形容詞 貴的

日常實用短句 *Useful Sentences*

- May I try on this pair of ear rings?
  我可以試試這對耳環嗎？
- I don't think they look good on me.
  我不覺得這個適合我。
- May I see this diamond ring?
  我可以看看這個鑽石戒指嗎？
- Is there a warranty?
  有保固嗎？
- These earrings look good on you.
  你戴這副耳環很好看。
- The pearl necklace looks very elegant.
  這條珍珠項鍊看起來非常高雅。
- It's the wrong size.
  尺寸不對。
- How much is the jade bracelet?
  這個玉手鐲多少錢？
- It's over our budget.
  這超出我們的預算。
- Can you show me the pearl earrings on the left?
  可以讓我看看左邊那副珍珠耳環嗎？

學習++ *More Tips*

「discount」是「折扣、優惠」的意思。如：「Can you give me a special discount?」（可以給我特別優惠嗎？）或是「Is it possible to discount this pearl necklace?」（這條項鍊可以給個折扣嗎？），更具體一點的話，可說：「I'd like to have at least a discount of ten percent.」（我想至少要打個九折吧。）。

28 盛裝打扮

TRACK 068.

實境對話 Conversation

A: How come you ***get up*** so early today?

B: I have to. I am going to a party at noon.

A: But it's only seven a.m.!

B: I know. But I need to make a lot of ***preparations*** for the party.

A: ***Such as***?

B: I have to ***put on makeup*** and decide what to wear.

A: ***I see***.

B: Right! I need to make myself look perfect.

A: 妳今天怎麼這麼早就起床啦？

B: 我必須早起。我中午要去參加一個聚會。

A: 不過現在才早上七點耶！

B: 我知道。但我得為了派對做很多準備呢。

A: 譬如說？

B: 我得化妝，還要選衣服。

A: 原來如此。

B: 沒錯！我得讓自己看起來很完美。

核心詞彙 Words&Phrases

get up	[gɛt ʌp]	片語 起床
preparation	[ˌprɛpəˋreʃən]	名詞 準備
such as	[sʌtʃ æz]	片語 譬如
put on makeup	[pʊt ɑn ˋmekˌʌp]	片語 化妝
I see	[aɪ si]	片語 我懂了

日常實用短句 Useful Sentences

- The dress code is business casual.
  服裝規定是輕鬆又不失專業形象的上班穿著風格。
- That necklace suits you nicely.
  那條項鍊跟你很搭。
- This dress is very stylish.
  這件洋裝很時髦。
- Betty looks awful in that pink scarf.
  貝蒂圍那條粉紅色圍巾真是太難看了。
- My boots are made of real leather which is very soft and comfortable.
  我的靴子是又軟又舒服的真皮做的。
- There's a dinner party at Tina's home. The invitation said dress formal.
  蒂娜家辦了一個晚宴。邀請卡上註明穿著要正式。
- All I need is a belt to make this dress look formal.
  我只需要一條皮帶讓我的裙子看起來正式一點。
- Joanna wore a bright sundress at Vicky's engagement party.
  喬安娜在薇琪的訂婚宴上穿了一件背心裙。
- Don't you think that dress is a little old-fashioned?
  你不覺得那件洋裝有點過時了嗎？
- I think David is overdressed.
  我認為大衛打扮得太超過了。

學習++ More Tips

「It takes someone to do...」是表示「某人花多少時間做⋯⋯」的常用句型，如：「It took her the whole morning to decide what to wear.」（她花了整個早上的時間決定要穿什麼衣服。），也可以說「She spent the whole morning deciding what to wear.」（她花了整個早上的時間決定要穿什麼衣服。）。

29 參加聚會

TRACK 069.

實境對話

Conversation

A: Hey, Lily, you look gorgeous today!

B: Thank you, George. You look ***handsome***, too. The party is ***wonderful***, isn't it?

A: Quite right! By the way, I haven't seen John yet. Didn't he come with you?

B: No. He had something ***urgent*** to ***deal with***. And where is your ***wife***?

A: She's ***over there*** chatting with her sisters.

B: Oh, I see her. Would you excuse me? Let me go there and say hello to them.

A: OK. Enjoy!

A: 嘿，莉莉，你今天看起來美極了！

B: 謝謝，喬治。你也很英俊。這個聚會很棒，不是嗎？

A: 沒錯！對了，我還沒有看到約翰呢，他沒跟妳一起來嗎？

B: 沒有，他有緊急的事情要處理。你太太在哪裡呢？

A: 她在那邊和她的姐妹們聊天呢。

B: 噢，看到了。失陪一下好嗎？我過去跟她們打個招呼。

A: 好的，玩得愉快喔。

核心詞彙

Words&Phrases

handsome	[ˋhænsəm]	形容詞 帥氣的
wonderful	[ˋwʌndəfəl]	形容詞 棒、美好的
urgent	[ˋɝdʒnt]	形容詞 緊急的
deal with	[dil wɪð]	片語 處理
wife	[waɪf]	名詞 老婆

over there	[ˋovɚ ðɛr]	片語 在那裡

日常實用短句 Useful Sentences

- The class reunion is next week!
  同學會是下個禮拜。
- Haven't seen any of my college classmates for a long time.
  很久沒見到我任何一個大學同學了。
- I am looking forward to the company gathering today.
  我很期待今天的公司聚會。
- Where will the reunion take place?
  會議在哪裡舉行？
- You haven't changed a bit since last time I saw you.
  從上一次見面到現在你都沒什麼變。
- I wonder if my close friends will attend the party.
  我想知道我的好朋友們會不會參加這次的派對。
- I am anxious to find out what everyone is up to.
  我迫不及待想知道大家都在幹嘛。
- I can hardly wait to catch up with my friends.
  我等不及跟朋友們見面啦。
- We should get together more often.
  我們應該更常聚在一起。
- I have got new clothes to wear to the gathering.
  我準備了新衣服為了聚會的時候穿。
- We had such a blast at the party.
  我們在派對上都玩得很盡興。
- What have you been doing lately?
  你最近都在幹嘛？

學習++ More Tips

「See you in a bit.」是表示「待會見」的口語用法。而常用的「See you later.」或是「Catch you later.」反而不是表示「待會見」，卻是表示「下次見。」的意思，因此在使用上需要特別留意。

30 放學或下班後回家 TRACK 070.

實境對話 Conversation

A: Honey, what shall we eat for ***supper***?

B: What about something special?

A: Like what?

B: Like fruit salad.

A: Only fruit salad.

B: Yes. I want to lose weight. My colleagues said that I look a little ***chubby*** lately.

A: I don't think so, honey. You have an ***attractive figure***!

B: Really? Well, in that case, I'll make curry beef stew ***served with*** rice for supper.

A: 親愛的，我們晚餐要吃什麼呢？

B: 吃點特別的東西怎麼樣？

A: 像是什麼呢？

B: 比如說水果沙拉。

A: 只吃水果沙拉嗎？

B: 沒錯。我想減肥。同事們說我最近看來有點胖嘟嘟的。

A: 寶貝兒，我可不這麼認為。你身材很迷人啊！

B: 真的嗎？那麼我決定燉咖哩牛肉配飯當晚餐。

核心詞彙 Words&Phrases

supper	[ˋsʌpɚ]	名詞 晚餐
chubby	[ˋtʃʌbɪ]	形容詞 圓胖的
attractive	[əˋtræktɪv]	形容詞 迷人的
figure	[ˋfɪgjɚ]	名詞 體態
serve with	[sɝv wɪð]	片語 供應

日常實用短句 Useful Sentences

- Go wash your hands. Dinner will be ready soon.
  去洗手，晚餐很快就準備好了。
- I've made some jelly butter sandwiches. They are on the table.
  我做了一些果醬三明治，放在桌子上。
- How was your day?
  你今天過得怎樣？
- Did you have a good time at school?
  你在學校過得開心嗎？
- I have to take a shower first.
  我要先洗澡。
- Brush your teeth before going to bed.
  睡覺前要刷牙。
- Set the table, please.
  請把餐具擺好。
- I enjoy family dinner time.
  我很喜歡家人聚在一起的晚餐時間。
- Shall we go out for a walk?
  我們能出去散步一下嗎？
- Help me with the dishes.
  幫我洗碗盤。
- Let's watch the movie on HBO.
  來看 HBO 的電影吧。

學習++ More Tips

「chubby」指的是「豐滿、圓胖」的意思，而「fat」這個字則通常較帶有貶意。如：「Look at that cute chubby baby!」（看那個胖嘟嘟的可愛嬰兒！），「Move your fat ass over, will you?」（把你的大屁股移過去一點好嗎？）。

PART❸日常生活篇

你都記住了嗎？

從各篇「日常實用短句」裡整理出外國人常用的單字和片語，如果背起來了，就在前方空格打個勾吧！

- ☐ cozy
  形容詞 舒適的
- ☐ hitch a ride
  片語 搭便車
- ☐ drop me off
  片語 讓我下車
- ☐ lung cancer
  名詞 肺癌
- ☐ quit smoking
  片語 戒菸
- ☐ give me a hand
  片語 幫我一個忙
- ☐ get lost
  片語 迷路
- ☐ intersection
  名詞 十字路口
- ☐ block
  名詞 街區
- ☐ stand
  動詞 忍受
- ☐ rip-off
  名詞 冒牌貨
- ☐ nag
  動詞 不斷嘮叨
- ☐ registered mail
  名詞 掛號郵件
- ☐ deposit
  動詞 存錢
- ☐ withdraw
  動詞 領錢
- ☐ get a grip
  片語 抓緊
- ☐ lean on
  片語 倚靠
- ☐ health insurance card
  名詞 健保卡
- ☐ registration fee
  名詞 掛號費
- ☐ dizzy
  形容詞 頭暈的
- ☐ teeth implant
  名詞 植牙
- ☐ local anaesthesia
  名詞 局部麻醉
- ☐ be allergic to
  片語 過敏
- ☐ side effect
  名詞 副作用
- ☐ pain killer
  名詞 止痛藥
- ☐ ointment
  名詞 藥膏

- ☐ laundromat
  名詞 自助洗衣店
- ☐ fabric softener
  名詞 柔軟精
- ☐ drying machine
  名詞 烘乾機
- ☐ haircut
  名詞 剪頭髮
- ☐ fringe
  名詞 瀏海
- ☐ digital camera
  名詞 數位相機
- ☐ shopping cart
  名詞 購物推車
- ☐ toothpaste
  名詞 牙膏
- ☐ coupon
  名詞 折價券
- ☐ go hiking
  片語 健行
- ☐ major in
  片語 主修
- ☐ go jogging
  片語 慢跑
- ☐ sit-up
  名詞 仰臥起坐
- ☐ push-up
  名詞 伏地挺身
- ☐ recreation center
  名詞 活動中心
- ☐ swimming party
  名詞 泳池派對
- ☐ soft drink
  名詞 軟性飲料
- ☐ appetizer
  名詞 開胃菜
- ☐ lotion
  名詞 乳液
- ☐ lip gloss
  名詞 唇蜜
- ☐ skin tone
  名詞 膚色
- ☐ mascara
  名詞 睫毛膏
- ☐ eye cream
  名詞 眼霜
- ☐ wrinkle
  名詞 皺紋
- ☐ ear rings
  名詞 耳環
- ☐ diamond ring
  名詞 鑽石戒指
- ☐ warranty
  名詞 保固
- ☐ bracelet
  名詞 手鐲
- ☐ budget
  名詞 預算
- ☐ engagement party
  名詞 訂婚宴
- ☐ be made of
  片語 以……做成
- ☐ sundress
  名詞 背心裙
- ☐ old-fashioned
  形容詞 過時的
- ☐ overdressed
  形容詞 過分打扮的

Part 4 各類話題篇－音檔連結

因各家手機系統不同，若無法直接掃描，
仍可以至以下電腦雲端連結下載收聽。
（https://tinyurl.com/54wzdwru）

PART 4

各類話題篇

01 天氣

TRACK 071.

實境對話

Conversation

A: What a ***stuffy*** hot day!
B: I can not ***stand*** this kind of ***weather*** anymore!
A: What weird weather!
B: It's probably due to the so called ***EI Nino*** effect.
A: The TV said that today we might have rain.
B: Don't you believe the weather ***forecasts***?
A: It's always wrong.
B: But you'd better bring an ***umbrella*** with you.

A: 好悶熱的天氣啊！
B: 我受不了這麼熱的天！
A: 很奇怪的天氣。
B: 大概是所謂的聖嬰現象吧！
A: 電視上說今天可能會下雨。
B: 氣象預報可以相信嗎？
A: 嗯，經常是錯誤的。
B: 不過還是把傘帶著吧！

核心詞彙

Words&Phrases

stuffy	[ˋstʌfɪ]	形容詞 悶熱的
stand	[stænd]	動詞 忍受
weather	[ˋwɛðɚ]	名詞 天氣
El Nino	[ɛl nɪno]	名詞 聖嬰現象
forecast	[ˋforˋkæst]	名詞 預報
umbrella	[ʌmˋbrɛlə]	名詞 雨傘

日常實用短句 Useful Sentences

- It's raining cats and dogs outside.
  現在外面正下著傾盆大雨呢。
- We had a thunder shower yesterday.
  昨天有雷陣雨。
- It started drizzling.
  開始下毛毛雨了。
- It's getting warmer and warmer, isn't it.
  天氣越來越熱了，不是嗎？
- I prefer cloudy days to rainy days.
  我喜歡陰天勝過雨天。
- We have a dry climate in winter here.
  我們這裡冬天氣候乾燥。
- I just can't stand the heat in this country.
  我就是無法忍受這個國家的炎熱。
- We were drenched to the skin in the rain.
  我們在雨中淋得全身都溼透了。
- It's quite sultry during the summer in my city.
  我住的城市夏天相當悶熱。
- According to the weather forecast, it will rain this afternoon.
  根據氣象預報，今天下午會下雨。
- It's so damp that it's likely to rain in a minute.
  天氣好潮濕，可能馬上就要下雨了。

學習++ More Tips

外國人也喜歡用天氣作為談天的開場白：「It's a beautiful day today.」（今天天氣很棒。），「It is pouring outside.」（外面下著傾盆大雨。）。其他形容天氣的詞還有「raining」（下雨）、「sunny」（晴天）、「cloudy」（多雲、陰天）、「misty」（有霧的）等。

02 電視節目

TRACK 072.

實境對話

Conversation

A: What kinds of TV ***program*** do you like?

B: I like watching ***new*** programs.

A: Why do you like to watch that kind of program?

B: I think keeping myself informed of the ***latest*** world news is very important.

B: What programs do you like most?

A: The Discovery ***Channel*** on ***cable*** TV is the one I like most.

A: It's full of ***knowledge*** and is a very good ***educational*** channel.

A: 你喜歡什麼樣的電視節目？
B: 我喜歡新聞節目。
A: 你為什麼喜歡看那類節目呢？
B: 我認為保持對國際新聞的動態了解是非常重要的。
B: 你最喜歡什麼節目呢？
A: 我最喜歡看有線電視的發現頻道。
A: 因為它充滿知識性，是很好的教育頻道。

核心詞彙

Words&Phrases

program	[ˋprogræm]	名詞 節目
news	[njuz]	名詞 新聞
latest	[ˋletɪst]	形容詞 最新的、最近的
channel	[ˋtʃænl̩]	名詞 頻道
cable	[ˋkebl̩]	名詞 有線電視
knowledge	[ˋnɑlɪdʒ]	名詞 知識
educational	[ˋɛdʒuˋkeʃənl̩]	形容詞 教育性的

日常實用短句 Useful Sentences

- Are you watching the soap opera again?
  你又在看那齣肥皂劇啦？
- He is so engrossed in the serial.
  他對那部連續劇好入迷。
- I can't wait to watch the next episode.
  我等不及要看下一集了。
- Would you mind tuning the television to Channel 21?
  你介意把電視轉到 21 頻道嗎？
- Can I watch the Simpson's on Channel 25?
  我可以看 25 頻道的辛普森家庭嗎？
- Would you stop switching the channels?
  你可以不要再切換頻道了嗎？
- Stay tuned.
  不要轉台。
- What's on Channel 55 at the moment?
  現在 55 頻道在播放什麼？
- I just love the host of this variety show.
  我真喜歡這個綜藝節目的主持人。
- There seems to be more and more talk shows these days.
  最近談話性節目好像越來越多了。
- Do we have to watch TV news right now?
  我們現在一定要看電視新聞嗎？

學習++ More Tips

當有人問起「What's your favorite TV program?」（你最喜歡看什麼電視節目？），你可以回答說：「My favorite TV program is the variety shows.」（我最喜歡的電視節目是綜藝節目。），或是美國流行的「talk show」（脫口秀）、「MTV」（音樂頻道）或是「sports channel」（運動頻道）。

03 嗜好

TRACK 073.

實境對話

Conversation

A: What are your hobbies?
B: I like ***music***.
A: Can you ***play*** any kind of ***musical instrument***?
B: I can ***play the piano***, but I'm not very good at it.
B: How about you?
A: I know nothing about any musical instrument.
A: But I have a ***collection*** of many ***different*** CDs and ***records***.

A: 你的興趣是什麼？
B: 我喜歡音樂。
A: 你會彈什麼樂器嗎？
B: 我會彈鋼琴，但不是很在行。
B: 你呢？
A: 我完全不懂樂器。
A: 但我蒐集了許多不同的 CD 和錄音帶。

核心詞彙

Words&Phrases

music	[ˋmjuzɪk]	名詞 音樂
play	[ple]	動詞 彈奏
musical instrument	[ˋmjuzɪkḷ ˋɪnstrəmənt]	名詞 樂器
play the piano	[ple ðə pɪˋæno]	片語 彈鋼琴
collection	[kəˋlɛkʃən]	名詞 收集
different	[ˋdɪfərənt]	形容詞 不同的
record	[ˋrɛkɚd]	名詞 錄音帶

日常實用短句 Useful Sentences

- The man has a hobby of collecting Barbie dolls.
  那個男人有收集芭比娃娃的嗜好。
- It is my mother's hobby to play cards.
  我媽媽的嗜好就是打牌。
- He is fond of culinary art.
  他很喜歡烹飪。
- Reading science fictions is one of my brother's hobbies.
  看科幻小說是我哥哥的嗜好之一。
- Samantha is lost in her reading again.
  莎蔓姍又專注在她的閱讀中了。
- Playing mahjong is a common hobby of my family.
  打麻將是我家人共同的嗜好。
- Smoking is one of the worst hobbies of my father.
  抽菸是我爸爸最糟糕的嗜好之一。
- Is there any bad hobby that you're trying to get rid of?
  你有任何想要改掉的不良嗜好嗎？
- It is not easy to correct one's bad hobby.
  要改正一個人的不良嗜好並不容易。
- What hobbies do you and your friends have in common?
  你跟你的朋友有什麼共同的嗜好？
- All of us like to make airplane models.
  我們所有人都喜歡做飛機模型。

學習++ More Tips

想要問及別人的嗜好，你可以說：「What's your hobby?」（你的興趣是什麼？），或是問說：「What do you do in your leisure time?」（你閒暇時做什麼？），Are you interested in sports?（你對運動有興趣嗎？）。

04 運動

TRACK 074.

實境對話 Conversation

A: Mr. Lin, what's your ***favorite sport***?
B: My favorite sport is ***tennis***.
A: What is the most popular sport in Taiwan?
B: ***Baseball*** is the most popular one in Taiwan.
A: In our ***country***, we prefer ***soccer*** to baseball.
B: If it is convenient for you, how about we go to watch the ***professional*** baseball game together tomorrow?
A: I would be glad to.

A: 林先生，你喜歡什麼運動？
B: 我最喜歡網球。
A: 在台灣最受歡迎的運動是什麼呢？
B: 棒球在我國非常盛行。
A: 我們國家則喜歡足球甚於棒球。
B: 方便的話，我們明天一起去看職棒比賽如何？
A: 我很樂意。

核心詞彙 Words&Phrases

favorite	[ˋfevərɪt]	形容詞 最愛的
sport	[sport]	名詞 運動
tennis	[ˋtɛnɪs]	名詞 網球
baseball	[ˋbesˋbɔl]	名詞 棒球
country	[ˋkʌntrɪ]	名詞 國家
soccer	[ˋsɑkɚ]	名詞 足球
professional	[prəˋfɛʃən!]	形容詞 專業的

日常實用短句 *Useful Sentences*

- He is a good swimmer.
  他是游泳好手。
- Can you teach me how to swim backstroke?
  你可以教我游仰式嗎？
- Shall we go mountain climbing?
  我們去爬山好嗎？
- She practiced gymnastics when she was in high school.
  她高中時練過體操。
- You can do yoga almost everywhere.
  你幾乎在任何地方都能做瑜珈。
- My father plays golf really well.
  我爸爸高爾夫球真的打得很好。
- Jogging in the morning is a good way to start a day.
  早上慢跑是展開一天的好方法。
- I prefer exercising outdoors to working out in the gym.
  我喜歡在戶外運動勝過在健身房健身。
- A marathon runner should have good physical strength.
  一個馬拉松賽跑選手要有很好的體力。
- Don't you know that heel-and-toe walking has become a fad?
  你不知道競走已經變成一種時尚了嗎？

學習++ *More Tips*

外國人是相當重視運動的，比方說是「swimming」（游泳）、「volley ball」（排球）、「tennis」（網球），或是男生熱中的「baseball」（棒球）、「football」（美式足球）、「basketball」（籃球）等等，都是大家茶餘飯後聊天的好話題。

05 男與女

TRACK 075.

實境對話

Conversation

A: Mr. Smith, What's your ***impression*** of Japanese ladies?

B: Japanese ladies are very kind and cute.

A: Mr. Tsurumi, What's your ***opinion*** of American girls?

C: They are ***open-minded*** and ***healthy***.

A: In Japan, There are three ***so called*** "***beauty*** cities".

B: Where are they?

A: Niigata, Akita and Aomori.

B: Let's arrange a "looking for beauty" trip!

A: 史密斯先生，你對日本女性有何看法？

B: 日本的女性很親切而且可愛。

A: 鶴見先生，你對美國女性的看法呢？

C: 她們很開朗活潑以及有健康的形象。

A: 在日本有所謂出美女的三大都市。

B: 在哪裡呢？

A: 新瀉、秋田及青森。

B: 我們安排一個尋美人之旅吧！

核心詞彙

Words&Phrases

impression	[ɪm`prɛʃən]	名詞 印象
opinion	[ə`pɪnjən]	名詞 看法
open-minded	[`opən`maɪndɪd]	形容詞 思想開明
healthy	[`hɛlθɪ]	形容詞 健康的
so called	[so kɔld]	片語 所謂的
beauty	[`bjutɪ]	名詞 美女

日常實用短句 Useful Sentences

- Joseph is really into that woman.
  約瑟夫真的很喜歡那個女人耶。
- Is he ready for a new relationship?
  他準備好談新戀情了嗎？
- He fell in love with the woman at first sight.
  他對那女人一見鍾情。
- How do I know if he's the one?
  我該如何知道他是不是我的真命天子？
- What do you think of one-night stand?
  你對一夜情有什麼看法？
- I dumped him.
  我把他甩了。
- Hey, the man over there is giving you the eye.
  嘿，那邊那個男人在對妳放電耶。
- Sarah is giving her boyfriend the silent treatment.
  莎拉正在跟她男友冷戰。
- Are you seeing anyone?
  你有固定的對象嗎？
- I'm still available.
  我還沒死會呢。
- You've got to have your eyes wide open.
  你的眼睛要張大一點。

學習++ More Tips

「She is a beautiful girl.」（她是一個美麗的女孩。）、「She is so pretty.」（她真的好漂亮。）、「She looks so wild.」（她看起來好狂野。）……都是男生形容女生的時候用的一些詞。女生形容男生則會說「He is a handsome boy.」（他是一個帥哥。）、「He is so cute.」（他好可愛。），或是「He is so masculine.」（他好有男人味！）等。

06 選課程

TRACK 076.

實境對話

Conversation

A: What's the matter? You look puzzled.

B: There are so many ***courses*** on this form. I don't know which ones to take.

A: What's the usual course ***load***?

B: About four or five courses. And between twelve to twenty hours of class per week.

A: It's a good idea to see your ***advisor*** before you make any decisions, to see whether your ***schedule*** is ***manageable***.

B: Oh, you ***reminded*** me!

A: 怎麼了？你看起來很困惑。

B: 這張表上有那麼多門課。我不知道要選什麼。

A: 通常大概要修多少課？

B: 大概四到五門課。每星期十二到二十小時的課。

A: 你做任何決定前，最好見見你的指導老師，看看你選的有沒有辦法應付。

B: 喔，你提醒了我！

核心詞彙

Words&Phrases

course	[kors]	名詞 課程
load	[lod]	名詞 負擔、裝載
advisor	[əd`vaɪzɚ]	名詞 指導老師
schedule	[`skɛdʒul]	名詞 時間表
manageable	[`mænɪdʒəbl̩]	形容詞 可管理控制的
remind	[rɪ`maɪnd]	動詞 提醒

日常實用短句 Useful Sentences

- Is Educational Psychology an optional course?
  教育心理學是門選修課嗎？
- I think it should be an obligatory course.
  我想它應該是必修課。
- I want to sign up for Dr. Lee's class.
  我想選修李教授的課。
- Dr. Lee's class is full.
  李教授的課額滿了。
- Dr. Sophie's class is always very popular.
  蘇菲教授的課總是很受歡迎。
- I heard that it's a Mickey Mouse course.
  我聽說那是營養課程。
- Fundamental Accounting is a required course for me.
  基礎會計學是我的必修科目。
- How many credits are you taking this semester?
  你這學期修多少學分呢？
- How many courses are you taking this semester?
  你這學期修幾門課呢？
- Does the professor take attendance every class?
  這個教授每堂課都會點名嗎？
- Have you cleared the prerequisites?
  你已經修過先修科目了嗎？
- I am thinking about dropping this course.
  我正在考慮要退選這門課。

學習++ More Tips

在國外的課程有美制的「semester」（一學年兩學期）、英制的「quarter」（一學年四學期），而「學期」的英文則是「term」，「This is the final term of this school year.」（這是這學年的最後一學期。）。

07 圖書館借書

TRACK 077.

實境對話

Conversation

A: Excuse me. I would like to find a book. How can I start?

B: The computer on that desk has a ***database*** with a record of all the books in this library, and the shelves they are on. You just follow the directions on the screen, and ***key in*** the information about the book you'd like to find.

A: I'm not sure of the correct name of the book, but only the ***author*** and the ***publisher***.

B: It doesn't matter. As long as you know some key words of the names of the books, the program will ***search*** for all the related books for you.

A: 抱歉。我想找一本書。要怎麼開始？

B: 那張桌上的電腦有資料庫，包含所有這座圖書館裡的書，以及所放置的書架。只要照著螢幕上的指示做，輸入你想找的書的資料就可以了。

A: 我不太確定那本書的正確名稱，只知道作者和出版者。

B: 沒關係。只要知道書名的幾個關鍵字，電腦程式會幫你找到所有相關的書。

核心詞彙

Words&Phrases

database	[ˋdetəˋbes]	名詞 資料庫
key in	[ki ɪn]	片語 鍵入
author	[ˋɔθɚ]	名詞 作者
publisher	[ˋpʌblɪʃɚ]	名詞 出版社
search	[sɝtʃ]	動詞 搜尋

日常實用短句 *Useful Sentences*

- You need a student ID to enter the school library.
  你要有學生證才能進入學校圖書館。
- I don't know how to find the book I'm looking for.
  我不知道該怎麼找我想借的書。
- You can search for the book and reserve it on the library website.
  你可以在圖書館網站上搜尋並預訂那本書。
- It is convenient to use self checkout machine.
  用自動借書機真方便。
- The self checkout machine is on the first floor of the Main Library.
  自動借書機位在總圖一樓。
- What if I want to renew due dates?
  如果我想要延長到期日該怎麼做呢？
- You can use self checkout machine to renew due dates if there isn't a reservation placed by other user.
  如果沒有其他人預約，你可以利用自動借書機延長到期日。
- You cannot borrow books when you hold overdue books.
  如果你有逾期未還的書，就不能借書。
- Only senior students, graduates can borrow journals.
  只有大四生和研究生可以借閱期刊。

學習++ *More Tips*

去「library」（圖書館）借書時別忘了要記得「the returning date」（還書的時間），別讓「librarian」（圖書管理員）跟你說：「Your book is overdue.」（你的書過期了。），那可是要罰錢的喔！

08 交報告

TRACK 078.

實境對話

Conversation

A: I'm working hard on my ***term paper***. At least 20 pages or 4000 words on Basic Biology.

A: I have to ***turn*** it ***in*** before Wednesday.

B: Otherwise?

A: Otherwise, I cannot pass this course.

B: You must have done a lot of research on your ***topic***, haven't you?

A: Of course. We have to discuss the topic we'd like to do with the ***professor***, and then start doing the research, both in the library and in the ***lab***.

A: 我正在努力寫期末報告。至少二十頁，或四千字的基本生物學報告。

A: 我必須在星期三前交報告。

B: 否則呢？

A: 否則就無法通過這門課。

B: 你對你的題目一定做了很多研究了吧？

A: 當然。必須先和教授討論我們要做的題目，然後開始做研究，包括圖書館裡找書和實驗室的研究。

核心詞彙

Words&Phrases

term paper	[tɝm ˋpepɚ]	名詞 學期研究報告
turn in	[tɝn ɪn]	片語 繳交
topic	[ˋtɑpɪk]	名詞 題目
professor	[prəˋfɛsɚ]	名詞 教授
lab	[læb]	名詞 實驗室

日常實用短句 Useful Sentences

- I need to hand in my Sociology paper by next Friday.
  我必須在下週五前繳交社會學報告。
- Don't sweat it.
  別擔心！
- You still have plenty of time to work on it.
  你還有很多時間可以寫。
- I need to go to the library to collect as many useful data as possible.
  我必須去圖書館盡可能收集多一點資料。
- I have to stay up finishing my term paper tonight.
  我今晚得熬夜趕報告。
- I'm afraid that I can't finish it before the deadline.
  我很擔心沒辦法在繳交期限內完成。
- My professor will flunk me if I hand it in late.
  如果我遲交，我的教授會把我當掉。
- Don't forget to list references in full at the end of your essay.
  別忘了在論文最後面列出全部的參考書目。
- It is nearly finished.
  就快完成了。
- It's done!
  完成了！
- I hope I can get an A this time.
  我希望這次可以拿優等。

學習++ More Tips

外國的學生常常需要找資料寫「report」（報告），你常常會聽到說「I have a paper due on Monday.」（我星期一要交一份報告。）。當然報告也分好多種，如「written reports」（手寫的報告）、「oral report」（口頭報告）等。

09 打工

TRACK 079.

實境對話

Conversation

A: This semester, I have the good ***fortune*** to work in our department office.

B: Will it ***occupy*** much of your time?

A: No. Since it is a job in the department office, all the teachers and other ***administrators*** are quite ***considerate*** of me. They all know I need to study, too.

B: What do you do there?

A: It's quite easy: I change the announcement on the ***bulletin board***, for example; I act as a support for the lower classes lab courses, and I answer the phone.

A: 這學期我獲得一個好機會，在系辦公室工作。

B: 會不會佔用你很多時間？

A: 不會。因為是系辦的工作，老師和其他行政人員對我都非常體貼。他們全都知道我需要念書。

B: 你在那裡做什麼？

A: 很簡單，譬如：換佈告欄裡的公告、支援低年級的實驗課，以及接電話。

核心詞彙

Words&Phrases

fortune	[ˋfɔrtʃən]	名詞 幸運
occupy	[ˋɑkjəˋpaɪ]	動詞 佔據
administrator	[ədˋmɪnəˋstretɚ]	名詞 行政人員
considerate	[kənˋsɪdərɪt]	形容詞 體貼的
bulletin board	[ˋbulɪtɪn bord]	名詞 佈告欄

日常實用短句 Useful Sentences

- My part-time job makes me very tired.
  我的兼差工作把我累慘了。
- I'm looking for a part-time job.
  我正在找打工機會。
- You can check the bulletin board.
  你可以看一下佈告欄。
- Can you keep up your grades while having a part-time job?
  你能一邊打工一邊保持成績嗎？
- My part-time job doesn't interfere with my studies.
  我打工不會影響課業。
- How many hours a week do I work?
  我一週要工作幾小時？
- What's the hourly pay?
  時薪是多少呢？
- The work pays fairly.
  這份工作待遇不錯。
- I need to work my way through college.
  我必須半工半讀唸大學。
- The work takes a maximum of three nights a week.
  這份工作一週最多只要工作三個晚上。
- Any kind of job is fine as long as I don't have to work for more than fifteen hours a week.
  只要是一週工作時數不超過 15 小時的工作都可以。

學習++ More Tips

國外的小孩很獨立，往往很小就開始找「part-time jobs」（打工）來賺取「pocket money」（零用錢），他們找的工作有「baby sitting」（臨時的保母）、「lawn mowing」（割草）、「tutoring」（家教），或是「car washing」（洗車）。

10 考試

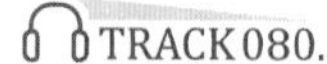
TRACK 080.

實境對話 Conversation

A: Would you close your books? The ***exam*** is now begin. Please remember to ***write down*** your name and school number. If the name or the school number is missing, the ***score*** will not be ***recorded***.

B: How long do we have?

A: 90 minutes. If you finish the paper earlier, you can leave the room. But you have to stay in the room for at lease 30 minutes.

B: Excuse me. My paper is not ***well-copied***. I cannot read several questions.

A: Let me give you another paper. Here you are.

A: 請把書本闔上。考試開始了。記得寫名字和學號。如果沒有名字和學號，就無法登記成績。

B: 要考幾分鐘？

A: 九十分鐘。如果你們早一點寫完，可以離開教室。不過至少要三十分鐘以上才能離開。

B: 抱歉。我的考卷印得不好。有幾題看不清楚。

A: 我幫你換一張。這裡。

核心詞彙 Words&Phrases

exam	[ɪgˋzæm]	名詞 考試
write down	[raɪt daʊn]	片語 寫下來
score	[skor]	名詞 成績
record	[rɪˋkɔrd]	動詞 紀錄
well-copied	[wɛlˋkɑpɪd]	形容詞 印清楚的

日常實用短句 Useful Sentences

- How did you find the quiz?
  你覺得這次的隨堂測驗如何？
- I found it difficult.
  我覺得很難。
- I ran out of time and didn't finish.
  考試時間到了，可是我沒答完。
- Don't be late; otherwise you'll miss the quiz.
  別遲到了，否則你會錯過隨堂測驗。
- I didn't do well on any of my exams in the midterm.
  我期中考沒有一科是考得好的。
- I need to prepare for the finals in advance this time.
  我這次要提前準備期末考。
- I hope I won't flunk the final exam.
  我希望我期末考不會被當掉。
- Long hours of study makes me sick and tired.
  長時間的 K 書讓我十分厭倦。
- My math teacher gives us a quiz every other day.
  我的數學老師每兩天就給我們一次隨堂小考。
- He passed in English, but failed in geography.
  他英文及格了，但是地理不及格。
- I screwed up my finals.
  我的期末考考砸了。
- I have finals next week. So I have to hit the books.
  我下週有期末考，所以，我得發憤讀書。

學習++ More Tips

「exam」是「examination」的縮寫，是「考試」的意思。一般比較小的考試可以用「test」或是「quiz」這個字。考試的類型除了一般的「term exam」（段考），還有「oral exam」（口試）、「written test」（筆試），還有「pop quiz」則是老師在沒有預警之下給的考試。

11 八卦

TRACK 081.

實境對話

Conversation

A: Hey, Mary! Have you heard that there is another handsome man ***pursuing*** Jane?

B: Linda, you are ***gossiping*** again!

A: No, I am serious. I've seen him!

B: OK. Tell me more about him. Is he more handsome than the guy called Jimmy?

A: Definitely! He is as cool as Nicolas Cage.

B: Really? In that case, I don't think Jane can ***match*** him in ***appearance***.

A: That's true. But it is her warm ***personality*** that makes her attractive.

A: 嘿，瑪麗！你聽説又一個英俊的男人在追求珍嗎？
B: 琳達，你又開始八卦了！
A: 不是啦，我是認真的。我還見過他！
B: 好吧。多講講他的事。他有比那個叫做吉米的傢伙帥嗎？
A: 當然了！他就像尼可拉斯凱吉一樣酷。
B: 真的喔？那樣的話，我覺得珍在外形上可配不上他。
A: 那倒是真的。不過讓她有吸引力的是她那熱情的個性。

核心詞彙

Words&Phrases

pursue	[pɚˋsu]	動詞 追求
gossip	[ˋgɑsəp]	動詞 八卦
match	[mætʃ]	動詞 相配
appearance	[əˋpɪrəns]	名詞 外表
personality	[ˋpɝsn̩ˋælətɪ]	名詞 個性

日常實用短句 *Useful Sentences*

- She is such a gossip.
  她真是個愛八卦的人哪！
- It's fun to read the gossip column.
  讀八卦專欄很有意思。
- Where did you get that information?
  你是從哪兒得到這個消息的？
- Why are you so interested in scandals about your boss?
  你為什麼對老闆的流言蜚語如此感興趣？
- Stop gossiping with your neighbors.
  別再跟你的鄰居們說長道短了。
- I heard that Mary has hooked a rich man.
  我聽說瑪莉釣到一個有錢人。
- Mary had a liposuction when she was twenty.
  瑪莉二十歲時曾動過抽脂手術。
- You won't believe this. Jack is dating Cynthia tonight.
  你一定不會相信的。傑克今天晚上要跟辛西亞約會耶。
- I overheard that Mary is going to marry a rich old man.
  我無意間聽到瑪莉即將跟一個有錢的老男人結婚了。
- Those girls are gossiping about everyone again.
  那些女生又在講每個人的八卦了。
- It seems that they will never get tired of it.
  她們似乎永遠都講不累。

學習++ *More Tips*

一般要開始蜚短流長時，都會用「Have you heard about...?」（你有沒有聽說……？），或是「Do you know that...?」（你知道……嗎？）來做開場白，以引起對方的興趣。如：「Have you heard that Jane is dating a married man?」（你有沒有聽說珍在跟一個有婦之夫交往？）。

12 約會

TRACK 082.

實境對話

Conversation

A: Hi, Sarah. How was your ***date*** last Sunday?

B: Not bad.

A: Tell me all the ***details***. What is he like?

B: He is smart, ***humorous***, gentle and ***cultivated***. In addition, he has his own business.

A: Sounds nice. Is there anything you ***dislike*** about him?

B: Well, he's a little ***conceited***. And I feel that he's kind of ***unreliable***.

A: Well, forget it then. There is always someone better.

A: 嗨，莎拉！你上周日的約會怎麼樣啊？

B: 還不錯唷。

A: 跟我說全部的細節啦。他是個什麼樣的人？

B: 聰明、幽默、溫文儒雅。除此之外，還有自己的事業。

A: 聽起來很不錯嘛。他有沒有什麼地方是你不喜歡的呢？

B: 這個嘛，他有點自負，而且我覺得他有點不可靠。

A: 呃，那就算了。總會有更好的人。

核心詞彙

Words&Phrases

date	[det]	名詞 約會
detail	[ˋditel]	名詞 細節
humorous	[ˋhjumərəs]	形容詞 幽默的
cultivated	[ˋkʌltəˋvetɪd]	形容詞 有教養的
dislike	[dɪsˋlaɪk]	動詞 不喜歡
conceited	[kənˋsitɪd]	形容詞 自負的
unreliable	[ˋʌnrɪˋlaɪəbl̩]	形容詞 可靠的

日常實用短句 Useful Sentences

- It's our first date.
  這是我們第一次約會。
- I'm kind of nervous about it.
  我有點緊張。
- Don't screw it up.
  別搞砸了。
- What should I wear?
  我應該穿什麼好呢？
- This is my treat.
  由我請客。
- I'm on the way.
  我已經在來的路上了。
- I'll probably be late for a while.
  我可能會遲到一會兒。
- I will wait for you by the fountain.
  我會在噴水池旁邊等你。
- How many times have you dated the guy?
  你跟那傢伙約會幾次了？
- We had a romantic candlelit dinner last night.
  我們昨晚享用了一個浪漫的燭光晚餐。

學習++ More Tips

「What is he like?」是在問「他人怎麼樣？」，詢問的重點在「個性、外型」等等，如：「He's humorous and thoughtful.」（他既幽默又體貼。），如果是問「What does he like?」則是在問「他喜歡什麼？」，如：「He likes sports and music.」（他喜歡運動和音樂。）。

13 地震

TRACK 083.

實境對話

Conversation

A: The ***earthquake*** that ***struck*** Haiti last month was so terrible. Hundreds of thousands of people were killed in the ***disaster***.

B: And ***countless*** homes were ***destroyed***.

A: Yes, I am afraid that it will take a very long time to ***ease*** the pain.

B: That's right. What if an earthquake occurs here? What should we do?

A: Never hide yourself under the table. You'd better run to the open space or stay next to the bed or a ***pillar***.

A: 上個月襲擊海地的地震實在是太可怕了。數十萬人都在這次災難中喪生了。

B: 無數的家園也被毀了。

A: 是啊。恐怕需要很長時間去撫平創傷了。

B: 沒錯。要是這裡發生地震呢？我們該怎麼做？

A: 絕對不要躲在桌子底下。你最好跑到開放的空間或是待在床或柱子的旁邊。

核心詞彙

Words&Phrases

earthquake	[ˋɝθˋkwek]	名詞 地震
strike	[straɪk]	動詞 襲擊
disaster	[dɪˋzæstɚ]	名詞 災難
countless	[ˋkaʊntlɪs]	形容詞 無數的
destroy	[dɪˋstrɔɪ]	動詞 毀壞
ease	[iz]	動詞 減輕、緩和

pillar	[ˋpɪlɚ]	名詞 柱子

日常實用短句 Useful Sentences

- Was that an earthquake?
  剛剛那個是地震嗎？
- Where is the epicenter of the earthquake?
  這場地震的震央在哪裡？
- What was the magnitude of the earthquake?
  那場地震規模多大？
- The whole building was shaking.
  整棟建築物都在搖晃。
- Don't panic.
  別驚慌。
- Don't worry. It was only an aftershock after the main earthquake.
  別擔心。剛剛那個只是主震之後的餘震。
- A felt earthquake occurred in Hualian this afternoon.
  今天下午在花蓮發生了一起有感地震。
- There were thousands of casualties in the disaster.
  這場災難中有數以千計的傷亡人數。
- Scientists are still unable to forecast where and when will an earthquake occur.
  科學家們目前仍無法預測地震會在何時何地發生。

學習++ More Tips

「protect... from...」是「保護……免受（傷害）」的意思，「from」後面可接名詞或是動名詞，如：「A helmet can protect your head from harm.」（安全帽可以保護你的頭免受傷害。），或「The mother tried to protect her son from being abused by his father.」（那個母親試圖保護兒子不讓爸爸虐待。）。

14 房奴

TRACK 084.

實境對話

Conversation

A: I am getting married and I am planning to buy a house ***on loan***.

B: Happy for your marriage and ***sorrow*** for your becoming a ***mortgage slave***.

A: I have no choice. We need a house to live in after we get married.

B: Do you know Peter? He is a ***typical*** mortgage slave. He is completely ***stressed out*** by the heavy mortgage loan.

A: I wish the ***government*** could do something.

A: 我要結婚了，正打算貸款買房呢。

B: 為你結婚而高興，卻也為了你即將成為房奴而悲哀。

A: 我別無選擇啊。我們結婚後需要有個房子住啊。

B: 你認識彼得嗎？他就是個典型的房奴。沉重的抵押貸款簡直把他壓得喘不過氣來。

A: 但願政府能為此種情況想點辦法。

核心詞彙

Words&Phrases

on loan	[ɑn lon]	片語 貸款
sorrow	[`sɑro]	形容詞 悲哀
mortgage	[`mɔrgɪdʒ]	名詞 抵押借款
slave	[slev]	名詞 奴隸
typical	[`tɪpɪkḷ]	形容詞 典型的
stress out	[strɛs aʊt]	片語 壓力大到幾乎無法承受
government	[`gʌvənmənt]]	名詞 政府

日常實用短句 Useful Sentences

- I had no option but to buy a house of my own.
  我別無選擇，只好買了自己的房子。
- It will take him twenty years to pay off the mortgage.
  他得花二十年才能還清貸款。
- Maybe it's not a good idea to buy our own house.
  也許買個屬於自己的房子並不是個好主意。
- What can we do if we don't want to be a mortgage slave?
  如果我們不想當房奴，該怎麼做呢？
- That's why many youngsters choose to stay with their parents.
  這就是為什麼許多年輕人選擇和父母同住。
- They can't afford the mortgage payments with their slender earnings.
  他們微薄的薪水負擔不起貸款。
- It's difficult for them to make ends meet.
  要他們收支平衡很難。
- Can the government do something about it for us?
  政府能不能幫我們想想辦法呢？
- How about renting an apartment instead of buying a house of your own?
  租一間公寓而不買自己的房子如何？
- Take care. Don't overwork yourself.
  保重啊！別工作過度了。

學習++ More Tips

「stressed out」表示「因心理緊張而被壓垮的」之意。如：「Most mortgage slaves are stressed out by their monthly loan payments.」（大部分的房奴都被每個月需要支付的貸款壓得喘不過氣來。）、「I'm totally stressed out!」（我壓力大到喘不過氣來了。）。

15 減肥

TRACK 085.

實境對話

Conversation

A: Look! I am getting ***fatter***, aren't I?

B: ***To be honest***, you do look a little ***plump***, but not fat.

A: I know I have ***put on*** more ***weight***. None of my clothes ***fit*** me well. I have to lose some weight!

B: What do you ***plan*** to do?

A: I'll eat fruit ***instead of*** snacks.

B: That's all?

A: Well, what do you suggest?

B: I think you should exercise more.

A: 看！我又變胖了是吧？

B: 坦白講，你看起來有些豐滿，但不是很胖啦。

A: 我知道我又胖了，我的衣服都穿不下啦。我得減肥了！

B: 你打算怎麼做呢？

A: 比如吃水果來代替吃零食。

B: 就這樣？

A: 那你建議我怎麼做呢？

B: 我認為你應該多運動。

核心詞彙

Words&Phrases

fatter	[ˋfætɚ]	形容詞（fat 的比較級）更胖
to be honest	[tu bi ˋɑnɪst]	片語 老實說
plump	[plʌmp]	形容詞 胖嘟嘟的
put on weight	[pʊt ɑn wet]	片語 增加體重
fit	[fɪt]	動詞 合身

plan	[plæn]	動詞 計畫
instead of	[ɪnˋstɛd ɑv]	片語 代替

日常實用短句 *Useful Sentences*

- I need to go on a diet.
  我得節食了。
- I can't squeeze myself in my jeans.
  我擠不進我的牛仔褲。
- Everything in my closet is too small for me now.
  我衣櫥裡的所有東西現在對我來說都太小了。
- Look at my abdomen.
  看我的小腹！
- You have put on some weight lately, haven't you?
  你最近胖了，是不是？
- Sally tries to lose her extra weight by skipping meals.
  莎莉試著靠不吃飯來減掉多餘的體重。
- Most diet pills are illegal.
  大部分的減肥藥都是不合法的。
- How do I calculate my BMI?
  我要如何計算我的身體質量指數？
- You don't need to lose weight. You are skinny already.
  你不需要減肥吧。你已經骨瘦如柴了。
- Oh, my! I've got love handles.
  噢，我的老天啊！我的腰部都是贅肉！

學習++ *More Tips*

「put on weight」是表示「增加體重」的意思，也可以說成「gain weight」；相反地，「lose weight」就是「減重」的意思。如：「She is trying to lose the extra weight she gained last month.」（她正試圖減掉上個月增加的多餘體重。）。

PART❹各類話題篇

你都記住了嗎？

從各篇「日常實用短句」裡整理出外國人常用的單字和片語，如果背起來了，就在前方空格打個勾吧！

- ☐ rain cats and dogs
  片語 下傾盆大雨
- ☐ a thunder shower
  名詞 雷陣雨
- ☐ drizzle
  動詞 下毛毛雨
- ☐ sultry
  形容詞 悶熱的
- ☐ damp
  形容詞 潮濕的
- ☐ soap opera
  名詞 肥皂劇
- ☐ engrossed
  形容詞 全神貫注的
- ☐ serial
  名詞 連續劇
- ☐ episode
  名詞 連續劇的一集
- ☐ stay tuned
  片語 別轉台
- ☐ variety show
  名詞 綜藝節目
- ☐ talk show
  名詞 脱口秀
- ☐ science fiction
  名詞 科幻小説
- ☐ in common
  片語 共同的
- ☐ marathon
  名詞 馬拉松
- ☐ heel-and-toe walking
  名詞 競走
- ☐ fad
  名詞 一時的流行
- ☐ fall in love
  片語 戀愛
- ☐ one-night stand
  名詞 一夜情
- ☐ dump
  動詞 甩掉
- ☐ silent treatment
  名詞 冷戰、沉默相待
- ☐ optional course
  名詞 選修課
- ☐ obligatory course
  名詞 必修課
- ☐ Mickey Mouse course
  名詞 營養學分
- ☐ required course
  名詞 必修課
- ☐ take attendance
  片語 點名

- □ prerequisite
  名詞 必要條件、前提
- □ overdue
  形容詞 過期的
- □ stay up
  片語 熬夜
- □ deadline
  名詞 截止期限
- □ flunk
  動詞 （使）不及格
- □ reference
  名詞 參考資料
- □ part-time
  形容詞 兼差的
- □ quiz
  名詞 測驗
- □ run out of
  片語 用完
- □ finals
  名詞 期末考
- □ in advance
  片語 提前
- □ screw up
  片語 搞砸
- □ column
  名詞 專欄
- □ scandal
  名詞 醜聞、流言蜚語
- □ hook
  動詞 引人上鉤
- □ liposuction
  名詞 抽脂手術
- □ date sb.
  片語 與某人約會
- □ get tired of
  片語 厭倦
- □ on the way
  片語 在路上
- □ candlelit dinner
  名詞 燭光晚餐
- □ epicenter
  名詞 震央
- □ magnitude
  名詞 震級
- □ panic
  動詞 驚慌
- □ aftershock
  名詞 餘震
- □ casualty
  名詞 傷亡
- □ disaster
  名詞 災難
- □ afford
  動詞 買得起
- □ make ends meet
  片語 使收支相抵
- □ instead of
  片語 代替
- □ overwork oneself
  片語 使工作過度
- □ squeeze
  動詞 擠
- □ diet pill
  名詞 減肥藥
- □ calculate
  動詞 計算
- □ love handles
  名詞 腰部贅肉

Part 5 出國旅遊篇－音檔連結

因各家手機系統不同，若無法直接掃描，仍可以至以下電腦雲端連結下載收聽。

（https://tinyurl.com/2p8ek4ca）

PART 5

出國旅遊篇

01 訂購機票

TRACK 086.

實境對話

Conversation

A: Hello. I would like to reserve one ***round-trip*** tickets to Tokyo. I'd like to leave October 17th, and return October 24th.

B: Let me check the ***availability***. May I have your name, please?

A: My name is Fang Kuo-Lung.

B: No problem, there are enough seats. The ***flight*** number is EG204 ***departing*** CKS Airport at 10:30 in the morning, ***arriving*** Narita Airport at 14:20 the same day. Please come here about one week prior to departure, to pay and to collect your ticket. Thank you.

A: 你好！我想要訂一張去東京的來回機票。去程 10 月 17 日，回程 10 月 24 日。

B: 我看一下目前的機位情形，請問你的名字是？

A: 我的名字是方國隆。

B: 沒有問題，還有機位，航班編號 EG204 上午 10:30 由中正機場出發，當天下午 14:20 抵達成田機場。請於大約兩小時前到達機場辦理報到手續，而且大約一週前來開票並付款，謝謝！

核心詞彙

Words&Phrases

round-trip	[ˋraʊnd͵trɪp]	形容詞 來回的
availability	[ə͵veləˋbɪlətɪ]	名詞 可得到的東西
flight	[flaɪt]	名詞 班機

depart	[dɪˋpɑrt]	動詞 啟程
arrive	[əˋraɪv]	動詞 到達

日常實用短句 Useful Sentences

- Could you get me a ticket to New York?
  可以給我一張到紐約的票嗎？
- What time should I check in?
  我該什麼時候報到？
- When is the flight to Hong Kong?
  去香港的飛機是什麼時候？
- Is it a direct flight?
  是直飛的嗎？
- You need to transfer at Tokyo.
  你必須在東京轉機。
- You need to be in the airport three hours before departure time.
  你必須在起飛前三個小時到機場。
- How much is the ticket?
  票多少錢？
- Do you have seat available for flight BE208?
  BE208 次班機還有位子嗎？
- Sorry, sir. The flight to Los Angeles is fully booked.
  先生不好意思，去洛杉磯的班機已經客滿。
- How long is the flight from Taipei to New York?
  從台北到紐約要飛多久？

學習++ More Tips

「book」原本是「書」的意思，但在這裡當作動詞用「to book a plane ticket」（訂飛機票）。有些人在訂購票的時候，通常會指定坐走道或是窗口座位，那麼你就可以說：「I want a window seat.」（我要窗口的座位。），「I want an aisle seat.」（我要走道座位。）。

02 機場報到

TRACK 087.

實境對話

Conversation

A: Good morning. This is the ***check-in*** counter for CX205 to Hong Kong.

B: Here are my ***passport*** and ticket.

A: How many pieces of luggage do you have?

B: Only this one.

A: Please put it here.

B: It's 28 kilos. I'm afraid it's ***overweight***

A: Umm, You can either take out something or pay the ***excess baggage*** charges.

B: Oh. I'd rather pay. Where should I pay?

A: The counter over there, and please come back with your receipt.

A: 早安，這是 CX205 號班機飛香港的手續櫃檯。
B: 我的護照和機票。
A: 你有幾件行李？
B: 只有這一件。
A: 請把它放在這裡。
B: 二十八公斤。大概超重了。
A: 嗯，你可以選擇把一些東西拿出來，或者付行李超重費。
B: 哦，我付錢好了。要到哪裡付？
A: 那邊的櫃檯，付款後請拿收據回來。

核心詞彙

Words&Phrases

check-in	[ˋtʃɛkˏɪn]	名詞 報到
passport	[ˋpasˏport]	名詞 護照
overweight	[ˋovɚˏwet]	形容詞 超重的

excess	[ɪkˋsɛs]	名詞 超額
baggage	[ˋbægɪdʒ]	名詞 行李

日常實用短句 Useful Sentences

- I'd like to check in.
  我要辦理報到手續。
- Where is the Eva Air counter?
  長榮航空櫃台在哪？
- May I have your passport and ticket, please?
  可以給我你的護照和機票嗎？
- How many bags do you want to check in?
  你要帶幾件行李？
- Could you give me a window seat?
  可以給我靠窗的座位嗎？
- I'd like an aisle seat.
  我要一個靠走道的位置。
- Please put your baggage on the scale, Miss Yung.
  楊小姐，請把你的行李放到磅秤上。
- Here's your ticket, your boarding pass and the tag of your baggage.
  這是你的機票、登機證和行李吊牌。
- How do I get to Gate 78?
  我要怎麼去 78 號登機門？
- You can get there by a shuttle bus.
  你可以搭接駁車。

學習++ More Tips

「excess」是「多餘的、超量」的意思，而它的形容詞「excessive」則是「過多的、極度的」的意思，如：「The price at this restaurant is excessive.」（這家餐廳的價錢真是貴！）、「She takes an excessive interest in cosmetics.」（她對化妝品特別的熱衷。）。

03 準備登機

TRACK088.

實境對話

Conversation

A: Here are your boarding passes. The ***gate*** number is 9. Boarding time is 10:00. Please don't forget to pay your ***departure fee***.

B: Thank you.

C: (***Announcement***) Attention ***passengers***, flight EG204 departing from Taipei to Tokyo is ready for boarding. ***First of all***, I would like to invite those passengers traveling with ***infants*** or in business class, please come forward and ***queue*** for boarding.

A: 這是你們的登機證，登機門是 9 號，登機時間是 10:00，請別忘了買機場稅。

B: 謝謝。

C: （廣播）各位旅客您好，現在請搭乘往東京的 EG204 的旅客準備登機，先請嬰幼兒同行或商務艙的旅客到前面來依序登機。

核心詞彙

Words&Phrases

gate	[get]	名詞 登機門
departure fee	[dɪ`pɑrtʃɚ fi]	名詞 機場稅
announcement	[ə`naunsmənt]	名詞 廣播通知
passenger	[`pæsn̩dʒɚ]	名詞 旅客
first of all	[fɝst ɑv ɔl]	片語 首先
infant	[`ɪnfənt]	名詞 嬰幼兒
queue	[kju]	動詞 排隊

日常實用短句 Useful Sentences

- Please follow the line.
  請排隊。
- When can I start to check in?
  我什麼時候可以開始辦理登機手續？
- Wow, you have a lot of baggages.
  哇，你有好多行李。
- I forgot to bring my passport.
  我忘記帶護照了。
- I can't catch the flight.
  我趕不上飛機。
- The airport is crowded.
  機場人很多。
- Your baggage is overweight.
  你的行李超重了。
- When is the boarding time?
  登機時間是什麼時候？
- Do you have any luggage to check in?
  你有任何行李要托運嗎？
- I have a carry-on luggage.
  我有一個要帶上飛機的行李。
- What's the baggage allowance?
  免費行李托運量是多大？
- I'm afraid that your passport is expired.
  恐怕你的護照已經到期了。

學習++ More Tips

搭飛機前最重要的就是要「confirm the ticket」（確定機位），並詢問飛機是否有「delay」（誤點），或是「on time」（準時）。到了機場就要拿機票與護照去換取你的「boarding pass」（登機證）。不要為了其中的一個小缺失而沒搭上飛機喔！

04 機上用餐

TRACK089.

實境對話 Conversation

A: (Announcement) Dear passengers, in 10 minutes, we will start to ***offer*** our lunch service, you may see the menu, there are fish fillet and curry chicken for you to choose from. Due to ***limited*** amounts, we may not be able to satisfy your ***requirements***.

A: Excuse me, for the ***convenience*** of the passengers behind you, please bring your seat to an ***upright position***.

A: Sir, would you like to have fish or chicken?

B: Fish, please.

A: （廣播）各位旅客，再過十分鐘，我們將提供今天的午餐，請各位可以參考菜單，有魚排和咖哩雞，因為份數有限，若有不能滿足您的要求之處，請包涵。

A: 對不起，為了方便後面乘客的用餐，請您豎直椅背。

A: 先生，您要吃魚或雞？

B: 給我魚好了。

核心詞彙 Words&Phrases

offer	[ˋɔfɚ]	動詞 提供
limited	[ˋlɪmɪtɪd]	形容詞 有限的
requirement	[rɪˋkwaɪrmənt]	名詞 要求
convenience	[kəˋvinjəns]	名詞 方便
upright	[ˋʌp,raɪt]	形容詞 挺直的
position	[pəˋzɪʃən]	名詞 方位、姿勢

日常實用短句 Useful Sentences

- May I have some water, please?
  可以給我些水嗎？
- When do you serve breakfast?
  你們什麼時候提供早餐？
- What would you like to drink?
  你想喝什麼？
- Soda, please.
  蘇打水，謝謝。
- What can I have for dinner?
  晚餐可以吃什麼？
- We have pork with rice and chicken noodles.
  我們有豬肉飯和雞肉麵。
- I'd like pork with rice, please.
  請給我豬肉飯。
- Would you like some coffee or tea?
  你想要咖啡或茶嗎？
- May I have orange juice?
  我可以要柳橙汁嗎？
- Sorry, I'm a vegetarian.
  不好意思，我吃素。
- Can I have some more bread?
  我可以要多一點麵包嗎？
- I need a sandwich, please.
  請給我一個三明治。

學習++ More Tips

「Veggie」是「vegetarian」的口語的表達方法，若你是素食主義者，在購買飛機票的時候就要先跟售票員說：「I want to order a vegetarian meal.」（我要訂一份素食餐。）。

05 機上服務

TRACK 090.

實境對話

Conversation

A: Excuse me, Miss. Could I have something to drink? I am a little ***thirsty***.

B: What would you like to drink, juice or ***milk***?

A: Can I have a ***beer***?

B: Sorry, sir, but we don't ***provide*** beer or alcohol on this plane.

A: Well, please give me ***a glass of*** fruit juice then.

B: All right. Would you like something ***else***?

A: Some cookies, please.

B: Sure. Wait a moment, please.

A: 打擾一下，小姐。我能點些喝的嗎？我有點口渴了。

B: 您想喝什麼？果汁還是牛奶呢？

A: 我能喝罐啤酒嗎？

B: 很抱歉，先生。本班機並不提供啤酒或含酒精飲料喔。

A: 噢，那請給我一杯果汁吧。

B: 可以。您還要其他的嗎？

A: 麻煩給我一些餅乾吧。

B: 請您稍等。

核心詞彙

Words&Phrases

thirsty	[ˋθɝstɪ]	形容詞 口渴的
milk	[mɪlk]	名詞 牛奶
beer	[bɪr]	名詞 啤酒
provide	[prəˋvaɪd]	動詞 提供
a glass of	[ə glæs ɑv]	片語 一杯
else	[ɛls]	副詞 其他、另外

日常實用短句 Useful Sentences

- Please help me put my baggage up in the cabin.
  請幫我把行李放在上面。
- Could you give me a blanket, please?
  可以給我一張毛毯嗎？
- I have a headache. Can I have some water?
  我頭痛，可以給我些水嗎？
- Please fasten your seatbelt.
  請繫好你的安全帶。
- Do you have Chinese newspaper?
  有中文報紙嗎？
- Do you sell duty free items?
  有賣免稅商品嗎？
- Here's the earphone.
  耳機在這裡。
- Excuse me, could you show me to seat 16F?
  不好意思，請問 16F 是哪一個座位？
- Sorry, I pushed the service button by mistake.
  不好意思，我不小心按到服務鈴。
- The lavatory is now vacant.
  廁所現在無人使用。
- Yes, I will need the immigration form.
  是的，我需要入境表格。
- When does the movie start?
  電影什麼時候開始？

學習++ More Tips

在飛機上需要請空服員服務時，可以善用「May I have...?」或是「Could you give me...?」（可以請你給我……嗎？）這兩個句型。如：「May I have one more blanket?」（我可以多要一條毯子嗎？），或「Could you give me another headset?」（可不可以給我另一個耳機呢？）。

06 通關審查

TRACK 091.

實境對話

Conversation

A: May I see your passport? Anything you want to ***declare***?

B: No.

A: Do you have any ***cigarettes*** or ***alcohol*** with you?

B: Only two ***bottles*** of ***wine***. It's within the ***tax-free*** limit.

A: What's this?

B: It's a gift for my friend.

A: Fine, go this way, please.

A: 請出示你們的護照，有需要申報的東西嗎？

B: 沒有。

A: 有帶香菸或酒嗎？

B: 有兩瓶酒，但在免稅範圍之內。

A: 這件是什麼呢？

B: 這些是送給朋友的禮物。

A: 好，沒問題，請這邊走。

核心詞彙

Words&Phrases

declare	[dɪˋklɛr]	動詞 申報
cigarette	[ˋsɪgəˏrɛt]	名詞 香菸
alcohol	[ˋælkəˏhɔl]	名詞 酒精
bottle	[ˋbɑtl̩]	名詞 瓶
wine	[waɪn]	名詞 酒
tax-free	[ˋtæksˏfri]	形容詞 免稅的

日常實用短句 Useful Sentences

- Can you tell me which line to follow?
  你可以告訴我要排哪條線嗎？
- Take out the laptop and put it in the box.
  請把膝上型電腦拿出來放在盒子裡。
- Place containers with liquid or gel inside a quart-size clear zip-top bag.
  把裡面有液體或膠狀的容器放在一個中型的透明夾鏈袋裡。
- Take off your coat and shoes and put them in the box.
  脫掉你的外套和鞋子，把它們放在盒子裡。
- Passport and tickets, please.
  請拿出護照和機票。
- Walk through the security gate, please.
  請走過這個安全門。
- Open the bag, please. I'd like to check what the circle stuff is in your bag.
  請打開這個包包，我想要檢查你包包裡這個圓狀物是什麼。
- Sorry, you can't have any liquid with you.
  不好意思，你不能帶任何液狀物體。
- Take off your belt. Test again.
  脫掉你的皮帶，再走一次。
- I'm afraid I need to take a thorough look in your bag.
  恐怕我要檢查一下你的包包了。
- You need to pass through the green line.
  你要通過綠色的那條線。

學習++ More Tips

「declare」在這裡是「申報」的意思；其他的用法是當作「宣告」，或是「聲稱」的意思。「I declare that he elected.」（我宣佈他當選了。）、「Mary declared that she was right. 」（瑪莉聲稱她是對的。）。

07 兌換

TRACK 092.

實境對話

Conversation

A: Excuse me. I'd like to ***exchange*** some money.

B: Ok, please fill out this ***form***.

A: May I use ***traveler***'s ***checks*** here?

B: Yes, you can.

A: I'd like to exchange ***USD***$1500 into Japanese ***Yen***.

B: Yes, please ***sign*** here.

A: Here is ¥195,000 ***in total***. Thanks!

A: 不好意思！我想要換錢！

B: 好的，請填寫這張表格。

A: 這裡可以用旅行支票嗎？

B: 可以。

A: 我想將 1500 美金換成日幣。

B: 好，請在這裡簽名。

A: 全部日幣十九萬五千元，謝謝！

核心詞彙

Words&Phrases

exchange	[ɪksˋtʃendʒ]	動詞 兌換
form	[fɔrm]	名詞 表格
traveler	[ˋtrævlɚ]	名詞 旅行者
check	[tʃɛk]	名詞 支票
USD	[ju ɛs di]	名詞 美金
Yen	[jɛn]	名詞 日幣
sign	[saɪn]	動詞 簽名
in total	[ɪn ˋtotl̩]	片語 總共

日常實用短句 Useful Sentences

- Where can I change money?
  我可以在哪裡換錢？
- At the bank.
  在銀行。
- I'd like to change some NT dollars into US dollars.
  我想要把一些台幣換成美鈔。
- Where do I get the information about today's exchange rate?
  哪裡可以知道今天的匯率？
- Is there any commission?
  要收手續費嗎？
- How much do you charge for the commission?
  手續費怎麼算？
- How would you like your change?
  你想怎麼換？
- I'd like five $100 bills, and ten $ 10 bills.
  我要五張百元鈔，十張十元鈔。
- Could you please give me some small change?
  你可以給我一些小額的零錢嗎？
- No problem.
  沒問題。
- I need some traveler's checks.
  我需要一些旅行支票。
- Do I have to sign each check?
  我要在每張支票上簽名嗎？

學習++ More Tips

出國在外都必須換當地錢或是帶「traveler's check」（旅行支票），或是隨身帶著一兩張「credit card」（信用卡），就可以免去許多麻煩了。

08 轉機

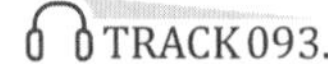

實境對話 Conversation

A: I am going to ***transfer*** in Hong Kong. Could you tell me where to get the ***formalities done***?

B: ***Sure***. Please go to the Transfer Counter.

A: Well, so will I get another boarding pass?

B: That's right, miss.

A: OK. ***One more*** thing. How do I deal with my ***luggage***?

B: Your luggage will be transferred ***onto*** your next plane.

A: 我要在香港轉機，可以請您告訴我要去哪裡辦手續嗎？
B: 當然。請您到轉機櫃檯那兒去辦理。
A: 那麼，我會拿到另一張登機證囉？
B: 沒錯，小姐。
A: 好的。還有一件事。我要如何處理我的行李呢？
B: 您的行李將會轉送到您下一班飛機上。

核心詞彙 Words&Phrases

transfer	[træns`fɚ]	動詞 轉換
formality	[fɔr`mælətɪ]	名詞 手續
done	[dʌn]	形容詞 完成的
sure	[ʃur]	副詞 當然
one more	[wʌn mor]	片語 再一
luggage	[`lʌgɪdʒ]	名詞 行李
onto	[`ɑntu]	介係詞 在……之上

日常實用短句 *Useful Sentences*

- Where is the Eva Air transfer desk?
  長榮航空的轉機櫃檯在哪？
- I have to transfer the flight to New York.
  我必須轉機去紐約。
- Do you have the boarding pass for the next flight?
  你有下一個班機的登機證嗎？
- You can go to the flight connection counter; they will direct you to the right gate.
  你可以去轉機櫃檯，他們會告訴你正確的登機門在哪裡。
- What is your flight number?
  你的班次是多少？
- Where do I go to catch my connecting flight?
  我要去哪裡轉搭下一班飛機？
- Flight 18 is delayed due to bad weather condition.
  因為天候不佳，18 次班機延誤。
- I have been waiting for 2 hours to catch my next flight.
  我已經等我的下一班飛機兩個小時了。
- When will the transit flight take off?
  轉機的班機什麼時候會起飛？
- All of the connecting passengers are requested to proceed to Gate 76.
  所有轉機的旅客被要求前往 76 號登機門。
- Can I get on the earlier flight instead?
  我可以換成早一點的班機嗎？

學習++ *More Tips*

「One more thing.」表示「還有一件事。」用於接續原本以為已經結束的話題之後，作為提醒或補充，如：「Your boarding time will be at 7:30. And one more thing, don't forget to keep your baggage claim tag.」（你的登機時間是在 7:30 分。還有一件事，別忘了保留行李提領單。）。

09 入境

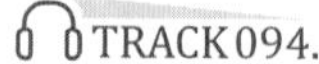
TRACK094.

實境對話 Conversation

A: Could you show me your passport and ***declaration*** form, please?
B: OK. Here you are.
A: What's the ***purpose*** of your visit?
B: I am here for ***business trip***.
A: OK. Is that your ***suitcase***? Would you mind if I open it?
B: Of course not! ***Go ahead***.
A: Very well. Thanks for your ***cooperation***. Here is your passport.

A: 請您出示您的護照和海關申報表好嗎？
B: 好的。給您。
A: 可以告訴我您來這裡的目的嗎？
B: 我來這兒出差。
A: 好。那是您的手提箱嗎？您介意我把手提箱打開嗎？
B: 當然不介意！請便吧。
A: 很好。謝謝您的合作。這是你的護照。

核心詞彙 Words&Phrases

declaration	[ˏdɛkləˋreʃən]	名詞 申報
purpose	[ˋpɝpəs]	名詞 目的
business trip	[ˋbɪznɪs trɪp]	名詞 出差
suitcase	[ˋsutˏkes]	名詞 公事包
go ahead	[go əˋhɛd]	片語 請便、先走
cooperation	[koˏɑpəˋreʃən]	名詞 合作

日常實用短句 Useful Sentences

- Passport, please.
  請給我看護照。
- Here you are.
  在這裡。
- How long will you stay here?
  你要在這裡待多久？
- I will stay here for a month.
  我會待一個月。
- What's your purpose of this trip?
  你這次來的目的是什麼？
- Visiting my friends.
  拜訪朋友。
- Where are you from?
  你從哪裡來？
- Do you have any family members or friends travelling with you?
  你有任何家人或朋友和你一起來嗎？
- Where are you going to stay?
  你要住哪裡？
- I'll stay at my relative's place.
  我會住在親戚家。
- Have you ever been to New York?
  你有去過紐約嗎？

學習++ More Tips

一般在海關都會被問及旅行的目的，只要將旅行的目的套用在「I am here for...」（我是來這裡……的）的句型即可，如：「I am here for business trip.」（我是來這裡出差的。），或「I am here for sightseeing.」（我是來這裡觀光的。）。

10 領取行李

TRACK 095.

實境對話

Conversation

A: I can't find my baggage. Could you help me?

B: ***Calm down*** miss. Can you tell me your flight number?

A: I ***flew*** CA956 from Taipei.

B: OK. Could you ***describe*** your baggage?

A: One black suitcase and a dark blue ***backpack***.

B: Pleas give me your baggage claim ***tag*** and fill out this form. I'll check it for you ***at once***. Ah...here it is!

A: Thank Goodness! I really appreciate your help.

A: 我找不到我的行李。您能幫幫我嗎？

B: 小姐，先冷靜一下。能告訴我您乘坐的班機號碼嗎？

A: 我是搭乘從台北起飛的 CA956 班機。

B: 好的。可以描述一下您的行李嗎？

A: 一個黑色手提箱和一個深藍色背包。

B: 請給我您的行李領取牌，然後填一下這張表。我馬上幫您查詢。喔……找到啦！

A: 謝天謝地！真的非常感謝您的幫助。

核心詞彙

Words&Phrases

calm down	[kɑm daʊn]	片語 冷靜
flew	[flu]	動詞 （fly 的過去式）飛
describe	[dɪˋskraɪb]	動詞 描述
backpack	[ˋbækˏpæk]	名詞 背包
tag	[tæg]	名詞 吊牌
at once	[æt wʌns]	片語 馬上

日常實用短句 Useful Sentences

- Where is the baggage claim?
  行李提領處在哪？
- Which carousel is for flight AA106?
  AA106 班機的行李輸送帶是哪一個？
- How can I get to the baggage claim?
  我要怎麼去行李提領處？
- I'm waiting for my luggage.
  我在等我的行李。
- What color is your baggage?
  你的行李是什麼顏色的？
- It's white and black with dots.
  是黑白的，上面有點點。
- I lost my baggage.
  我的行李不見了。
- What does it look like?
  它長什麼樣子？
- It is a red hard shell suitcase.
  是紅色硬殼的手提箱。
- Where can I get a baggage trolley?
  哪裡有行李推車？
- Can you help me get my baggage? It's too heavy.
  你可以幫我拿行李嗎？實在太重了。
- Excuse me. This is my luggage.
  不好意思，這是我的行李。

學習++ More Tips

找不到行李時，必須告知地勤人員你的飛機班次，以利查詢行李下落，因此「I flew (flight number) from (place).」（我是搭乘從（某地）起飛的（班次號碼）班機。）是個很重要的句型。如：「I flew JA356 from Kaohsiung.」（我是搭乘高雄起飛的 JA356 次班機。）。

11 | 海關、出關

TRACK 096.

實境對話

Conversation

A: Show me your ***custom*** declaration form, please.
B: Here you are.
A: Could you let me know what's in your luggage?
B: There are some ***clothes*** and ***several*** books.
A: Do you have anything to declare?
B: No. I ***merely*** bought a ***scarf*** for myself. May I ***leave*** now?
A: Yes, you can go now.
B: Thank you. Bye!

A: 請出示您的海關申報表。
B: 給您。
A: 可不可以告訴我，您的行李裡面裝什麼？
B: 只有一些衣服和幾本書。
A: 您有應該申報的東西嗎？
B: 沒有。我只是給自己買了條圍巾。我現在可以走了嗎？
A: 是的，您可以走了。
B: 謝謝。再見！

核心詞彙

Words&Phrases

custom	[ˋkʌstəm]	名詞 海關
clothes	[kloz]	名詞 衣物
several	[ˋsɛvərəl]	形容詞 幾個的
merely	[ˋmɪrlɪ]	副詞 僅僅
scarf	[skɑrf]	名詞 圍巾
leave	[liv]	動詞 離開

日常實用短句 Useful Sentences

- Peggy is going through the customs.
  珮姬正走出海關。
- I have nothing to declare.
  我沒有什麼要申報的。
- These are gifts for my friends.
  這是要給我朋友的禮物。
- Where should I pay the tax?
  我要在哪裡繳稅？
- Can I have a tax refund?
  我可以退稅嗎？
- Do you have the declaration form?
  你有申報表格嗎？
- No. I have nothing to declare.
  不，我沒有什麼要申報的。
- You need to fill out a declaration form.
  你需要填寫申報表格。
- Please follow the line if you have anything to declare.
  如果你有東西要申報請排這條線。
- Is that meat product?
  那是肉製品嗎？
- We need to check the bag.
  我們必須檢查包包。
- Would you tell me how to fill the declaration form, please?
  你可以告訴我怎麼填這個申報表格嗎？

學習++ More Tips

「declare」是「申報（納稅品）」的意思。出海關時，海關會例行詢問：「Do you have anything to declare?」（你有要申報的東西嗎？），如果沒有，則回答：「I have nothing to declare.」（我沒有需要申報的東西。）就可以了。

12 預定房間

TRACK 097.

實境對話 Conversation

A: Good afternoon. I'd like to ***book*** a ***double room*** from August 18 for four ***nights***.

B: May I have your name, sir?

A: John Williams.

B: Could I ***ask*** when you will arrive?

A: I'll get there by five o'clock on ***August*** 18.

B: OK. We'll have the ***room*** ready for you, See you ***then***.

A: Thank you. Good bye.

A: 午安。我想訂一間雙人房，從 8 月 18 日起住四個晚上。
B: 請給我您的大名好嗎？
A: 約翰威廉。
B: 可以請問您什麼時候到達嗎？
A: 我將會在 8 月 18 號那天五點之前到達。
B: 好的。我們會為您將房間準備好的。到時候見。
A: 謝謝你。再見。

核心詞彙 Words&Phrases

book	[bʊk]	動詞 預訂
double room	[ˋdʌbl̩ rum]	名詞 雙人房
night	[naɪt]	名詞 夜晚
ask	[æsk]	動詞 問
August	[ɔˋgʌst]	名詞 八月
room	[rum]	名詞 房間
then	[ðɛn]	副詞 那時

日常實用短句 Useful Sentences

- I've made a reservation.
  我有訂房。
- May I have your name, please?
  可以告訴我你的名字嗎？
- How can I help you?
  有什麼可以為您效勞嗎？
- Can I book a single room for three nights?
  我可以訂三個晚上的單人房嗎？
- Do you have your reservation number?
  你有訂房號碼嗎？
- We don't have any single room available at this time.
  現在我們沒有空的單人房了。
- How much is the double room?
  雙人房多少錢？
- Sorry sir, we're fully booked.
  先生不好意思，我們都客滿了。
- Do you have any vacancies this weekend?
  你們這個周末有空房嗎？
- I need a room with sea view.
  我要一個海景房間。
- May I see the double room first?
  我可以先看一下雙人房嗎？
- OK, I'll take the double room.
  好，我要一間雙人房。

學習++ More Tips

打電話向飯店訂房時，最重要的就是要將時間日期和屬意的房型正確傳達給訂房人員，如：「I'd like to reserve a single room for September 10. 」（我要訂 9 月 10 日那天一間單人房。），或是「I need a suite from October 11 to October 15.」（我 10 月 11 日至 10 月 15 日需要一間套房。）。

13 租車

TRACK 098.

實境對話

Conversation

A: Could I have a look at your ***pamphlet***?

B: Yes, please do.

A: I would like to ***rent*** this type of car starting today for 5 days.

B: Do you prefer ***automatic*** or ***standard***?

A: I prefer automatic.

B: Could I take a look at your international ***driver's license***?

A: Here you are. May I drop the car off in Osaka?

B: Yes, you can. But you need to pay an ***additional*** charge.

A: 可否讓我看一下你們的手冊？

B: 是，請看。

A: 我想租這款車，從今天起 5 天時間。

B: 你喜歡自排還是手排的？

A: 我要自排的。

B: 我可以看一下你的國際駕照嗎？

A: 這就是，我可以在大阪還車嗎？

B: 可以，但是你要付額外的費用。

核心詞彙

Words&Phrases

pamphlet	[`pæmflɪɪt]	名詞 小冊子
rent	[rɛnt]	動詞 租
automatic	[ˏɔtə`mætɪk]	名詞 自排
standard	[`stændɚd]	名詞 手排、標準
driver's license	[`draɪvɚs `laɪsn̩s]	名詞 駕照
additional	[ə`dɪʃənl̩]	形容詞 額外的

日常實用短句 *Useful Sentences*

- Good morning, sir. I'd like to rent a van.
  早安，先生。我想要租一台車。
- Do you have driver's license?
  你有駕照嗎？
- How many days would you like to rent the car for?
  你要租幾天？
- What kind of options do you have?
  有什麼可以選的？
- What is the daily rental rate?
  租一天多少錢？
- Where should I return the car?
  我應該在哪裡還車？
- Do I need to pay the deposit?
  要付訂金嗎？
- Do I have to fill up the gas when I return the car?
  還車前要加滿油嗎？
- Can I see the car first?
  可以先看一下車嗎？
- Here's the rental agreement.
  這是租約。

學習++ *More Tips*

外出旅行若是也有車子代步，而你的方向感也不錯的話，那麼肯定是方便多了。在機場或是旅館都會有「Car Rental Service」（租車服務），你可以依自己的喜好與需要租「mini van」（休旅車）、「Jeep」（吉普車）或是拉風的「convertible」（敞篷車）。

14 問路

TRACK 099.

實境對話

Conversation

A: Excuse me. I am afraid I ***got lost***. Could you tell me where I am now?

B: This is ***downtown*** area. Where do you want to go?

A: I want to return to my ***hotel***– Holiday ***Inn***.

B: Oh, it's a little far from here.

A: Could you tell me how to get ***back*** there ***as soon as possible***?

B: I think you'd better ***take a taxi*** in case you get lost again.

A: 打擾一下。我恐怕迷路了。您能告訴我我現在在哪裡嗎？
B: 這裡是市中心。您想去哪裡呢？
A: 我想回我住的酒店——假日酒店。
B: 喔，那裡離這裡有點遠哦。
A: 可不可以請您告訴我如何儘快回到那兒去呢？
B: 我想為了以防你又迷路，你最好還是搭計程車吧。

核心詞彙

Words&Phrases

get lost	[gɛt lɔst]	片語 迷路
downtown	[ˌdaʊnˋtaʊn]	名詞 市區
hotel	[hoˋtɛl]	名詞 酒店
inn	[ɪn]	名詞 小旅館
back	[bæk]	副詞 回原處
as soon as possible	[æz sun æz ˋpɑsəbl̩]	片語 越快越好
take a taxi	[tek ə ˋtæksɪ]	片語 搭計程車

日常實用短句 Useful Sentences

- I'm lost.
  我迷路了。
- Could you tell me how to get to the Ritz Hotel?
  可以告訴我麗緻酒店怎麼走嗎？
- Just go down the street and it's on your left.
  只要往這條路走就可以在左邊看到了。
- It's on the corner of 5th Street and First Road.
  就在第五街和第一路的路口
- What's the landmark in this area?
  這個區域的地標是什麼？
- I have no sense of directions.
  我沒有方向感。
- You can take Bus 5 to the Mall.
  你可以搭5號公車去購物中心。
- How can I get to the department store?
  我要怎麼去百貨公司？
- You can get there by subway.
  你可以搭地鐵去。
- Can you help me?
  你可以幫我嗎？
- Where are we?
  我們在哪裡？
- I'm looking for the library.
  我在找圖書館。

學習++ More Tips

問路時，在請教前往地方的方位之後，最好加問一句：「Is there any landmark?」（有什麼地標嗎？），對方便會回答如：「Yes, there is a big fountain next to the mall.」（有的，購物中心旁邊有一個大噴水池。），有了一個醒目的大標的物，對於正確找到地點將相當有幫助。

15 旅館

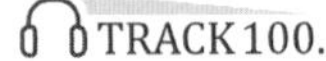

實境對話 Conversation

A: Welcome!

B: Excuse me. We did not ***make a reservation***.

A: Just two of you? How many nights do you want to stay?

B: Yes, only two of us. We ***plan*** to stay 5 nights.

A: Ok, please fill out this form for me.

B: Is that ok?

A: Yes, that's fine. Your room number is 1234. Here is your ***key***. Please ***use*** the ***elevator*** over there.

A: 歡迎光臨！

B: 對不起，我們沒有事先預訂。

A: 您們兩位嗎？請問要停留幾個晚上呢？

B: 是的，只有兩位。我們預備要住 5 個晚上。

A: 好的，請填寫這份表格。

B: 這樣子填寫可以了嗎？

A: 這樣就可以了。房間號碼 1234，這是房間的鑰匙。請利用那邊的電梯。

核心詞彙 Words&Phrases

make a reservation	[mek ə ˌrɛzɚˋveʃən]	片語 預訂房間
plan	[plæn]	動詞 計畫
key	[ki]	名詞 鑰匙
use	[juz]	動詞 使用
elevator	[ˋɛləˌvetɚ]	名詞 電梯

日常實用短句 *Useful Sentences*

- What time will you serve the breakfast?
  你們幾點供應早餐？
- Here is your key card.
  這是你的房卡。
- Where can I have the breakfast?
  我要在哪裡吃早餐？
- You may have the breakfast on the third floor.
  你可以在三樓吃早餐。
- The bellboy will take your baggage to your room.
  服務生會幫你把行李拿到房間。
- The breakfast will be served from 6 a.m. to 10 a.m..
  早餐時間是早上六點到十點。
- Can I have one more bathrobe, please?
  可以再給我一件浴衣嗎？
- Please give me a morning call at 5:30 am tomorrow.
  明天早上五點半請打電話叫醒我。
- Do you have laundry service?
  有洗衣服務嗎？
- Can you fix the hair dryer?
  可以修一下這個吹風機嗎？
- How can I make an international call?
  我要怎麼打國際電話？
- The air conditioner in my room doesn't work.
  我房間裡的空調壞了。

學習++ *More Tips*

除了餐廳需要「make a reservation」（預約）之外，訂飯店旅館也都需要「make a reservation」。你在訂房間時也別忘了要先詢問「When can I check in?」（我何時可以住進來？）和「When is the check-out time?」（什麼時候需要退租旅館？）。

16 給小費

TRACK 101.

實境對話

Conversation

A: Excuse me! Can I have the ***bill***, please?

B: ***Here*** is your bill. That'll be $195.

A: Will you ***give*** me a receipt?

B: ***Surely***, sir.

A: Good. Here is 200 ***dollars***. You can ***keep*** the change.

B: Thank you, sir. You're so ***generous***. Here's the receipt.

A: Okay.

A: 不好意思，請給我帳單好嗎？
B: 給您帳單。一共是 195 元。
A: 您會給我收據嗎？
B: 當然會的，先生。
A: 好，這是兩百元。零錢當小費吧。
B: 謝謝。先生，您真慷慨。這是發票，請收好。
A: 好的。

核心詞彙

Words&Phrases

bill	[bɪl]	名詞 帳單
here	[hɪr]	名詞 這裡
give	[gɪv]	動詞 給
surely	[ˋʃurlɪ]	副詞 當然
dollar	[ˋdɑlɚ]	名詞 美元
keep	[kip]	動詞 保留
generous	[ˋdʒɛnərəs]	形容詞 大方慷慨的

日常實用短句 Useful Sentences

- How much do I need to pay for the tips?
  我需要付多少小費？
- You can leave the tip on the pillow.
  你可以把小費留在枕頭上。
- Five dollars should be good enough for tips.
  五塊錢應該就夠當小費了。
- Check, please.
  我要結帳。
- Don't forget to tip the bellman.
  不要忘了給服務生小費。
- The waiter is very kind and helpful.
  服務生很好心也幫很多忙。
- You need to give the waitress about 15% for tips.
  你必須給女服務員 15% 當小費。
- He had a bad attitude. Save the tips.
  他的態度很糟，把小費省下來吧。
- It is reasonable.
  這是很合理的。
- Thanks for your tips.
  謝謝你的小費。
- You gave too much tips.
  你給太多小費了。
- You must pay in cash.
  你一定要付現。

學習++ More Tips

很多人都會以為「receipt」和「invoice」是一樣的東西，事實上「receipt」指「收據」，是「買方付費之後，賣方給的已付款證明」；而「invoice」指的是「發票」，是「賣方開立給買方的收費通知」。前者與後者的差別在於「已付費」和「未付費」，必須弄清楚。

17 逛遊樂園

TRACK 102.

實境對話

Conversation

A: It's such a ***large amusement park***, isn't it?
B: Yes. It is the largest one in the city.
A: Where shall we buy the ***admission*** tickets?
B: Oh, the ***ticket window*** is over there. Let's go to the back of the line.
A: What is the most ***exciting*** amusement ***facility*** here?
B: It should be the ***roller coaster***.
A: Let's try that first.

A: 這個遊樂園可真大啊。是吧？
B: 是啊。這是這個城市最大的遊樂園了。
A: 我們去哪裡買入場票呢？
B: 噢，售票口在那裡。我們去排隊吧。
A: 這裡最刺激的遊樂設施是什麼呢？
B: 應該是雲霄飛車吧。
A: 我們就先去玩那個吧。

核心詞彙

Words&Phrases

large	[lɑrdʒ]	形容詞 大的
amusement park	[əˋmjuzmənt pɑrk]	名詞 遊樂園
admission	[ədˋmɪʃən]	名詞 入場券
ticket window	[ˋtɪkɪt ˋwɪndo]	名詞 售票口
exciting	[ɪkˋsaɪtɪŋ]	形容詞 刺激的
facility	[fəˋsɪlətɪ]	名詞 設施
roller coaster	[ˋrolɚ ˋkostɚ]	名詞 雲霄飛車

日常實用短句 Useful Sentences

- Where can I buy the tickets?
  我要在哪裡買票？
- Line up, please.
  請排隊。
- You are not tall enough to take the ride.
  你不夠高不能搭這個。
- I want to ride the ferries wheel.
  我想搭摩天輪。
- I think I will skip the hunted house.
  我想我還是不要去鬼屋好了。
- It's scary.
  好恐怖。
- The queue at the rollercoaster is extending to the gate.
  雲霄飛車的隊伍已經排到門口了。
- Disneyland is one of my favorite amusement parks.
  迪士尼樂園是我最愛的遊樂園之一。
- A day pass will be a better choice.
  一日票是個不錯的選擇。
- Let's stand in line.
  我們來排隊吧。
- I'm too old to ride the merry-go-round.
  我太老了，不適合搭旋轉木馬。
- We played the Bumper Car twice today.
  我們今天玩了兩次碰碰車。

學習++ More Tips

「roller coaster」指的是「雲霄飛車」，如：「I dare not ride on the roller coaster.」（我不敢玩雲霄飛車。），其他常見的遊樂設施有：「bumper car」（碰碰車）、「ferris wheel」（摩天輪）、「merry-go-round」（旋轉木馬）等。

18 攝影留念

TRACK 103.

實境對話

Conversation

A: ***What a*** beautiful ***view***! Why don't we ***take a picture*** here?

B: Good idea. Let me take a picture for you.

A: All right. I'd like to have a picture with the ***flower garden*** in the ***background***.

B: That's good! Would you like to ***stand by*** the ***tulips***?

A: Sure.

B: OK. Now ***say cheese***. Done!

A: 多美的風景啊！我們為什麼不在這裡拍張照呢？
B: 好主意。我幫你拍一張吧。
A: 好的。我想照一張以花園為背景的照片。
B: 好啊！你要不要站在鬱金香旁邊呢？
A: 好啊。
B: 好，現在笑一下。拍好了！

核心詞彙

Words&Phrases

What a...!	[hwɑt ə]	片語 多麼……!
view	[vju]	名詞 風景
take a picture	[tek ə `pɪktʃɚ]	片語 拍照
flower garden	[`flauɚ `gɑrdn̩]	名詞 花園
background	[`bæk͵graund]	名詞 背景
stand by	[stænd baɪ]	片語 站在……旁邊
tulip	[`tjuləp]	名詞 鬱金香
say cheese	[se tʃiz]	片語 笑一個

日常實用短句 Useful Sentences

- Could you please take a picture for us?
  你可以幫我們拍張照嗎？
- Just press this button.
  按這個鈕就好。
- We should have a picture together.
  我們應該一起拍一張。
- Smile.
  微笑。
- Say cheese.
  笑一個。
- Can I take a picture with you, Miss Wu?
  吳小姐，我可以和你拍一張嗎？
- We have to find a nice background.
  我們要找一個漂亮的背景。
- Wow, a new camera.
  哇，新相機耶！
- Is there a video recording function?
  有錄影功能嗎？
- It's a digital camera.
  這是數位相機。
- It's dark here. Turn on the flash.
  這裡太暗了，開閃光燈。
- Hold that pose.
  保持那個姿勢。

學習++ More Tips

「take a picture」是表示「拍照」的意思，也可以說成「take a photo」，如：「Let me take a picture of you two.」（我來幫你們兩個拍一張照吧！）、「We should have a picture taken together.」則是表示（我們應該一起拍張照。）。

19 買紀念品

TRACK 104.

實境對話

Conversation

A: Good morning. I'd like to buy some souvenirs for my friends. Would you ***recommend*** something good for me?

B: How about ***handicrafts*** or special ***costumes***?

A: ***Sounds*** good. Could you show me the red ***hat*** over there?

B: Here you are. It's a very unique hat that you can't find anything like this ***elsewhere***.

A: Good. I'll ***take*** it.

A: 早安。我想給我的朋友們買些紀念品。您可不可以給我推薦些好東西？

B: 手工藝品或特色服飾如何？

A: 聽起來不錯。您能讓我看看那邊那頂紅色的帽子嗎？

B: 您看看。這個帽子非常獨特，您在別的地方找不到像這樣的東西。

A: 很好。我買了。

核心詞彙

Words&Phrases

recommend	[ˏrɛkəˋmɛnd]	動詞 推薦
handicraft	[ˋhændɪˏkræft]	名詞 手工藝品
costume	[ˋkɑstjum]	名詞 服飾
sound	[saʊnd]	動詞 聽起來
hat	[hæt]	名詞 帽子
elsewhere	[ˋɛlsˏhwɛr]	副詞 在別處
take	[tek]	副詞 拿走

日常實用短句 Useful Sentences

- Wow, everything in the store is on sale.
  哇，這間店的每一樣東西都在特價。
- Let's buy some souvenirs at the gift shop.
  我們去禮品店買一些紀念品吧。
- I'll take the cup, please.
  我要買這個杯子。
- How much is the cup?
  這個杯子多少錢？
- Excuse me. Can I have one more of this?
  不好意思，我可以再多買一個嗎？
- Sorry. They're sold out.
  抱歉，這個賣光了。
- This is the last one.
  這是最後一個。
- Could you wrap it as a gift?
  你可以把它包成禮物嗎？
- I'll get it for you.
  我買給你。
- I'll get Tom and Mary some T-shirts as souvenirs.
  我要買一些T恤給湯姆和瑪莉當紀念品。
- That's a good idea.
  這是個好主意。
- That is a real bargain.
  這真的很划算。

學習++ More Tips

為家人買紀念品或小禮物時，不妨告訴店員：「I am looking for something that I can get for my family.」（我要找些可以送給家人的禮物。），因為是要送人的禮物，所以買好之後，別忘了告訴店員：「Please warp it as a gift.」（請把它包成禮物。）。

20 返程回家

TRACK 105.

實境對話

Conversation

A: Good morning, Mrs. Green. I am leaving. Thank you so much for everything.

B: It's my ***pleasure***. Why not stay ***longer***?

A: I ***wish*** I could, but the school will ***begin*** in two weeks.

B: Oh. I hope you can come again next year. Please give my best ***regards*** to your family.

A: Thanks a lot. Let's ***keep in touch***.

B: Sure. Have a ***safe trip***.

A: 早上好，格林太太，我要走了。謝謝您為我所做的一切。
B: 這是我的榮幸嘛。為什麼不再待一段時間呢？
A: 我也希望，不過學校兩星期後就要開學了。
B: 噢，我希望你明年能夠再來。請幫我向你的家人問好。
A: 多謝。我們要保持連絡喔。
B: 當然囉。祝你一路順風。

核心詞彙

Words&Phrases

pleasure	[ˋplɛʒɚ]	名詞 榮幸
longer	[ˋlɔŋgɚ]	形容詞 （long 的比較級）更久
wish	[wɪʃ]	動詞 希望
begin	[bɪˋgɪn]	動詞 開始
regard	[rɪˋgɑrd]	名詞 問候、致意
keep in touch	[kip ɪn tʌtʃ]	片語 保持聯絡
safe	[sef]	形容詞 安全的
trip	[trɪp]	名詞 旅程

日常實用短句 Useful Sentences

- I had a great trip in US.
  我在美國玩得很開心。
- It's time to go home.
  是時候該回家了。
- I'll visit again with my family.
  我會再跟我的家人一起來。
- Thank you so much for letting me visit.
  非常謝謝你讓我來拜訪。
- I can't wait to go home.
  我等不及要回家了。
- I hope you have a chance to visit again.
  我希望你有機會可以再來。
- What's the greatest part of your trip?
  你的旅行中最好玩的是哪一部分啊？
- Don't forget your belongings.
  不要忘了你的隨身物品。
- I really enjoyed myself in Europe.
  我在歐洲真的玩得很開心。
- It's so nice to be home.
  回到家真好。
- Who will pick you up at the airport?
  誰會去機場接你？
- I wish you could stay longer.
  我希望你可以待久一點。

學習++ More Tips

「give one's regards to...」是表示「向……問候」之意。道別時，禮貌上都會請對方代為問候對方的父母或家人，如：「Please give my regards to your parents.」（請代我問候你的父母。），或是：「Please send my best regards to your family.」（請代我問候你的家人。）

PART ❺ 出國旅遊篇

你都記住了嗎？

從各篇「日常實用短句」裡整理出外國人常用的單字和片語，如果背起來了，就在前方空格打個勾吧！

- □ check in
  片語 報到
- □ direct flight
  名詞 直飛班機
- □ window seat
  名詞 靠窗的位子
- □ aisle seat
  名詞 靠走道的位子
- □ scale
  名詞 磅秤
- □ boarding pass
  名詞 登機證
- □ shuttle bus
  名詞 接駁車
- □ crowded
  形容詞 擁擠的
- □ overweight
  形容詞 超重的
- □ carry-on
  形容詞 可隨身攜帶的
- □ expired
  形容詞 到期的
- □ vegetarian
  名詞 素食者
- □ cabin
  名詞 客艙
- □ fasten
  動詞 扣緊
- □ duty free
  形容詞 免稅的
- □ service button
  名詞 服務鈴
- □ by mistake
  片語 錯誤地
- □ lavatory
  名詞 廁所
- □ vacant
  形容詞 空著的、未被佔用的
- □ immigration form
  名詞 入境表格
- □ laptop
  名詞 膝上型電腦
- □ zip-top bag
  名詞 拉鏈袋
- □ take off
  片語 脫掉、起飛
- □ security gate
  名詞 安全門
- □ exchange rate
  名詞 匯率
- □ commission
  名詞 佣金

- ☐ traveler's check
  名詞 旅行支票
- ☐ delayed
  形容詞 延遲的
- ☐ due to
  片語 由於
- ☐ proceed
  動詞 繼續進行、著手
- ☐ baggage claim
  名詞 行李提領處
- ☐ carousel
  名詞（機場的）行李輸送帶
- ☐ Customs
  名詞 海關
- ☐ fill out
  片語 填寫
- ☐ make a reservation
  片語 預訂
- ☐ single room
  名詞 單人房
- ☐ rental
  形容詞 出租的
- ☐ fill up the gas
  片語 把油加滿
- ☐ rental agreement
  名詞 租約
- ☐ sense of directions
  名詞 方向感
- ☐ bellboy
  名詞 旅館大廳的服務生
- ☐ bathrobe
  名詞 浴衣
- ☐ morning call
  名詞 叫醒服務
- ☐ hair dryer
  名詞 吹風機
- ☐ international call
  名詞 國際電話
- ☐ air conditioner
  名詞 空調冷氣
- ☐ tip
  名詞 小費
- ☐ pay in cash
  片語 付現
- ☐ line up
  片語 排隊
- ☐ ferries wheel
  名詞 摩天輪
- ☐ hunted house
  名詞 鬼屋
- ☐ day pass
  名詞 一日票
- ☐ merry-go-round
  名詞 旋轉木馬
- ☐ bumper car
  名詞 碰碰車
- ☐ video recording
  名詞 錄影
- ☐ turn on
  片語 打開
- ☐ flash
  名詞 閃光燈
- ☐ gift shop
  名詞 禮品店
- ☐ bargain
  名詞 便宜貨
- ☐ belonging
  名詞 隨身物品

Part 6 職場會話篇－音檔連結

因各家手機系統不同，若無法直接掃描，
仍可以至以下電腦雲端連結下載收聽。
（https://tinyurl.com/mr3hm5pm）

PART 6

職場會話篇

01 面試禮儀

TRACK 106.

實境對話 Conversation

A: Ted, I have a job ***interview*** next Monday. Could you give me some ***suggestions***?
B: Like what?
A: How do I make a good ***impression*** on the interviewers?
B: First of all, you should be ***modestly*** dressed.
A: Oh, I see. What else?
B: Don't be late. Act ***spontaneous***, but be ***well prepared***.
A: I know. Thank you very much for your useful ***advice***.

A: 泰德，我下週一有個工作面試。你能給我些建議嗎？
B: 比如說？
A: 我該如何給面試官一個好印象呢？
B: 首先，你應該穿著得體。
A: 喔，我明白了。還有其他的嗎？
B: 別遲到。表現自然，但是要準備周全。
A: 我知道了。非常感謝你有用的建議。

核心詞彙 Words&Phrases

interview	[ˋɪntɚˏvju]	名詞 面試
suggestion	[səˋdʒɛstʃən]	名詞 建議
impression	[ɪmˋprɛʃən]	名詞 印象
modestly	[ˋmɑdɪstlɪ]	副詞 適度地
spontaneous	[spɑnˋtenɪəs]	形容詞 自發地、自然地
well prepared	[wɛl prɪˋpɛrd]	片語 準備好的、準備周全的
advice	[ədˋvaɪs]	名詞 建議

日常實用短句 Useful Sentences

- I appreciate this opportunity of interview.
  我很感謝有這個面試的機會。
- Here is my thorough resume.
  這是我完整的履歷表。
- What should I wear for my job interview?
  我該穿什麼去面試工作？
- Do I have to wear a makeup?
  我應該化妝嗎？
- You'd better arrive there fifteen minutes earlier.
  你最好早個十五分鐘到。
- Don't be late for your interview.
  面試別遲到了。
- Don't criticize your past employer.
  不要批評你以前的雇主。
- Don't speak ill of your ex-supervisor.
  不要說前主管的壞話。
- This outfit is too casual for the job interview.
  穿這件衣服去面試工作太隨便了。
- Should I wear a tie?
  我應該繫條領帶嗎？

學習++ More Tips

「make an impression」是「留下印象」的意思，如：「How do I make a good impression on the interviewers?」（我該如何給面試官留下好印象？）、「The interviewee made a good impression on all the interviewers.」（該面試者給所有面試官都留下了好印象。）。

02 介紹同事

TRACK 107.

實境對話 Conversation

A: Good morning, everyone! Let me ***introduce*** your ***new*** colleague, Lucy. Lucy, this is Mary, the ***Director*** of ***Customer Service*** Department.

B: Hello, Lucy, I am Mary, how do you do?

C: How do you do, Mary?

A: As ***others*** are not in the office ***at present***, I'll introduce them to you later.

C: OK. So shall I ***get started*** now?

A: 大家早安！讓我為你們介紹新同事露西。露西，這是瑪麗，客服部主管。

B: 露西，我是瑪麗，你好。

C: 你好，瑪麗。

A: 因為其他人現在不在辦公室裡，我稍後再介紹他們給你認識。

C: 好的。那我現在開始工作了嗎？

核心詞彙 Words&Phrases

introduce	[ˌɪntrəˋdjus]	動詞 介紹
new	[nju]	形容詞 新的
director	[dəˋrɛktɚ]	名詞 主管
customer service	[ˋkʌstəmɚ ˋsɝvɪs]	名詞 客戶服務
other	[ˋʌðɚ]	代名詞 其餘的
at present	[æt ˋprɛzn̩t]	片語 現在、目前
get started	[gɛt stɑrtɪd]	片語 開始

日常實用短句 Useful Sentences

- The office is expecting you.
  公司的人都在等你了。
- Let me introduce some of our staffs here.
  讓我為你介紹這裡的一些同事。
- I hope you can get a good idea of everyone in our department.
  希望你能好好的認識認識本部門的同仁。
- Let me introduce your fellow workers to you.
  我帶你來認識一下工作夥伴們。
- Sitting at the center of the office is our supervisor.
  坐在辦公室中間的那位是我們的頂頭上司。
- This is Alex Chang, a very respectable senior staff in our office.
  這位是艾力克斯張，是我們辦公室很值得尊敬的一位前輩。
- Mike is the part-time assistant of our department.
  麥可是我們部門的助理工讀生。
- I hope you will enjoy working with us.
  希望我們能共事愉快。
- Nice to have you join our team.
  很高興你加入我們的團隊。
- I think I have introduced everyone.
  我想我已經介紹過每個人了。
- Is there anyone who hasn't been introduced to?
  還有人沒有被介紹到嗎？

學習++ More Tips

「introduce A to B」是「把 A 介紹給 B 認識」的意思。如：「Allow me to introduce our new secretary to you all.」（容我向大家介紹我們的新祕書。），如果要請人做自我介紹，可以說：「Would you briefly introduce yourself to your fellow workers?」（你可以簡短地向你的同事們做個自我介紹嗎？）。

03 公司介紹

TRACK 108.

實境對話 Conversation

A: The company was ***set up*** in 2001. We have 23 ***branch offices*** in major cities.

B: What business ***are*** we ***specializing in***?

A: We are dealing in ***manufacturing*** electric appliances and exporting them to 20 countries around the world.

B: Oh, what's our ***annual*** business ***gross***?

A: We have a ***turnover*** of seven million dollars a year.

A: 我們公司成立於 2001 年。我們在各個主要城市有 23 家分公司。

B: 我們公司主要做哪方面的生意呢？

A: 我們主要從事電器產品的製造，並將產品外銷至世界上二十個國家。

B: 喔，我們每年總營業額有多少啊？

A: 我們每年的總營業額有七百萬美元。

核心詞彙 Words&Phrases

set up	[sɛt ʌp]	片語 創立
branch office	[bræntʃ ˋɔfɪs]	名詞 分公司
be specialize in	[be ˋspɛʃəl͵aɪz ɪn]	片語 專門從事……
manufacture	[͵mænjəˋfæktʃɚ]	動詞 製造
annual	[ˋænjuəl]	形容詞 每年的
gross	[gros]	名詞 總額
turnover	[ˋtɝn͵ovɚ]	名詞 營業額

日常實用短句 Useful Sentences

- It is a great pleasure having you all visit our company.
  承蒙各位造訪本公司，實屬榮幸。
- May I say a few words about our company so that you can get a picture of what our business is?
  容我稍微談談本公司，好讓各位了解我們的業務，好嗎？
- Our company was founded in 1950.
  本公司創立於 1950 年。
- We are one of the oldest companies in our country.
  我們是國內歷史最悠久的公司之一。
- We are considered to be one of the most reliable agents in Asia.
  我們是亞洲公認最值得信賴的代理商之一。
- We currently have six branches across the nation.
  我們在全國各地有六個分公司。
- We are dealing in exporting ready-to-wears.
  我們經營成衣外銷。
- We are specializing in importing European dining utensils.
  我們專門進口歐洲餐具。
- Please feel free to ask us any questions during your visit.
  訪問期間有任何問題，請儘管發問。

學習++ More Tips

「specialize in...」為「專攻、專門從事」的意思，如：「We have been specializing in exporting household appliances for many years.」（我們已經從事出口家電用品多年。）。另外「deal in」也是「經營、交易」之意，如：「We have been dealing in importing clothes for years.」（我們已經營進口服飾多年。）。

04 瞭解工作

TRACK 109.

實境對話

Conversation

A: Judy, would you please make a ***brief*** introduction of the office work?

B: OK. We ***are*** mainly ***responsible for*** the office ***routine***, such as making arrangements for meetings, making plans and ***sorting*** the files and documents.

A: I see. I hope I could ***adapt*** myself to the work as soon as possible.

B: I believe you can. If you have any questions, do not ***hesitate*** to ask.

A: Thank you very much.

A: 茱蒂，可以請您簡單介紹一下辦公室的工作嗎？

B: 好的。我們主要負責像是會議的準備工作、制定計劃以及整理檔案和文件等辦公室例行事務。

A: 我明白了，我希望我能盡快適應這個工作。

B: 我相信你可以的。如果你有任何問題，可以隨時提出來。

A: 非常感謝你。

核心詞彙

Words&Phrases

brief	[brif]	形容詞 簡短的
be responsible for	[be rɪˋspɑnsəbḷ fɔr]	片語 為……負責
routine	[ruˋtin]	名詞 例行事務
sort	[sɔrt]	動詞 分類
adapt	[əˋdæpt]	動詞 適應
hesitate	[ˋhɛzə͵tet]	動詞 猶豫

日常實用短句 Useful Sentences

• What is a sales assistant responsible for?
業務助理要負責什麼工作內容？
• Do I need to clock in and clock out?
我上下班必須打卡嗎？
• We will work in shift next month.
我們下個月要輪班工作。
• I am working on the morning shift today.
我今天上早班。
• Your job will involve several business trips a month.
你的工作每個月必須出差幾次。
• You will be in charge of the office administration.
你將負責辦公室行政。
• Talk to me if you need any assistance while working here.
在這裡工作時，若需要任何協助都可以找我。
• You will be personal assistant to General Manager.
你會是總經理的個人助理。
• It is normal to take on an additional shift every day.
每天加班是很正常的。
• All personnel need to undergo an annual performance review.
所有員工都要接受年度績效考核。
• Thank you for your thorough explanation.
謝謝你完整的說明。

學習++ More Tips

在為他人做說明或解釋時，因為擔心對方還有疑問卻不好意思提出，所以通常會告訴對方：「Please do not hesitate to ask if you have any questions.」（如果你有任何問題，請不要客氣，儘管問。），或是「Feel free to ask me if you have further questions.」（如果有進一步的問題想問，請不要客氣。）。

05 請同事幫忙

TRACK110.

實境對話

Conversation

A: Hi, Ian! Are you ***busy*** now?

B: ***Not really***. What's the matter?

A: Could you ***translate*** the ***contract*** for me? The manager needs it by 4 p.m. today. But I am afraid I can't manage all things by myself.

B: All right. I'll do it ***right away***.

A: Thank you so much. I will ***repay*** your ***kindness***.

B: No problem.

A: 嗨，伊恩。你現在忙嗎？

B: 不會啊。什麼事？

A: 請你幫我翻譯一下這份合約好嗎？經理今天下午四點前就要。不過我怕我一個人沒辦法應付所有的事。

A: 好的。我馬上就做。

B: 真是太感謝你了。我會報答你的恩惠的。

A: 小事一樁啦。

核心詞彙

Words&Phrases

busy	[ˋbɪsɪ]	形容詞 忙碌的
not really	[nɑt ˋrɪəlɪ]	片語 不會、不完全是
translate	[træsnˋlet]	動詞 翻譯
contract	[ˋkɑntrækt]	名詞 合約
right away	[raɪt əˋwe]	片語 馬上、立刻
repay	[rɪˋpe]	動詞 回報
kindness	[ˋkaɪndnɪs]	名詞 好心

日常實用短句 Useful Sentences

- Do you have a minute?
  能耽擱你一下嗎？
- Please do me a favor.
  請幫我個忙。
- Can you come over and check my computer?
  可以過來看一下我的電腦嗎？
- I have problem operating this fax machine.
  我不會操作這台傳真機。
- Would you mind helping me photocopy this document?
  你介意幫我影印這份文件嗎？
- My server is down.
  我的伺服器壞了。
- Can you show me how to change the cartridges?
  你能示範怎麼換墨匣給我看嗎？
- I have no clue what it is.
  我完全搞不懂這是什麼。
- Thank you very much for your help.
  真是謝謝你的幫忙。
- What can I do without you!
  沒有你我該怎麼辦哪！
- You are genius!
  你真厲害！
- Leave it to me!
  包在我身上！

學習++ More Tips

「No problem.」是「沒問題」的意思，可以用來回應他人的道謝，表示「小事一樁」。其他可以用來回應他人道謝的用語還有：「Don't mention it.」（不用客氣。）、「My pleasure.」（我很樂意。）或是「Anytime.」（我隨時都可以幫忙。）。

06 約訪客戶

TRACK 111.

實境對話

Conversation

A: Hello, Mr. White. This is Jim from NOC Company. There is something that I want to ***discuss*** with you. I ***wonder*** if I could pay you a visit tomorrow morning.

B: Ur... I am afraid that I have to ***attend*** a ***meeting*** tomorrow morning.

A: So what time will be ***convenient*** for you?

B: Can you come to my ***office*** next Monday?

A: All right. I'll be there around nine thirty.

B: OK. Ill be waiting for you then.

A: 懷特先生，您好。我是 NOC 公司的吉姆。我有些事想跟您討論一下。不知道我明天上午是否可以去拜訪您。

B: 呃……恐怕明天上午我得參加一個會議。

A: 那麼，您什麼時間方便呢？

B: 你下週一能來我辦公室嗎？

A: 好的。我大約九點半到那裡。

B: 好，到時我等你。

核心詞彙

Words&Phrases

discuss	[dɪˋskʌs]	動詞 討論
wonder	[ˋwʌndɚ]	動詞 想知道
attend	[əˋtɛnd]	動詞 參與
meeting	[ˋmitɪŋ]	名詞 會議
convenient	[kənˋvinjənt]	形容詞 方便的
office	[ˋɔfɪs]	名詞 辦公室

日常實用短句 Useful Sentences

- Could we make an appointment within this week?
  我們這週內可以約個時間嗎？
- When is the most convenient time for you?
  你最方便的時間是什麼時候？
- Could we reschedule our appointment?
  我們可以改個時間嗎？
- I'd like to pay you a visit in person.
  我想親自過去拜訪您。
- My schedule is pretty tight this week.
  我這週行程很滿。
- Can I schedule you for an appointment on Friday?
  我可以跟你排定週五碰面嗎？
- Does that work for you?
  這時間你可以嗎？
- We'll come to you.
  我們過去你那裡。
- We'll see you in a little while.
  我們待會兒見。
- The rest of this week doesn't look good for me.
  這禮拜接下來的幾天我都沒辦法。
- May I have thirty minutes of your time this week to show you our new product line?
  這星期可以佔用您三十分鐘的時間向您介紹我們的新系列產品嗎？

學習++ More Tips

「pay someone a visit」意指「拜訪」。如：「I'd like to pay you a visit to discuss our contract.」（我想去拜訪您，討論我們的合約問題。），如果是要詢問登門拜訪的時間，可以說：「When is the best time for me to pay you a visit in your office?」（我何時到您的公司去拜訪您最好呢？）。

07 接待客戶

實境對話 Conversation

A: Good afternoon, sir. What can I do for you?

B: I am John Brown. I want to see your ***General Manager***.

A: Our General Manager is ***having a meeting*** right now. It should be over in 15 minutes. Would you mind waiting for a ***while***?

B: Not at all. I'll wait for him.

A: You may ***browse through*** the ***magazines*** while you wait if you want.

B: OK. Thank you.

A: 先生，午安。能為您做些什麼嗎？

B: 我是約翰布朗。我想見你們總經理。

A: 我們總經理現在正在開會。會議應該會在十五分鐘內結束。您介意稍等一會兒嗎？

B: 一點也不。我會等他。

A: 您可以一邊等一邊隨意瀏覽雜誌。

B: 好的。謝謝你。

核心詞彙 Words&Phrases

General Manager	[ˋdʒɛnərəl ˋmænɪdʒɚ]	名詞 總經理
have a meeting	[hæv ə ˋmitɪŋ]	片語 開會
while	[hwaɪl]	名詞 一段時間
browse	[braʊz]	動詞 瀏覽
through	[θru]	介係詞 通過
magazine	[ˌmægəˋzin]	名詞 雜誌

日常實用短句 Useful Sentences

- We are so glad that you can come today.
  很高興今天您能過來。
- It's a great pleasure having you here.
  您能過來真是太讓人高興了。
- Thank you for taking time to visit our company.
  謝謝您撥冗來造訪我們公司。
- Sorry to have kept you waiting.
  抱歉讓您久等了。
- Welcome! How may I help you today?
  歡迎！今天需要什麼服務呢？
- Do you care for a cup of tea of coffee?
  您想喝杯茶或咖啡嗎？
- Would you like to browse through our catalogue first?
  你想先花幾分鐘大致看一下我們的目錄嗎？
- This is the brochure regarding the product you're interested in.
  這是與您有興趣的產品相關的手冊。
- Let me grab a couple of samples for you.
  讓我去幫您拿些樣品過來。
- Here are some samples for you to try out.
  這是讓您試用的樣品。
- We will be happy to help you with any questions.
  我們很樂意協助您任何問題。

學習++ More Tips

接待來訪的客戶時，通常會先詢問對方是否有事先約好，如「Do you have an appointment with Mr. Louise?」（您與路易斯先生有約嗎？），或是「Is Mr. Louise expecting you?」（路易斯先生知道您要來嗎？）。

08 做簡報

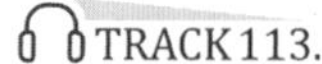

實境對話

Conversation

A: So that is how I am going to give my ***presentation***. What do you think?

B: ***Pretty good***. Your ***slides*** give good ***illustration***.

A: Is there anything I should ***improve on***?

B: Maybe you could ***highlight*** each ***key point*** on the slides.

A: Good idea. That will definitely make the presentation ***clearer***.

B: That's right. Good luck to you!

A: 這就是我將做簡報的方式。你覺得怎麼樣？

B: 很好。你的投影片提供很不錯的說明。

A: 有我應該要改進的地方嗎

B: 或許你可以在投影片上強調每一個重點。

A: 好主意。這樣絕對會讓簡報更加條理分明。

B: 沒錯。祝你好運！

核心詞彙

Words&Phrases

presentation	[ˌprizɛnˋteʃən]	名詞 簡報
pretty good	[ˋprɪtɪ gʊd]	片語 非常好
slide	[slaɪd]	名詞 投影片
illustration	[ɪˌlʌsˋtreʃən]	名詞 說明
improve on	[ɪmˋpruv ɑn]	片語 改進
highlight	[ˋhaɪˌlaɪt]	動詞 強調
key point	[ki pɔɪnt]	名詞 重點
clearer	[ˋklɪrɚ]	形容詞 （clear 的比較級）更清楚

日常實用短句 Useful Sentences

- Please make your presentation brief.
  報告請簡短。
- I need a meeting room for 8 to 10 people.
  我需要一間可以容納 8 至 10 人的會議室。
- Please have the projector ready.
  請把投影機準備好。
- Do you need a speakerphone?
  你需要喇叭擴音器嗎？
- I'll use slides as a visual aid.
  我會用幻燈片作為視覺輔助工具。
- Please have Ms. Chen make arrangements for our presentation.
  請陳祕書為我們的簡報做一下準備工作。
- Please give us an outline of your presentation.
  請給我們你的簡報的大綱。
- I will focus on the short term solution.
  我會集中做短期解決方案的報告。
- Where did you get the statistic data?
  這個數據資料是從哪裡來的？
- Thanks for your briefing.
  謝謝你的簡報。
- Now I would like to entertain your questions.
  接下來歡迎各位發問。

學習++ More Tips

「presentation」指「簡報」，而「give a presentation」就是「做簡報」的意思。如：「I will give a presentation on the project for the board of directors this week.」（本週我將為董事會做這個計畫的簡報。）。

09 產品介紹

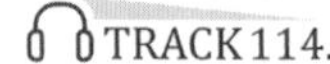

實境對話 Conversation

A: This is our new ***product***.

B: Would you please give me some brief introduction? What ***advantages*** does it have?

A: It has great ***performance*** especially in data ***memorization***. It can take in 10,000 ***bytes*** of information in a second.

B: That's ***amazing***. Could you give me a ***brochure*** on this product?

A: Of course! This brochure gives a thorough introduction of this product. Please take a look.

A: 這些是我們的新產品。

B: 你能簡單為我介紹一下嗎？它有什麼優點？

A: 它具有優異的性能，尤其是在記憶資料這方面。它在一秒內能存取 10,000 個資訊。

B: 那可真了不起呢。可以給我這個產品的宣傳冊嗎？

A: 當然！這本手冊提供此產品完整的介紹。請您過目。

核心詞彙 Words&Phrases

product	[ˋprɑdəkt]	名詞 產品
advantage	[ədˋvæntɪdʒ]	名詞 優勢
performance	[pɚˋfɔrməns]	名詞 表現
memorization	[ˏmɛməˋrɪzeʃən]	名詞 記憶
byte	[baɪt]	名詞 （電算）位元組
amazing	[əˋmezɪŋ]	形容詞 令人吃驚的
brochure	[broˋʃur]	名詞 手冊

日常實用短句 Useful Sentences

- We have just marketed our new product.
  我們已經推出了新產品。
- The quality of our products is our main strength.
  產品的品質就是我們主要的優勢。
- This 5 in 1 fax machine is easy to use.
  這台五合一傳真機操作容易。
- It is very light in weight.
  它十分輕巧。
- It gives better colors and sounds.
  它能輸出更好的色彩和音質。
- It has better durability.
  它的耐久性較佳。
- The market price for this camera is about half the price of other video cameras.
  這台相機的市價是其他攝影機的一半。
- It is sensational in many respects including price, quality and portability.
  它在許多方面包括價格、品質及方便攜帶性，都很讓人心動。
- It will unquestionably satisfy consumers' needs.
  它絕對會滿足消費者的需求。
- I'm sure it will be well-received by consumers.
  我相信它會受到消費者的喜愛。
- We're considering exporting it to Western Europe.
  我們考慮將它外銷至西歐各國。

學習++ More Tips

「advantage」是指「優勢、優點」之意。向他人介紹產品時，一定要提出該產品優於其他產品的特色，才能吸引顧客，如：「This product has the advantage of a good durability.」（這產品具有良好耐久性的優勢。）。

10 詢問報價

TRACK 115.

實境對話

Conversation

A: Hello, I've browsed your ***website*** and I am very interested in your camera, AF230. May I have the ***quotation*** for this ***camera***?

B: The best price we can offer you is $350 for each camera.

A: Is it possible to offer us a ***special discount*** if it's a large order?

B: Certainly. But it depends on the amount you order.

A: Well, I can't ***make a decision*** yet. I would let you know once we decide to ***place an order***.

A: 您好，我瀏覽過貴公司的網站，並且對您們 AF230 型號的相機非常感興趣。可以給我這款相機的報價嗎？

B: 我們可以提供您的最低價格是每台 350 美元。

A: 假如訂貨數量大的話有沒有可能給我們特別優惠呢？

B: 當然可以，但這得依您的訂貨量而定。

A: 我現在還無法做決定。我們一旦決定下訂就告訴你。

核心詞彙

Words&Phrases

website	[ˋwɛb͵saɪt]	名詞 網頁
quotation	[kwoˋteʃən]	名詞 報價
camera	[ˋkæmərə]	名詞 相機
special discount	[ˋspɛʃəl ˋdɪskaʊnt]	名詞 特別優惠
make a decision	[mek ə dɪˋsɪʒən]	片語 做決定
place an order	[ples æn ˋɔrdɚ]	片語 下訂單

日常實用短句 Useful Sentences

- Thank you for your inquiry regarding the product.
  謝謝你詢問這項產品。
- Can I have your price schedule?
  可以給我價目表嗎？
- Can you formalize it in a quote?
  你可以正式報價嗎？
- What's the best price of the machine?
  這台機器最優惠的價格是多少？
- Can I have the lowest quotations for these head-sets and microphone?
  可以給我這套耳機和麥克風的最低報價嗎？
- I want to know the price for the multi-function printer with freight included.
  我想知道購買這台多功能印表機含運費是多少錢。
- I need a price list with specification.
  我需要一份有規格說明的價目單。
- Would you fax me the quotation?
  可以把估價單傳真給我嗎？
- Can you give us some discount?
  可以給我們折扣嗎？
- Is it possible to make a reduction of $100?
  有可能少算我一百美元嗎？
- I hope you can reduce the price on the bundle.
  我希望這一大堆東西你可以賣我便宜一點。

學習++ More Tips

想要對產品進行詢價時，可說：「We'd like to make an inquiry about this product.」（我們想要對這個產品進行詢價。），或是「We'd like to request the lowest quotations for this product.」（我們想要求你們給予這產品的最低報價。）。

11 給上司提建議

TRACK116.

實境對話 Conversation

A: Are there any ***further*** questions?

B: Yes, I think you might have ***ignored*** something at the meeting.

A: Oh? What would that be?

B: The transportation cost. ***In my opinion***, it might ***increase*** our ***budget*** to transport goods by railroad.

B: I think we'd better have our goods transported by sea. It'll save much cost.

A: It ***makes sense***. Do as you said.

A: 還有任何問題嗎？

B: 是的。我認為您在會議上可能忽略了一些事情。

A: 喔？你覺得我忽略了什麼呢？

B: 忽略的是運輸成本。在我看來，用鐵路運輸可能會增加我們的預算。

B: 我認為我們最好以海運發貨，這樣能節省很多成本。

A: 言之有理。就按你説的做吧。

核心詞彙 Words&Phrases

further	[ˋfɝðɚ]	形容詞 更多的
ignore	[ɪgˋnor]	動詞 忽略
in my opinion	[ɪn maɪ əˋpɪnjən]	片語 在我看來
increase	[ɪnˋkris]	動詞 增加
budget	[ˋbʌdʒɪt]	名詞 預算
make sense	[mek sɛns]	片語 有道理

日常實用短句 *Useful Sentences*

- May we have a word with you?
  我們可以跟您談談嗎？
- We have something to say regarding this project.
  我們對這個案子有些話要說。
- I suggest we get more reasonable overtime pay.
  我建議我們應拿更合理的加班費。
- A coffee machine might be a necessity in our office.
  我們辦公室可能需要一台自動咖啡機。
- A coffee break may help to refresh the staff in the afternoon.
  下午有休息時間也許可以幫助員工重新提起精神。
- We have to upgrade our software versions on the instant.
  我們必須立刻更新軟體版本。
- How about some incentive payments?
  發點獎勵金如何？
- The atmosphere in the office doesn't seem good.
  辦公室氣氛似乎不是很好。
- I really do hope we don't take on an additional shift so often.
  我真的希望我們不用那麼常加班。
- Is it possible that the company provide the staff with some educational programs?
  公司是否能提供員工一些教育課程？

學習++ *More Tips*

「in my opinion,...」是表示「在我看來，……」的意思，為欲闡述自己意見時所用的開頭語，如：「In my opinion, we should reduce our monthly office expenses.」（依我看來，我們應該減少每個月的辦公室支出。）。

12 請假

TRACK 117.

實境對話

Conversation

A: Could I ***ask for leave*** tomorrow?

B: Oh, why do you need to ask for leave?

A: My daughter is seriously ill. I need to ***look after*** her.

B: I am sorry to hear that. Fine, you can take a ***day off*** and take good care of your daughter. I will have someone ***sub*** for you tomorrow.

A: Thank you so much for your ***understanding***.

B: Don't mention it. I hope your daughter will ***get well soon***.

A: 我明天能請假嗎？

B: 喔，你為什麼需要請假呢？

A: 我女兒病得很厲害。我得照顧她。

B: 聽到這個消息很遺憾。好吧，你可以放一天假在家好好照顧你的女兒。我明天會找人來代你的。

A: 非常感謝您的體諒。

B: 不必客氣。希望你的女兒能早日康復。

核心詞彙

Words&Phrases

ask for leave	[æsk fɔr liv]	片語 請假
look after	[luk ˋæftɚ]	片語 照顧
day off	[de ɔf]	片語 休假
sub	[sʌb]	動詞 代替
understanding	[ˏʌndɚˋstændɪŋ]	名詞 理解、體會
get well soon	[gɛt wɛl sun]	片語 很快好起來

日常實用短句 *Useful Sentences*

- This is my absent note.
  這是我的假單。
- Do I need to fill out the absent form beforehand?
  我必須事先填請假單嗎？
- I am thinking to take my annual holidays next month.
  我打算下個月休年假。
- Jane is out of the office on maternity leave currently.
  珍目前正在放產假。
- I am wondering if I could ask for a leave of absence next Monday.
  我想知道我下週一是否可以請假。
- I have to ask for a sick leave this afternoon.
  我今天下午得請病假。
- I want to take a day off tomorrow.
  我明天想要休假。
- All incidents of sick leave require the doctor's notes.
  所有病假都需要醫生證明。
- Leave of absence for personal reasons require prior approval from your supervisor.
  請事假需要得到主管同意。
- I will be absent for a family funeral tomorrow.
  我明天要請喪假。
- An employee is entitled to 7 days' annual leave.
  員工享有七天的年假。

學習++ *More Tips*

「ask for leave」是表示「請假」的意思，如：「You don't look very well. Why don't you ask for a sick leave?」（你看起來很不舒服耶。為什麼不請個病假呢？）或「I'd like to ask for leave of absence for some person reasons.」（因為私人原因，我想要請事假。）。

13 調換部門

TRACK 118.

實境對話

Conversation

A: Well, I am wondering if I could work in another ***department***.

B: You want a ***transfer***, don't you?

A: ***Basically***, yes.

B: Can you tell me why you want a transfer?

A: I ***feel like*** doing something more ***challenging***, such as ***marketing***. Could I work in Marketing Department?

B: Well, I will take that into ***consideration***.

A: 是這樣，我想知道我可不可以去另外一個部門工作。

B: 你想調換部門，是嗎？

A: 基本上是這樣的。

B: 能告訴我為什麼想調部門嗎？

A: 我想做些較有挑戰性的工作，例如：行銷。我可以在行銷部工作嗎？

B: 嗯，我會考慮的。

核心詞彙

Words&Phrases

department	[dɪ`pɑrtmənt]	名詞 部門
transfer	[`trænsfɚ]	名詞 轉調
basically	[`besɪklɪ]	副詞 基本上
feel like	[fil laɪk]	片語 想要
challenging	[`tʃælɪndʒɪŋ]	形容詞 有挑戰性的
marketing	[`mɑrkɪtiŋ]	名詞 行銷
consideration	[kənsɪdə`reʃən]	名詞 考慮

日常實用短句 Useful Sentences

- What's wrong with your present job?
  你現在的工作有問題嗎？
- I will be transferred to Accounting Department from next month.
  我下個月起要調到會計部工作了。
- She was moved to the headquarters.
  她被調到總部去了。
- Sally will be my replacement.
  莎莉會接替我的工作。
- Have you heard about John's transfer?
  你聽說約翰調職的事了嗎？
- He put in for a transfer to another position.
  他申請調職。
- Unfortunately, I will be moved to the branch office.
  很不幸地，我要被調到分公司了。
- I hope we will stay in touch.
  希望我們能保持聯絡。
- Please give my replacement kind support and assistance.
  請給予接替我工作的人支持與協助。
- I've enjoyed working with you.
  很高興能與你共事。
- I heard that you will be posted to London.
  我聽說你要被調到倫敦去了。

學習++ More Tips

「take... into consideration」是「考慮某事」的意思。如：「Would you please take my request into consideration?」（能否請您考慮我的請求呢？），若要簡單的表示，也可以用「think about」這個片語，如：「I need a few days to think about it.」（我需要幾天的時間考慮一下。）。

14 代班

TRACK 119.

實境對話 Conversation

A: Hi. Lily. I wonder ***whether*** you will be ***on duty*** tomorrow.
B: No. Tomorrow will be my day off.
A: Well, ***here's the thing***. I ***am supposed to*** work the ***morning shift*** tomorrow, but I have to go pick up my mother at the airport.
B: You want me to ***cover*** for you, don't you?
A: Yes. Could you do me the favor?
B: Fine, I will sub for you tomorrow.
A: Thank you very much.

A: 嗨，莉莉。我想知道您明天要值班嗎？
B: 沒有啊。我明天休假。
A: 嗯，事情是這樣的，我明天應該輪值早班，但是我得去機場接我媽媽。
B: 你希望我幫你代班，對不對？
A: 是的，可以請你幫我這個忙嗎？
B: 好吧，我明天來替你代班。
A: 太感謝你了。

核心詞彙 Words&Phrases

whether	[ˋhwɛðɚ]	連接詞 是否
on duty	[ɑn ˋdjutɪ]	片語 值班
here's the thing	[hirz ðə θɪŋ]	片語 是這樣的
be supposed to	[be səˋpozd tu]	片語 應該……
morning shift	[ˋmɔrnɪŋ ʃɪft]	名詞 早班
cover	[ˋkʌvɚ]	動詞 頂替

日常實用短句 Useful Sentences

- Thanks for covering for me.
  謝謝你幫我代班。
- Would you take over my shift tomorrow?
  明天可以幫我代班嗎？
- Who is to substitute Mary?
  誰要代替瑪莉？
- He substitutes as our manager for the time being.
  他暫時代任我們的經理。
- Who is acting for Jane in this matter?
  這件事誰代理珍？
- Mr. Chen is ill today, so the assistant manager will be sitting in.
  陳先生今天生病，所以襄理今天會代理他。
- You should find someone to act for you while you're on maternity leave.
  你要找個人在你放產假期間代理你。
- Jack will be my agent while I am out of office.
  我不在辦公室的時候，傑克是我的代理人。
- Ms. Tailor will hold the fort for me while I'm gone.
  我不在的這段期間，泰勒小姐會代理我的職務。
- Please contact her if you need anything.
  有需要什麼，就找她吧。
- Is there anything I should especially pay attention to?
  有什麼我需要特別注意的事情嗎？

學習++ More Tips

「Here's the thing.」是美國人常用的口語，表示「事情是這樣的。」可以用來作為說明事情的開場白，如：「Well, here's the thing. I need you to cover for me tomorrow.」（嗯，事情是這樣的。我需要請你明天幫我代班。）。

15 上班遲到

TRACK120.

實境對話

Conversation

A: Steven, you are late for work again!

B: I am ***terribly*** sorry.

A: This is the third time this month. Can you give me an ***explanation***?

B: I just don't know what to say. I must have ***forgotten*** set up the ***alarm clock*** and ***overslept***.

A: ***Anyway***, I hope it won't ***happen*** again

B: Never, I ***promise***.

A: 史蒂芬，你上班又遲到了！

B: 真的非常抱歉。

A: 這是這個月你第三次遲到了吧。你能給我個解釋嗎？

B: 我真的不知道該說什麼。我一定是忘記設定鬧鐘了，結果睡過頭了。

A: 不管怎樣，我希望不要再發生這種事。

B: 不會了，我保證。

核心詞彙

Words&Phrases

terribly	[ˋtɛrəbḷɪ]	副詞 非常地
explanation	[ˋɛkspləˋneʃən]	名詞 解釋
forgotten	[fɚˋgɑtṇ]	動詞（forget 過去分詞）忘記
alarm clock	[əˋlɑrm klɑk]	名詞 鬧鐘
oversleep	[ˋovɚˋslip]	動詞 睡過頭
anyway	[ˋɛnɪˏwe]	副詞 無論如何
happen	[ˋhæpən]	動詞 發生
promise	[ˋprɑmɪs]	動詞 答應、承諾

日常實用短句 Useful Sentences

- Sorry I was late.
  抱歉我遲到了。
- What's your excuse this time?
  這次又是什麼理由？
- Stayed up again?
  又熬夜了？
- I will try my best to be punctual.
  我會盡量準時。
- An occasional late arrival is tolerable.
  偶爾遲到還可以。
- You missed the early morning meeting.
  你錯過早會了。
- Why didn't you leave home early?
  你為何不早點出門？
- You can't count on the traffic here.
  你不能相信這裡的交通狀況啊。
- I missed the bus.
  我錯過公車了。
- My car had a breakdown on the road.
  我的車子在路上拋錨了。
- I overslept myself.
  我睡過頭了。
- It won't happen again.
  不會再發生這種事了。

學習++ More Tips

「oversleep」指「睡過頭」，如：「Jack is late again. He must have overslept himself.」（傑克又遲到了，他肯定是睡過頭了。）；提醒他人不要睡過頭，可以說：「Go to bed earlier tonight in case you oversleep yourself tomorrow.」（今晚早點睡，免得明天睡過頭了。）。

16 要求加薪

TRACK 121.

實境對話

Conversation

A: Sarah, I ***am*** so ***frustrated by*** the fact that I am ***working*** so ***hard*** for so little!

B: Why don't you ask for a ***pay raise***?

A: How am I supposed to ***ask for*** a raise?

B: Well, first of all, you should make a ***list*** of all the things you've ***accomplished*** for the company.

A: ***And then***?

B: And you'd better arrange a specific time to discuss this with your boss.

A: 莎拉，我好沮喪，我如此努力工作卻只得到這一點薪水！
B: 你為什麼不要求加薪呢？
A: 我要怎麼要求加薪呢？
B: 首先，你應該把你為公司所達成的所有業績列舉出來。
A: 然後呢？
B: 然後你最好安排個特定的時間跟你的老闆討論一下。

核心詞彙

Words&Phrases

be frustrated by	[be ˋfrʌstretɪd baɪ]	片語 為……而沮喪
work hard	[wɝk hɑrd]	片語 努力工作
pay raise	[pe rez]	名詞 加薪
ask for	[æsk fɔr]	片語 要求
list	[lɪst]	名詞 清單
accomplish	[əˋkɑmplɪʃ]	動詞 完成
and then	[ænd ðɛn]	片語 然後

日常實用短句 Useful Sentences

- I am going to ask for a raise.
  我將要求加薪。
- I deserve a pay raise.
  我應該被加薪。
- You absolutely deserve a higher salary.
  你絕對值得更高的薪資。
- Are you going to sit around and wait for your boss to give you a raise?
  你打算坐著等你老闆來給你加薪嗎？
- Do you have any idea about typical salaries in your field?
  你知道你的工作領域一般薪資是多少嗎？
- You can get the information by using salary calculator tools on the net.
  你可以利用網路上的薪資計算工具來得到相關資料。
- Make a list of all the things you've accomplished for the employer.
  列出一張你為公司達成的業績清單。
- What will you do if you get turned down?
  如果被拒絕，你會怎麼做？
- Set up a time to meet with your boss.
  跟你的老闆約一個時間開會。
- You should show your boss how serious you are.
  你該讓你老闆知道你是認真的。

學習++ More Tips

「raise」指的是「加薪、加薪額」；「ask for a raise」就是「要求加薪」的意思。如：「I'm going to ask my boss for a pay raise.」（我要去找老闆要求加薪。），或「I think you should ask for a raise actively.」（我認為你應該主動要求加薪。）。

17 升職

TRACK 122.

實境對話

Conversation

A: I have good news for you, Betty.

B: Really? What is it?

A: You are ***promoted as*** the ***manager*** of the ***Planning*** Department!

B: What? Oh, I'm so ***overwhelmed*** that I don't know what to say.

A: You ***deserve*** it! And I'm sure you will ***prove*** to be a ***competent*** manager.

B: Thank you very much. I'll do my best!

A: 貝蒂，我有個好消息要告訴你。

B: 真的嗎？是什麼好消息呢？

A: 你被晉升為企劃部經理了！

B: 什麼？噢，我激動得不知道該說什麼了。

A: 你應得的！而且我相信你會證明自己是一個能幹的經理。

B: 非常感謝您。我會努力做到最好的！

核心詞彙

Words&Phrases

promote	[prəˋmot]	動詞 晉升
as	[æz]	介係詞 作為……
manager	[ˋmænɪdʒɚ]	名詞 經理
planning	[ˋplænɪŋ]	名詞 規劃
overwhelm	[ˏovɚˋhwɛlm]	動詞 使不知所措
deserve	[dɪˋzɝv]	動詞 應受、該得
prove	[pruv]	動詞 證明
competent	[ˋkɑmpətənt]	形容詞 能幹的

日常實用短句 Useful Sentences

- You definitely deserve it.
  你絕對應該被升職的。
- It was no surprise to me.
  我對你的升職一點都不感到意外。
- You are moving up in the world!
  你正在平步青雲哪！
- Congratulations on your promotion!
  恭喜你升官啦。
- Please accept my sincere felicitations.
  請接受我誠摯的祝賀！
- I am proud of you!
  我真為你感到驕傲。
- You will surely be able to fulfill the responsibilities of this important position.
  你絕對能夠勝任這個重要的職位。
- Shall we have a party?
  要不要開派對慶祝一下？
- Your hard work paid off.
  你的努力都值得了！
- Wish you every success in your new position.
  祝你在新的崗位上大獲全勝！
- Your new post sounds tough.
  你的新職位會很辛苦喔！

學習++ More Tips

「be promoted as...」是表示「被晉升為……」的意思，如：「I am happy to tell you that you have been promoted as the director of our HR Department.」（很高興告訴你，你已經被晉升為我們人資部的主任。）。

18 跳槽

TRACK 123.

實境對話

Conversation

A: Hi, Susan. You seem a little ***upset***. ***What's wrong*** with you?

B: I am not happy working here. I don't want to stay here anymore.

A: Do you want to ***quit***?

B: Yes. I am thinking about ***job-hopping*** to ABC Company.

A: But what makes you unhappy here?

B: My boss always ***makes light of*** my ***ability***. He never ***assigns*** me anything important.

A: 嗨，蘇珊。你看來有點沮喪哦。你怎麼了？
B: 我在這裡工作得不開心。我不想再待在這裡了。
A: 你想辭職嗎？
B: 是的。我正在考慮要跳槽到 ABC 公司去。
A: 不過，這裡為什麼讓你做得那麼不開心呢？
B: 我老闆總是輕視我的能力。他從不交代我任何重要的事。

核心詞彙

Words&Phrases

upset	[ʌpˋsɛt]	形容詞 沮喪的
What's wrong...?	[hwɑts rɔŋ]	片詞 ……怎麼了？
quit	[kwɪt]	動詞 辭職
job-hop	[dʒɑb hɑp]	動詞 跳槽
make light of	[mek laɪt ɑv]	片語 輕視
ability	[əˋbɪlətɪ]	名詞 能力
assign	[əˋsaɪn]	動詞 指派

日常實用短句 Useful Sentences

- I plan to change my job.
  我打算換工作。
- I found another job that pays better.
  我找到另一個薪水較高的工作了。
- I'm going to work in the Taipei Times.
  我要去台北時報工作了。
- I've wanted to change my job for a while.
  我已經想換工作好一陣子了。
- I intend to job-hop to that foreign company.
  我打算跳槽到那家外商公司。
- I was recruited by the famous publisher.
  我被那家有名的出版社挖角了。
- Is it the right time to job-hop?
  現在是跳槽的好時機嗎？
- Think before you leap.
  三思而後行哪！
- It's not good for your career in the long term.
  長期來看，對你的事業不是件好事。
- This is my new contact number.
  這是我新的聯絡電話。
- Let's keep in touch with each other.
  我們保持聯絡吧。
- We'll meet again someday!
  我們後會有期。

學習++ More Tips

「job-hop」是指「跳槽」的意思，如：「I'm thinking to job-hop to that computer company.」（我打算跳槽到那家電腦公司。）、「Patrick decided to job-hop to CTS company, one of their competitors.」（派崔克決定跳槽到CTS公司，那是他們公司的其中一個競爭對手。）。

19 辭職

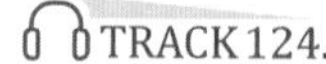
TRACK 124.

實境對話

Conversation

A: I've made a ***tough*** decision. Here's my ***resignation***.

B: Why did you make such a decision?

A: I've decided to ***accept*** a position in another company.

B: I am still ***confused***. Is there anything wrong with your work here?

A: To tell you the ***truth***, I think there isn't much ***room*** for me to ***improve*** in the company.

B: Fine. I wish you could get what you want in the new company.

A: 我已經做了一個艱難的決定。這是我的辭職信。
B: 你為什麼會做這樣的決定？
A: 我已經決定接受另外一家公司的職位了。
B: 我還是很困惑。你在這裡的工作有什麼問題嗎？
A: 說實話，我覺得這個公司沒有太多讓我提升的空間。
B: 好吧。希望你在新公司得到你想要的。

核心詞彙

Words&Phrases

tough	[tʌf]	形容詞 困難的
resignation	[ˏrɛzɪgˋneʃən]	名詞 辭呈
accept	[əkˋsɛpt]	動詞 接受
confused	[kənˋfjuzd]	形容詞 困惑的
truth	[truθ]	名詞 真相
room	[rum]	名詞 空間
improve	[ɪmˋpruv]	動詞 進步、提升

日常實用短句 Useful Sentences

- I quit.
  我不幹了。
- I have sent in my papers.
  我已經遞辭呈了。
- Here is my resignation.
  這是我的辭呈。
- I want to change my environment.
  我想換一下環境。
- I need to take a break.
  我需要休息一下。
- I want to expand my horizons.
  我想拓展我的視野。
- I think it's time for me to leave.
  我覺得是我該離開的時候了。
- I want to resign for some personal reason.
  因為私人因素，我想辭職。
- I'm sorry to bring up my resignation at this moment.
  很抱歉這個時候提出辭呈。
- This position is not suitable for me.
  這個職務不適合我。
- I need a certificate of releasing from the job.
  我需要離職證明。
- All good things must come to an end.
  天下無不散之筵席。

學習++ More Tips

提出辭呈時，通常必須給公司一個需要辭職的理由，如：「I don't think I am up to this job.」（我覺得我無法勝任這個工作。），或是「I think perhaps that job would be more suitable for me.」（我想那份工作可能更適合我。）。

20 解雇

實境對話 Conversation

A: You want to see me, boss?

B: Yes, Please answer my ***following*** questions ***honestly***. Are you always late for work? Do you have a habit of sleeping during ***working hours***?

A: Not very often. I can't ***deny*** that I might ***doze*** for a while from time to time.

B: Good. ***According to*** your ***attendance*** and your performance at work, I think I have to ask you to leave.

A: 老闆，您找我有事？

B: 是的。請誠實地回答我的問題。你是不是經常遲到？是不是有上班睡覺的習慣？

A: 不是很經常吧。我不能否認偶爾我可能會打打盹兒。

B: 很好。根據你的上班出席狀況還有工作表現，我想我必須請你離開。

核心詞彙 Words&Phrases

following	[ˋfɑləwɪŋ]	形容詞 下列的
honestly	[ˋɑnɪstlɪ]	副詞 誠實地
working hour	[ˋwɝkɪŋ aʊr]	名詞 工作時間
deny	[dɪˋnaɪ]	動詞 否定
doze	[doz]	動詞 打瞌睡
according to	[əˋkɔrdɪŋ tu]	片語 根據
attendance	[əˋtɛndəns]	名詞 出席

日常實用短句 Useful Sentences

- He's been put out to grass.
  他被解雇了。
- He's been removed from office.
  他被革職了。
- He was dismissed from his job.
  他被開除了。
- He's out of the saddle.
  他被解除職務了。
- The manager got replaced without early warning.
  該經理遭到無預警的撤換。
- He got the sack for being absent from work without leave.
  他因為曠職而捲鋪蓋了。
- They decided to relieve him from his post.
  他們決定把他予以解職。
- You can't lay off me without a reason.
  你不能無緣無故把我裁掉。
- It's nothing personal. It's business.
  這不是針對個人。這是公事公辦。
- I am out of work now.
  我沒工作了。
- Will I get redundancy pay?
  我會拿到遣散費嗎？

學習++ More Tips

通知他人被解雇，單刀直入的說法，如：「I think I have to ask you to leave.」（我想我必須請你離開。），也有較婉轉的表示法，如：「I'm sorry to tell you that your employment with the firm shall be terminated.」（很遺憾要告訴你，公司將解除對你的雇用。）。

PART❻職場會話篇

你都記住了嗎？

從各篇「日常實用短句」裡整理出外國人常用的單字和片語，如果背起來了，就在前方空格打個勾吧！

- ☐ opportunity
  名詞 機會
- ☐ resume
  名詞 履歷表
- ☐ criticize
  動詞 批評
- ☐ employer
  名詞 雇主
- ☐ casual
  形容詞 隨意的
- ☐ expect
  動詞 期待
- ☐ fellow
  名詞 夥伴、同事
- ☐ supervisor
  名詞 主管
- ☐ senior staff
  名詞 前輩
- ☐ assistant
  名詞 助理
- ☐ be founded in
  片語 建立於……
- ☐ reliable
  形容詞 可靠的
- ☐ agent
  名詞 代理商
- ☐ ready-to-wears
  名詞 成衣
- ☐ dining utensil
  名詞 餐具
- ☐ clock in and clock out
  片語 打卡
- ☐ work in shift
  片語 輪班
- ☐ in charge of
  片語 負責
- ☐ administration
  名詞 行政
- ☐ personal assistant
  名詞 私人助理
- ☐ personnel
  名詞 員工
- ☐ undergo
  動詞 接受
- ☐ annual performance review
  名詞 年度績效考核
- ☐ fax machine
  名詞 傳真機
- ☐ photocopy
  動詞 影印
- ☐ reschedule
  動詞 重新安排時間

□ product line
名詞 產品系列

□ catalogue
名詞 目錄

□ grab
動詞 抓取

□ try out
片語 試驗

□ speakerphone
名詞 喇叭擴音器

□ visual aid
名詞 視覺輔助工具

□ make arrangement
片語 做安排

□ outline
名詞 題綱、概要

□ focus on
片語 專心於……

□ statistic data
名詞 數據資料

□ market
動詞 上市

□ strength
名詞 長處

□ durability
名詞 耐久性

□ market price
名詞 市價

□ well-received
形容詞 評價高的

□ multi-function printer
名詞 多功能印表機

□ overtime pay
名詞 加班費

□ upgrade
動詞 升級

□ on the instant
片語 立即

□ take on an additional shift
片語 加班

□ absent
形容詞 缺席的

□ maternity leave
名詞 產假

□ sick leave
名詞 病假

□ approval
名詞 批准

□ annual leave
名詞 年假

□ post
動詞 調派

□ substitute
動詞 代替

□ hold the fort
片語 代為照料

□ excuse
名詞 理由

□ punctual
形容詞 準時的

□ tolerable
形容詞 可忍受的

□ count on
片語 依賴

□ breakdown
名詞 故障、損壞

□ oversleep oneself
片語 睡過頭

Part 7 景點＆文化篇－音檔連結

因各家手機系統不同，若無法直接掃描，仍可以至以下電腦雲端連結下載收聽。

（https://tinyurl.com/45kuthnu）

PART 7

景點&文化篇

向老外介紹旅遊

01 中國菜

TRACK 126.

實境對話

Conversation

A: My favorite ***dish*** is Peiking Duck. But like chicken feet and snake meat are really difficult for me to eat.

B: Does the so called Chinese ***Cuisine*** actually include many different types and styles?

A: Yes, China is a huge country with a very long history. Chinese Cuisine is just a ***catch-all*** name. It includes many varieties. Such as Taiwanese, Cantonese, Hu-Nan, Szechwan.

B: My mouth is ***watering*** now!

A: Are you hungry? How about going with me to the ***night market*** and having something to eat?

A: 我最喜歡吃北京烤鴨，但像雞腳和蛇肉則實在不敢吃。
B: 中國菜是否包含許多種類和形式呢？
A: 是的，中國是一個歷史悠久又廣大的國家，中國菜只是一個總稱，下面包括了像：台菜、粵菜、湘菜、川菜等等。
B: 我已經在流口水了。
A: 你餓了嗎？我們一起去夜市吃小吃如何？

核心詞彙

Words&Phrases

dish	[dɪʃ]	名詞 菜餚
cuisine	[kwɪˋzin]	名詞 菜餚
catch-all	[ˋkætʃˏɔl]	名詞 籠統的一類（或描述）
water	[ˋwɔtɚ]	動詞 流口水
night market	[naɪt ˋmɑrkɪt]	名詞 夜市

日常實用短句 Useful Sentences

- You must learn to use chopsticks.
  你得學著使用筷子。
- I've always wanted to try Beijing Duck.
  我一直都很想試試北京烤鴨。
- Do you agree that Chinese food is healthier and more tasteful than the Western food?
  你同意中國菜比西方菜更健康美味嗎？
- If you like hot spicy dishes, you will love Sichuan food for sure.
  如果你喜歡吃辣，那你一定會愛四川菜。
- Taiwan is famous for its traditional snacks.
  台灣以傳統小吃聞名。
- Have you tried Stinky Tofu before?
  你以前有吃過臭豆腐嗎？
- I like Cantonese cuisine, and Cantonese dim sum is my favorite.
  我很喜歡粵菜，而港式點心是我的最愛。
- You can never get tired of Chinese food because it is diversified.
  你永遠不會吃膩中國菜，因為它很多樣化。
- If you don't feel like to eat rice, you can also have noodles or dumplings.
  如果你不想吃飯，你也可以吃麵或水餃。
- We always have several dishes in a meal.
  我們一餐通常會吃好幾道菜。

學習++ More Tips

「water」當名詞用的時候是「水」的意思，而當動詞的時候就可以解釋成「澆水」； 當作形容詞就是「流口水」的意思。「Can I have a glass of water?」（我可以要一杯水嗎？）、「I am watering the flower.」（我在澆花）、「This cake is mouth watering.」（這蛋糕讓人想流口水。）。

02 茶藝

TRACK 127.

實境對話

Conversation

A: What a ***tiny teapot***! What's that for?

B: That's the teapot for a Chinese tea ***ceremony***.

A: Is tea very popular in Taiwan?

B: Yes, Bau-Tsung Tea, Oolong Tea, and ***Black Tea*** are the three most famous tea ***varieties*** in Taiwan.

A: Do you drink tea?

B: Yes, I do. But I only use ***tea bags***.

A: The tea ceremony is too ***troublesome*** for me.

A: 這麼小的茶壺是作什麼用的呢？
B: 這是中國茶藝所用的茶壺。
A: 茶在台灣很普及嗎？
B: 是的，包種茶、烏龍茶以及紅茶是台灣最有名的三種茶。
A: 你喝茶嗎？
B: 有啊，但是只喝茶包。
A: 茶藝對我而言太麻煩了。

核心詞彙

Words&Phrases

tiny	[ˋtaɪnɪ]	形容詞 小的
teapot	[ˋti͵pɑt]	名詞 茶壺
ceremony	[ˋsɛrə͵monɪ]	名詞 儀式
black tea	[blæk ti]	名詞 紅茶
variety	[vəˋraɪətɪ]	名詞 種類
tea bag	[ti bæg]	名詞 茶包
troublesome	[ˋtrʌbl̩səm]	形容詞 麻煩的

日常實用短句 Useful Sentences

- Jasmine scented tea is one of my favorite.
  茉莉香片是我最喜歡的茶之一。
- I prefer Longjin to Puerh.
  我喜歡龍井茶更勝普洱茶。
- Would you like some oolong tea before you order?
  點菜前要不要先喝點烏龍茶呀？
- Instead of soda or coke, we often have Chinese tea while having meals.
  我們吃飯時通常會喝中國茶，而非汽水或可樂。
- Tea plays an essential role in Chinese culture.
  茶在中華文化中扮演了重要的角色。
- People always show their respect to one another by offering a cup of tea.
  人們經常以敬茶的方式來表示對彼此的尊敬。
- In formal occasions, the younger generation should offer a cup of tea to the older generation.
  在正式場合，晚輩應該要向長輩敬茶。
- Going to restaurants and drinking tea is an important activity for family gatherings in Chiense society.
  在華人社會中，上餐館喝茶是家庭聚會的一個重要活動。
- We will pour tea for someone if we want to make serious apologies or to express thanks.
  如果我們想向某人正式道歉或表達感謝，便會替對方斟茶。
- You can also put a handful of tea leaves into a pot and pour in hot water.
  你也可以放一點茶葉在水壺裡，並倒入熱水。

學習++ More Tips

中國人講究茶藝，而外國人則注重「tea」（下午茶）。在下午茶的時候大家都會暫時放下手邊的事務，悠閒的來杯茶「a cup of tea」， 再配上一些「home-baked cookies」（手製餅乾），真的是在再愜意不過了！

03 節慶

TRACK 128.

實境對話

Conversation

A: What kinds of ***festivals*** do you have throughout the year in Taiwan?

B: ***Tomb*** Sweeping day is on the 5th of April. We pay ***respects*** to ***beloved*** ones who have passed away. The Dragon boat Festival is on the 5th day of the fifth lunar month. We eat ***glutinous*** rice tamales. The ghost Festival is on the 15th day of the 7th lunar month. The Mid-Autumn Festival is on the 15th day of the 8th ***lunar month***. We eat Moon-Cakes. And New Year is the first day of the first lunar month, which is the largest festival of the year.

A: 在台灣，你們一年中有些什麼主要節慶？

B: 清明節在國曆四月五日，是紀念已逝去的親人。端午節在農曆的五月初五，特色是吃粽子。中元節在農曆七月十五；而中秋節在農曆八月十五，特色是吃月餅。而新年是一年中最大的節慶，在農曆的正月初一。

核心詞彙

Words&Phrases

festival	[ˋfɛstəvḷ]	名詞 節慶
tomb	[tum]	名詞 墓碑、墳地
respect	[rɪˋspɛkt]	名詞 尊敬
beloved	[bɪˋlʌvɪd]	形容詞 心愛的
glutinous	[ˋglutɪnəs]	形容詞 黏稠的
lunar month	[ˋlunɚ mʌnθ]	名詞 農曆

日常實用短句 Useful Sentences

- Chinese New Year's Eve is the time for family reunions.
  中國新年的除夕是家人團聚的時刻。
- Each member of the family will gather together for the family reunion dinner.
  家庭裡的每個成員都會聚在一起吃年夜飯。
- It is our custom to eat stuffed dumplings on Lantern Festival.
  元宵節這天，吃湯圓是我們的習俗。
- On the Dragon Boat Festival, we eat rice dumplings and enjoy the dragon boat race.
  端午節這天，我們會吃粽子並欣賞龍舟賽。
- Tomb-sweeping Day is a time for us to remember and honor our deceased ancestors and family members.
  清明節是我們對已故的祖先和家人表達懷念和敬意的日子。
- The seventh lunar month is regarded as the Ghost Month.
  農曆七月被視為鬼月。
- Just as the West has Halloween, so does Taiwan have the Ghost Festival.
  就如同西方有萬聖節一樣，台灣也有中元節。
- Many people like to have a barbecue while enjoying the glorious full moon.
  很多人喜歡一邊賞月一邊烤肉。

學習++ More Tips

中國人在特別的節日都會有不同的食物，外國人也是，在「Halloween」（萬聖節）的時候會煮「pumpkin」（南瓜大餐）；「Thanksgiving」（感恩節）則會煮豐盛的「turkey」（火雞大餐）和一家人團聚吃晚餐喔！

04 故宮博物院

TRACK 129.

實境對話

Conversation

A: Could you briefly tell me about the National ***Palace*** Museum?

B: It's one of the four largest museums in the world. It was built in 1965.

B: It ***imitated*** the old Peiking palace and followed the traditional Chinese palace style.

B: It ***exhibits*** the ***unearthed*** relics and the royal collections from the New Stone Age to the Ching Dynasty.

A: Then, after having been through this museum, I can get a ***rough*** idea of Chinese 5000 years of history, culture and arts.

A: 你可不可以簡單地介紹一下故宮呢？

B: 故宮是世界四大博物館之一，建立於西元 1965 年。

B: 它是仿造北京的清故宮所建造的中國式的宮殿建築物。

B: 展覽的文物從新石器時代到清朝的出土物以及皇室收藏品。

A: 那麼參觀完這裡，就可以大概了解中國 5000 年的歷史，文化及藝術的內容了。

核心詞彙

Words&Phrases

palace	[ˋpælɪs]	名詞 皇宮
imitate	[ˋɪmə͵tet]	動詞 模仿
exhibit	[ɪgˋzɪbɪt]	動詞 展示
unearth	[ʌnˋɝθ]	動詞 從地下發掘出
rough	[rʌf]	形容詞 粗略的

日常實用短句 *Useful Sentences*

- National Palace Museum is both a gallery and a museum.
  故宮博物院是美術館也是博物館。
- There is a large collection of Chinese artifacts and works of art.
  那裡大量收藏著中國工藝及藝術品。
- The National Palace Museum is a very magnificent architecture.
  故宮博物院是個非常宏偉的建築物。
- It is located near Yangmingshan National Park and Shih Lin Night Market.
  它就位在陽明山國家公園和士林夜市附近。
- You can enter the Zhide Garden for free whenever you want to.
  你隨時都可以免費進入至德園。
- Almost everyone in Taiwan has been to National Palace Museum at least once.
  台灣幾乎所有人至少都去過故宮博物院一次。
- I visited the National Palace Museum for the first time when I was in elementary school.
  我第一次去故宮博物院是我小學的時候。
- It is an ideal place to take the students to a field trip.
  這是個帶學生做戶外教學的理想地點。
- The National Palace Museum is always filled with sightseers in peak season.
  故宮博物院在旅遊旺季總是擠滿了遊客。

學習++ *More Tips*

「brief」是「簡單」、「大略」的意思；「tell me briefly」（簡略的告訴我。），也可以說「tell me in brief」、「Give me a brief report.」（給我一個簡單的報告。）。

05 台灣的原住民

TRACK 130.

實境對話

Conversation

A: Taiwanese people are ***made up of*** four major groups of people; those are Fujian, Hakka, Mainlanders and Aborigines.

A: They are all Han people ***except for*** the ***Aborigines***. But the ***population*** of Aborigines is only about 300,000, 2% of the total population.

B: Is there any museum in Taiwan that I can visit to understand their ***cultures***?

A: Yes. In ***central*** Taiwan, near Sun-Moon Lake, there is a place called "Nine Peoples' Cultural Village".

A: 台灣人由四大族群所組成，即閩南人、客家人、外省人及原住民。

A: 除了原住民其他都是屬於漢民族。但原住民只佔了總人口的百分之二，約 30 萬人。

B: 在台灣有沒有什麼博物館可以了解他們的文化呢？

A: 有的。在台灣中部的日月潭附近有一個九族文化村。

核心詞彙

Words&Phrases

make up of	[mek ʌp ɑv]	片語 以……組成
except for	[ɪk`sɛpt fɔr]	片語 除了
aborigine	[æbə`rɪdʒəni]	名詞 原住民
population	[ˌpɑpjə`leʃən]	名詞 人口
culture	[`kʌltʃɚ]	名詞 文化
central	[`sɛntrəl]	形容詞 中央的

日常實用短句 Useful Sentences

- There are fourteen officially recognized aboriginal tribes and eleven unrecognized aboriginal tribes.
  被正式承認的原住民族有十四個，而未被正式承認的原住民族有十一個。
- The Bunun are best-known for their sophisticated polyphonic vocal music.
  布農族最為人所知的就是他們複雜的和弦聲樂。
- The Atayal have a custom of face tattooing.
  泰雅族有黥面的習俗。
- An important part of Paiwan culture is witchcraft.
  排灣族文化中很重要的一部分就是巫術。
- The Rukai live in the mountains of southern Taiwan.
  魯凱族居住於台灣南部的山上。
- The Amis are the largest tribal group in Taiwan.
  阿美族是台灣最大的部落族群。
- The Yami, native to Orchid Island, are good at making canoes.
  蘭嶼的原住民雅美族擅長製作獨木舟。
- The Thao, the smallest aboriginal groups in Taiwan, inhabit near the Sun Moon Lake.
  台灣最小的原住民族一邵族，居住在日月潭附近。
- It is generally acknowledged that Taiwanese aborigines are good at singing.
  台灣原住民很會唱歌是大家所公認的。
- Their exceptionally beautiful voice makes them gifted singers.
  他們得天獨厚的嗓音使他們成為有天賦的歌手。

學習++ More Tips

美國的原住民是我們俗稱的「Indians」（印地安人），但是這是不禮貌的說法，你應該說是「native Americans」，就等於是我們中文的「原住民」。

06 台北101大樓

TRACK 131.

實境對話

Conversation

A: What is that tower with a ***spire***?

B: Oh, that is Taipei 101.

A: It's pretty tall and spectacular.

B: Yes. It used to be the highest ***skyscraper*** in the world.

B: It ***combines*** finance, commerce, entertainment, shopping, and life and so on altogether. It's like a ***metropolis*** inside. And there's an ***observation deck*** on 89th floor with a charge of 400 NT dollars where you can see the whole Taipei.

A: 哇，那幢有個尖頂的高塔是什麼啊？

B: 喔，那是台北 101 大樓。

A: 真的好高、好壯觀啊！

B: 是啊！它曾經是全世界最高的摩天大樓。

B: 台北 101 大樓結合金融、商業、娛樂、購物、生活等用途，猶如大都會生活的縮影。在 89 樓還有觀景台，只要付台幣 400 元進去就可以看到整個大台北的景觀呢！

核心詞彙

Words&Phrases

spire	[spaɪr]	名詞 尖塔
skyscraper	[ˋskaɪˏskrepɚ]	名詞 摩天大樓
combine	[kəmˋbaɪn]	動詞 結合
metropolis	[məˋtrɑpl̩ɪs]	名詞 大都市
observation deck	[ˏɑbzɝˋveʃən dɛk]	名詞 觀景台

日常實用短句 Useful Sentences

- You can't miss the 101-floor skyscraper in Taipei.
  你不能錯過台北那棟 101 層樓的摩天大樓。
- It is the tallest building in Taiwan at present.
  它是台灣目前最高的建築物。
- How long does it take to go up to the top floor?
  要往上到頂樓要花多久時間啊？
- There are two fastest double-decker elevators which run at a speed of 37.5 mph.
  那兒有兩台速度最快的雙層電梯，每小時時速達 37.5 英里呢。
- If you get to visit Taipei 101, you can overlook the whole Taipei city from an outdoor observatory on the 89th floor.
  如果你能去台北 101，那麼你就能從 89 樓的室外觀景台俯瞰整個台北市。
- The outdoor observation deck is so far the highest in the world.
  戶外的觀景台目前是全世界最高的。
- There is another thing that makes Taipei 101 attractive.
  台北 101 還有另一個吸引人的地方。
- The biggest countdown party by year end in Taiwan is held in front of the city hall, which is only a few minutes walk from Taipei 101.
  台灣年終最大的倒數派對就是在離台北 101 只有幾分鐘路程之遙的台北市政府前舉行。

學習++ More Tips

「Have you ever been...?」是常用來詢問他人「你有去過（某地）嗎？」的句型，如：「Have you ever been to New York?」（你有去過紐約嗎？），或「Have you ever been up there?」（你有去過那上面嗎？）。

07 日月潭

TRACK 132.

實境對話

Conversation

A: One of my friends went to Sun Moon ***Lake*** last time when he visited Taiwan. He said that it was really amazing there.

B: Yeah, Sun Moon Lake, the largest lake in Taiwan, is a very famous ***spot***.

B: The lake is ***divided*** by Lalu Island. The eastern part of the lake is round like the sun and the western side is ***shaped*** like a ***crescent*** moon. That's where the name ***came from***.

B: And that place is as wonderful as its name.

A: Wow! I must go see it!

A: 上次我朋友來台灣去了日月潭，他說那裡非常的漂亮。
B: 是啊！日月潭是台灣最大的湖，也是很有名的觀光景點。
B: 潭面以拉魯島為界線，東側形狀如太陽，西側形狀如月亮，所以取名叫日月潭。
B: 而且那個地方就跟名字一樣漂亮呢！
A: 哇！那我一定要去瞧瞧！

核心詞彙

Words&Phrases

lake	[lek]	名詞 湖
spot	[spɑt]	名詞 景點
divide	[də`vaɪd]	動詞 分開
shaped	[ʃept]	形容詞 成某種形狀的
crescent	[`krɛsn̩t]	形容詞 新月形的
come from	[kʌm frɑm]	片語 來自……

日常實用短句 Useful Sentences

- How about spending a weekend holiday at Sun Moon Lake?
  要不要到日月潭去度週休假期呢？
- Sun Moon Lake is the largest natural lake in Taiwan.
  日月潭是台灣最大的天然湖。
- There are many hotels built by the lake.
  湖邊蓋了許多飯店。
- Would you like to take a boat ride on Sun Moon Lake?
  你想不想搭船遊日月潭啊？
- We can also take a bicycle ride around the Sun Moon Lake.
  我們還可以繞著日月潭騎腳踏車。
- The pleasure-boat is making a round-the-lake cruise.
  遊船正在做環潭航行。
- It's a very different experience to enjoy the landscape from a boat.
  從船上欣賞陸上風景別有一番滋味。
- It is good to get away from the city from time to time.
  偶爾遠離城市是很好的。
- The scene of the lake is really impressive.
  這湖景真教人印象深刻。
- Being in this beautiful scenery, I was touched beyond words.
  置身如此美景，讓我感動莫名。

學習++ More Tips

聽到他人對某地讚不絕口，一定會興起一股也想親眼去瞧瞧的念頭，這時候可以說：「I must go see it!」（我一定要去看看！），或是「I will definitely visit the place someday.」（我哪天絕對要去參觀那個地方。）。

08 高雄愛河

TRACK 133.

實境對話

Conversation

A: Did you ***grow up*** in Taipei?

B: No, Kaohsiung is my ***hometown***.

A: Really? What is fun in Kaohsiung?

B: When people mentioned Kaohsiung, they think of Love River. It used to be seriously ***polluted***; however, it is now clean and beautiful after river ***remediation*** and ***beautification*** construction.

B: And you must take the Love Boat. It is such a great enjoyment to enjoy the night view along the river on a boat.

A: 你是台北長大的嗎？

B: 不，我老家在高雄。

A: 真的嗎？高雄有什麼好玩的啊？

B: 大部分的人一提到高雄，就會想到愛河。它曾經飽受污染，但經過河川整治和美化工程之後，現在已經很乾淨、很漂亮了。

B: 而且一定要去搭愛之船。搭船沿著河欣賞夜景，真是一大享受呢！

核心詞彙

Words&Phrases

grow up	[gro ʌp]	片語 長大
hometown	[ˋhomˋtaʊn]	名詞 家鄉
polluted	[pəˋlutɪd]	形容詞 受汙染的
remediation	[rɪˏmidɪˋeʃən]	名詞 矯正
beautification	[ˏbjutɪfɪˋkeʃən]	名詞 美化

日常實用短句 Useful Sentences

- We can sit in an open-air café and sip a cup of coffee.
  我們可以找一間露天咖啡屋坐坐，並喝一杯咖啡。
- It only takes NT$50 to enjoy a 20 minutes leisurely and romantic cruise along the river.
  只要花台幣五十元就能享受二十分鐘悠閒浪漫的遊河。
- You should definitely experience the ride on the Love Boat if you've got plenty of time.
  如果你有足夠的時間，你絕對應該來一趟搭乘愛之船的體驗。
- It is a chance for you to get a close look at the river.
  這是你可以就近觀看這條河的機會。
- The stench of the Love River used to drive people away.
  愛河的惡臭曾經讓人們敬而遠之。
- But after the treatment, the Love River has been turned into a tourist attraction.
  但在整治之後，愛河已經搖身一變成為令人嚮往的觀光勝地。
- The once dying river is now alive again.
  曾經瀕死的河川現在又再度活躍起來。
- If you have a chance to visit Kaohsiung, make sure you pay an actual visit to the Love River.
  如果你有機會造訪高雄，一定要實地到愛河去看看。
- You can't claim to have been to Kaohsiung without visiting the Love River.
  沒有去過愛河，你就不能說你曾經去過高雄。

學習++ More Tips

「enjoyment」是「令人愉快之事、樂趣、享受」的意思。「It is such an enjoyment to...」這個句型，可以用來表達「……真是享受」的感嘆。如：「It is such an enjoyment to enjoy the night scenes from a boat.」（從船上欣賞夜景真是一大享受啊！）。

09 慈湖忠烈祠

TRACK 134.

實境對話

Conversation

A: Where is Cihu Building?

B: Cihu Building is the ***burial*** place of Chiang Kai-shek in Dasi Township of Taoyuan County. The lakeside scenery is ***fascinating***. And there are mountains all around so that we can see different ***scenery*** in different seasons.

B: And there is hourly ***rifle drill performed by*** tri-service honor guards. It is really great. By the way, you can also buy some souvenirs at Cihu ***Tourist*** Service Center next to the ***parking lot***.

A: 慈湖在哪裡呢？

B: 慈湖在桃園縣的大溪鎮，是先總統蔣公陵寢所在地。湖邊景色很美。而且四面環山，一年四季會有不同的風景喔！

B: 而且每個小時會有儀隊表演花式操槍，很精采呢！對了，你還可以去停車場旁的遊客服務中心，買一些紀念品回家。

核心詞彙

Words&Phrases

burial	[ˋbɛrɪəl]	形容詞 埋葬的
fascinating	[ˋfæsn̩ˏetɪŋ]	形容詞 迷人的、極美的
scenery	[ˋsinərɪ]	名詞 風景
rifle drill	[ˋraɪfl̩ drɪl]	名詞 刺槍術
perform by	[pɚˋfɔrm baɪ]	片語 表演
tourist	[ˋturɪst]	名詞 遊客
parking lot	[pɑrkɪŋ lɑt]	名詞 停車場

日常實用短句 Useful Sentences

- The entrance is guarded by the military police.
  入口由憲兵守衛著。
- The place was named Cihu by Chian Kai-shek because the scenery reminded him of his benevolent mother.
  這地方被蔣介石命名為「慈湖」，因為這裡的景致讓他想起了他慈祥的母親。
- It has beem the temporary resting place of Chiang Kai-shek since his death in 1975.
  這裡自 1975 年蔣介石死後就成了他暫時安息之地。
- It is not allowed to take photographs inside the mausoleum.
  在陵寢裡面是不能拍照的。
- Numerous visitors flock here to watch the ceremony for changing the guards.
  許多遊客成群而至就為了欣賞衛兵交接儀式。
- You can take photographs of the ceremony as souvenirs of your visit.
  你可以拍下儀式的照片以作為到此一遊的紀念品。
- There is also a souvenir shop in which you can buy figurines of the two Presidents.
  那裡還有一間紀念品商店，在那裡你可以買到兩蔣的小雕像。
- It is also a nice place to take the students for outdoor excursions.
  這裡同時也是帶學生來戶外遠足的好地點。

學習++ More Tips

「tourist service center」指的是「遊客服務中心」，提供遊客相關旅遊資訊，有些也兼具「gift shop」（禮品店）的功能。如果有人想買紀念品，不妨說：「Let's go see if there's anything we can get as souvenirs in the tourist service center.」（我們到遊客服務中心去看看有沒有什麼可以買來當紀念品的吧！）。

10 阿里山日出

TRACK 135.

實境對話

Conversation

A: How did you celebrate the New Year?

B: I went to see the first ***sunrise*** on Alishan with my boyfriend.

A: Oh, that is romantic.

B: Yeah. The sunrise scenery was really ***majestic***.

A: When did you have to get up in order to see the sunrise?

B: Very early. Actually, we didn't get much sleep the night before. We had to ***set off*** before four o'clock in the early morning in order to ***greet*** the first ***gleams*** of the day.

A: 妳今年跨年去哪裡玩啊？

B: 和我男朋友去阿里山上看今年第一道日出。

A: 喔，真浪漫。

B: 是啊，日出的景色真是非常壯麗呢。

A: 你們必須幾點起床，才能看到日出？

B: 非常早。事實上，我們前一晚根本沒怎麼睡。我們必須在清晨四點之前就出發，好迎接第一道曙光。

核心詞彙

Words&Phrases

sunrise	[ˋsʌn͵raɪz]	名詞 日出
majestic	[məˋdʒɛstɪk]	形容詞 壯麗的
set off	[sɛt ɔf]	片語 出發、動身
greet	[grit]	動詞 迎接
gleam	[glim]	名詞 閃光、微光

日常實用短句 Useful Sentences

- It is a place that you must pay a visit to once in your lifetime.
  那是你這一輩子一定要去一次的地方。
- It is known for its sunrise scenery.
  它因為日出景象而聞名。
- Tourists come here one after the other just to enjoy the scenery with their own eyes.
  遊客絡繹不絕地來到這裡就是為了親眼欣賞這風景。
- It is a marvelous experience to take the Alishan railway.
  搭阿里山小火車是個很特別的體驗。
- I've never seen such glorious scenery in my life.
  我這輩子從未看過如此壯麗的景色。
- I was so overwhelmed by the view that I couldn't speak a word.
  我深受震撼而無法言語。
- The golden sea of clouds was an unrivaled sight.
  那片金色的雲海是無與倫比的景色。
- It is a sight that will never be forgotten.
  那真是讓人難忘的景色。
- Don't forget to bring a camera with you because you will definitely want to photograph the scene.
  別忘了帶照相機，因為你絕對會想把那景色拍下來的。

學習++ More Tips

「the first gleams of the day」意指「第一道曙光」，也可以表示為「the first light of morning」（早晨第一道光）。要邀請他人一同看日出時，不妨說：「Let's go greet the first gleams of the day together.」（我們一起去迎接一天的第一道曙光吧。）。

11 香港迪士尼樂園

TRACK 136.

實境對話

Conversation

A: You must take your children to Hong Kong Disneyland.

B: Really? Is it ***worth*** going?

A: Of course! They will be happy to see so many Disney ***characters***, such as Mickey Mouse, Snow White and Winnie the Pooh.

A: ***In addition to*** the amusement facilities, there are lots of shows to watch and many different cuisines to ***choose from***. Also, you can buy Disney ***merchandise*** at their ***souvenir shops***.

A: 你一定要帶你的小孩去香港迪士尼樂園玩。

B: 真的嗎？那裡很值得去玩嗎？

A: 當然啊。他們看到那麼多迪士尼卡通人物，像是米老鼠、白雪公主和維尼小熊，一定會非常開心。

A: 除了遊樂設施之外，有很多的表演節目可以看，有許多不同的美食供你選擇。還有，你可以在紀念品店買到迪士尼商品喔。

核心詞彙

Words&Phrases

worth	[wɝθ]	形容詞 值得的
character	[ˋkærɪktɚ]	名詞 角色
in addition to	[ɪn əˋdɪʃən tu]	片語 除……之外
choose from	[tʃuz frɑm]	片語 選擇
merchandise	[ˋmɝtʃənˏdaɪz]	名詞 商品
souvenir shop	[ˋsuvəˏnɪr ʃɑp]	名詞 紀念品店

日常實用短句 Useful Sentences

- I'm taking my family to Hong Kong Disneyland.
  我要帶家人去香港迪士尼樂園。
- We are going to watch the Broadway-style shows.
  我們要去看百老匯風格的節目表演。
- And we will definitely enjoy the adventurous, thrilling rides.
  而且一定要去玩那些冒險刺激的遊樂設施。
- I had a picture with Princess Aurora, the Sleeping Beauty, in Fantasyland.
  我在夢幻仙境和睡美人歐羅拉公主合照。
- I bought a gift for you from the themed shop in the Disneyland.
  我在迪士尼樂園的主題商店買了一個禮物送你。
- We enjoyed the indoor rollercoaster in Tomorrowland. It was really exciting.
  我們在明日世界玩室內雲霄飛車。那真是太刺激了。
- We also got to interact with Stitch, my wife's favorite character, in Tomorrowland.
  我們在明日世界還跟我太太最喜歡的人物史迪奇互動呢。
- Actually, my wife and I had a fairy tale wedding in Hong Kong Disneyland.
  事實上，我和我太太是在香港迪士尼樂園舉行童話婚禮的。
- You can also book tickets to the Disneyland online.
  你也可以在線上預訂迪士尼樂園的門票。

學習++ More Tips

「be worth +V-ing」是表示「值得……」的片語，如：「Is the place worth visiting?」（那地方值得參觀嗎？），或「The amusement park is really worth going.」（這個遊樂園真的很值得一去。）。

12 鳥巢

TRACK 137.

實境對話

Conversation

A: I'm wondering if you have time this weekend. I'd like to go to the Bird's ***Nest*** with you.

B: What Bird's Nest? I've ***never*** heard of it.

A: You haven't heard of it? It's the National Stadium.

B: I get it! You mean the main stadium where the 29th Beijing ***Olympic*** Games was ***held***, right?

A: That's it! The National Stadium is so beautiful and spectacular ***on TV***. I'd like to see it ***in person***.

A: 我想知道妳這個週末有沒有空。我想找妳一起去鳥巢。

B: 什麼鳥巢？我從沒聽過。

A: 妳沒聽過？就是國家體育場啊。

B: 我知道了！你說的是舉辦第二十九屆北京奧運會的主體育場吧？

A: 沒錯！國家體育場在電視上看太美麗壯觀了！我想親自去看一下。

核心詞彙

Words&Phrases

nest	[nɛst]	名詞 巢
never	[ˋnɛvɚ]	副詞 永不
Olympic	[Iˋlɪmpɪks]	名詞 奧林匹克
hold	[hold]	動詞 舉辦
on TV	[ɑn ti vi]	片語 電視上
in person	[ɪn ˋpɝsn̩]	片語 親身

日常實用短句 Useful Sentences

- It was the main stadium for the 2008 Olympic Games.
  它是 2008 年奧運的主館場。
- It has a seating capacity of 80,000.
  它可容納八萬名觀眾。
- It is nicknamed the "Bird's Nest" because of its innovative grid formation.
  它被稱為「鳥巢」是因為它創新的格子結構。
- The most amazing part of the "Bird's Nest" is that it support its own weight without relying on any of the supporting structures.
  「鳥巢」最讓人感到驚奇的部分就是它完全沒有藉助任何支撐結構來支撐自己本身的重量。
- It was designed for use of the 2008 Summer Olympics and Paralympics.
  它是被設計作為 2008 年夏季奧運及殘障奧運之用的。
- It is very likely to be turned into a shopping and entertainment complex in the future.
  未來它很可能會成為一個集合購物及娛樂的綜合設施。
- The water used throughout and around the stadium is collected by the rainwater collector near the stadium.
  館場內及週遭所使用的水是附近的雨水收集器所收集而來的。
- The authorities are thinking to develop tourism as a major draw for the stadium.
  有關當局打算發展觀光業以作為體育場的主要規劃。

學習++ More Tips

「in person」是「親自」的意思，如：「I've always wanted to visit the museum in person.」（我一直以來都很想親自去參觀那間博物館。）；若要表示「親眼看」，可以用「with one's own eyes」這個片語，如：「I really want to see it with my own eyes.」（我真想親眼看看！）。

13 水立方

TRACK 138.

實境對話 Conversation

A: Have you ever been to Water ***Cube***?

B: You mean one of the landmark buildings of Beijing Olympic Games——the National ***Aquatics*** Center? It's so beautiful with blue gentle appearance, just like many water ***bubbles***.

A: It's ***fortunate*** that I got the ticket and watched Phelps' ***race*** there.

B: Phelps? The US ***athlete*** who won eight ***gold medals***? Wow, it must be very cool!

A: 你去過水立方嗎？

B: 你是指北京奧運的代表性建築之一的國家游泳中心嗎？它藍色的外觀很柔美很漂亮，就像有很多泡泡一樣。

A: 我很幸運的買到票，而且在那裡看了菲爾普斯的比賽。

B: 菲爾普斯？就是贏得八枚金牌的美國運動員？哇，那一定非常酷！

核心詞彙 Words&Phrases

cube	[kjub]	名詞 立方體
aquatics	[ə`kwætɪks]	名詞 水上運動
bubble	[`bʌbl̩]	名詞 泡泡
fortunate	[`fɔrtʃənɪt]	形容詞 幸運的
race	[res]	名詞 比賽
athlete	[`æθlit]	名詞 運動員
gold medal	[gold `mɛdl̩]	名詞 金牌

日常實用短句 Useful Sentences

- It is an alternative given name of the Beijing National Aquatic Center.
  它是北京國家游泳中心的別名。
- It was built for use of the swimming competitions of the 2008 Summer Olympics.
  它是被造來作為 2008 年夏季奧運游泳比賽之用的。
- It has a capacity of 6,000.
  它可以容納六千名觀眾。
- The building looks just like a rectangular box.
  這建築物看起來就像一個長方形的盒子。
- It embodies Green Olympics concept.
  它體現了綠色奧運的概念。
- There is a water park under construction inside the building.
  現在館內有一個水世界正在建構中。
- They are going to turn it into an indoor shopping arcade.
  他們要將它變成一個室內購物商場。
- This building looks even more beautiful at night.
  這建築物晚上看起來更美。
- The splendid night view of the Water Cube is stunning.
  水立方光彩奪目的夜景真是絕美。
- It is one of the most worth visiting tourist attractions in Beijing.
  它是北京最值得一遊的旅遊景點之一。

學習++ More Tips

「envy」是「羨慕」的意思，如：「I envy you your good luck to watch the game for free.」（我真羨慕你能免費看比賽的好運氣哪！）、「Don't envy me. Just pay a visit to the place yourself.」（別羨慕我了。親自到那裡去參觀就好了。）。

14 東方明珠塔

TRACK 139.

實境對話

Conversation

A: Hi, Victor! I heard that you went to Shanghai last week. How was your trip?

B: Quite good.

A: Did you visit any special places in Shanghai?

B: Of course! I went to the ***Oriental*** Pearl's ***Tower***.

A: That's the ***symbol*** of Shanghai. How tall is it?

B: It's the second highest tower in Asia with the ***height*** of 468 ***meters***.

B: It's really gorgeous, ***especially*** at night.

A: 嗨，維特！我聽説你上周去上海了。好玩嗎？

B: 非常不錯。

A: 你有參觀上海什麼特別的地方嗎？

B: 當然有啦！我去了東方明珠塔。

A: 那是象徵上海的地標呢。它有多高啊？

B: 它是亞洲第二高塔，有 468 公尺高。

B: 它真的美極了，尤其是在晚上。

核心詞彙

Words&Phrases

oriental	[͵orɪˋɛntl̩]	形容詞 東方的
tower	[ˋtauɚ]	名詞 塔
symbol	[ˋsɪmbl̩]	名詞 象徵
height	[haɪt]	名詞 高度
meter	[ˋmitɚ]	名詞 公尺、米
especially	[əˋspɛʃəlɪ]	副詞 特別地

日常實用短句 *Useful Sentences*

- It is a key tourist attraction in Shanghai.
  它是上海一個主要的旅遊景點。
- Before the Shanghai World Financial Center is built, it was once the tallest structure in China.
  在上海世界金融中心蓋好之前，它曾是中國最高的建築物。
- It attracts millions of visitors each year.
  它每年都吸引數百萬的遊客。
- If you're planning a romantic dinner with your significant other, you should definitely come here.
  如果你計畫和另一半來個浪漫晚餐，你更應該來這裡。
- You can overlook the landscape of Shanghai while enjoying your dinner.
  你可以一邊享用晚餐，一邊俯瞰上海風景。
- There are exhibition facilities, restaurants as well as a shopping mall.
  那裡有展場設備、餐廳還有一間購物中心。
- There is also a hotel called the Space Hotel between the two large spheres.
  在兩個大球體中間還有一間名為太空飯店的飯店。
- The tower has fifteen observatory levels.
  這座塔有 15 個觀景樓層。
- You can look down at the Shanghai City from the outdoor observation deck through the glass floor.
  你可以在觀景樓層透過玻璃地板俯瞰上海市。

學習++ *More Tips*

「symbol」是「象徵、標誌」的意思。每個城市幾乎都會有代表性的象徵物，如：「Taipei 101 is the symbol of Taipei.」（台北 101 大樓是象徵台北的標的物。）、「What's the symbol of your city?」（你們城市的象徵標的物是什麼呢？）。

15 萬里長城

TRACK 140.

實境對話 Conversation

A: I've dreamed of visiting the Great Wall ***since*** I was a child, now my dream is going to come true. I can hardly believe that!

B: I can understand. By the way, how much do you know about the Great Wall?

A: The Great Wall is a great ***miracle*** in China. It is one of the greatest ***engineering*** projects that ***created by human being***. Going to China without visiting the Great Wall is like going to Paris without visiting the Eiffel Tower.

B: I wish you had a wonderful time!

A: 我從小就夢想著去長城，現在我的夢想就要實現了，真不敢相信哪！

B: 我能理解。對了，關於長城你知道多少呢？

A: 長城是中國的一大奇蹟。它是人類創造的最偉大的建築工程之一。去中國不去長城就跟去巴黎卻不參觀艾菲爾鐵塔一樣。

B: 希望你玩得開心！

核心詞彙 Words&Phrases

since	[sɪns]	連接詞 自從
miracle	[ˋmɪrək!]	名詞 奇蹟
engineering	[ˏɛndʒəˋnɪrɪŋ]	名詞 工程
create by	[krɪˋet baɪ]	片語 ……創造的
human being	[ˋhjumən ˋbiɪŋ]	名詞 人類

日常實用短句 Useful Sentences

- The Great Wall is like a gigantic dragon.
  萬里長城就像一條巨龍。
- It winds up and down across deserts, grasslands, mountains and plateaus.
  它上下蜿蜒穿越沙漠、草原、山陵及高原。
- It is about 5,500 miles from east to west of China.
  由中國東至西約有五千五百英里長。
- It is one of the most appealing tourist attractions all around the world.
  它是世界上最吸引人的觀光勝地之一。
- It was listed as a World Heritage by UNESCO in 1987.
  它在 1987 年被聯合國教科文組織列為世界遺產。
- The Great Wall was built as a defense against invasions of the barbarians from the north.
  萬里長城是建來作為抵擋北方蠻族侵略的防禦物。
- The Great Wall became the world's largest military structure in the Ming dynasty.
  萬里長城在明朝時成為世界上最大的軍事建築。
- It is said to be the only human work that can be seen from the moon.
  據說它是從月球上唯一可以看到的人類建築工程。
- A visit to the Wall will give you a chance to better understand the history of China.
  去長城走一趟將會給你一個更了解中國歷史的機會。

學習++ More Tips

「dream of…」是表示「夢想……、渴望……」的片語，而「a dream comes true」就是「夢想成真」的意思。如：「I've dreamed of seeing the Yellow River with my own eyes since I was little. Now my dream comes true.」（我從小就夢想可以親眼看看黃河。現在我夢想成真了。）。

PART 7 景點＆文化篇

你都記住了嗎？

從各篇「日常實用短句」裡整理出外國人常用的單字和片語，如果背起來了，就在前方空格打個勾吧！

- ☐ for sure
  片語 確切地
- ☐ traditional snack
  名詞 傳統小吃
- ☐ tofu
  名詞 豆腐
- ☐ diversified
  形容詞 多變的、各種的
- ☐ role
  名詞 角色
- ☐ younger generation
  名詞 晚輩
- ☐ older generation
  名詞 長輩
- ☐ gathering
  名詞 集會、聚集
- ☐ tea leave
  名詞 茶葉
- ☐ reunion
  名詞 團聚
- ☐ stuffed dumpling
  名詞 湯圓
- ☐ rice dumpling
  名詞 粽子
- ☐ ancestor
  名詞 祖先
- ☐ be regarded as
  片語 視為……
- ☐ full moon
  名詞 滿月
- ☐ artifact
  名詞 手工藝品
- ☐ work of art
  名詞 藝術作品
- ☐ architecture
  名詞 建築
- ☐ for free
  片語 免費
- ☐ field trip
  名詞 校外教學
- ☐ peak season
  名詞 旺季
- ☐ tribe
  名詞 部落、種族
- ☐ best-known
  形容詞 最有名的
- ☐ sophisticated
  形容詞 複雜的
- ☐ tattoo
  名詞 刺青
- ☐ witchcraft
  名詞 巫術

□ canoe
名詞 獨木舟

□ at present
片語 現在、目前

□ countdown party
名詞 倒數派對

□ cruise
名詞 巡航

□ landscape
名詞 風景

□ from time to time
片語 有時、不時

□ open-air café
名詞 露天咖啡

□ sip
動詞 啜飲

□ stench
名詞 惡臭

□ tourist attraction
名詞 旅遊勝地

□ military police
名詞 憲兵

□ benevolent
形容詞 仁慈的

□ temporary
形容詞 暫時的

□ mausoleum
名詞 陵寢

□ figurine
名詞 小雕像

□ excursion
名詞 遠足

□ lifetime
名詞 終身

□ marvelous
形容詞 令人驚嘆的

□ overwhelm
動詞 征服

□ unrivaled
形容詞 無可比擬的

□ fairy tale
名詞 童話故事

□ stadium
名詞 體育場

□ capacity
名詞 容量

□ nickname
動詞 起綽號

□ under construction
片語 建構中

□ arcade
名詞 商場

□ splendid
形容詞 極好的

□ stunning
形容詞 絕色的

□ gigantic
形容詞 巨大的

□ appealing
形容詞 有魅力的

□ World Heritage
名詞 世界遺產

□ defense
名詞 防禦

□ invasion
名詞 入侵

□ dynasty
名詞 朝代

語研力 E066

生活美話帶著走：

實境模擬＋精準短句＋學習關鍵細節，練出自然流暢英語力

7大生活主題＋140篇情境會話＋1400個生活短句，英語會話能力三級跳！

作　　者　Tong Weng
顧　　問　曾文旭
出版總監　陳逸祺、耿文國
主　　編　陳蕙芳
文字校對　翁芯琍
封面設計　李依靜
內文排版　李依靜
法律顧問　北辰著作權事務所

印　　製　世和印製企業有限公司
初　　版　2022年05月
出　　版　凱信企業集團-凱信企業管理顧問有限公司
電　　話　（02）2773-6566
傳　　真　（02）2778-1033
地　　址　106 台北市大安區忠孝東路四段218之4號12樓
信　　箱　kaihsinbooks@gmail.com

定　　價　新台幣349元／港幣116元
產品內容　1書

總 經 銷　采舍國際有限公司
地　　址　235 新北市中和區中山路二段366巷10號3樓
電　　話　（02）8245-8786
傳　　真　（02）8245-8718

國家圖書館出版品預行編目資料

生活美語帶著走：實境模擬＋精準短句＋學習關鍵細節，練出自然流暢英語力／Tong Weng 著. -- 初版. -- 臺北市：凱信企業集團凱信企業管理顧問有限公司, 2022.05
面；　公分
ISBN 978-626-7097-11-3(平裝)

1.CST: 英語 2.CST: 會話

805.188　　111002872